Shadows & Tall Trees

Also by Michael Kelly
Songs From Dead Singers
Scratching the Surface
Ouroboros (With Carol Weekes)
Apparitions
Undertow & Other Laments
Chilling Tales: Evil Did I Dwell, Lewd I Did Live
Chilling Tales: In Words, Alas, Drown I
Shadows & Tall Trees, Vols. 1 - 7
Year's Best Weird Fiction, Vol. 1 (With Laird Barron)
Year's Best Weird Fiction, Vol. 2 (With Kathe Koja)
Year's Best Weird Fiction, Vol. 3 (With Simon Strantzas)
Year's Best Weird Fiction, Vol. 4 (With Helen Marshall)
Year's Best Weird Fiction, Vol. 5 (With Robert Shearman)
All the Things We Never See

Shadows & Tall Trees

UP UNDERTOW
PUBLICATIONS

Interior design and layout by Courtney Kelly
Title page decoration designed by Freepik
Proofreader: Carolyn Macdonell-Kelly

Contents

The Glassy, Burning Floor of Hell

Brian Evenson

IT BEGAN WITH Hekla's sister, who had always been, so she liked to style herself, a seeker. There was a workshop she was dying to attend, with a guru of sorts, concerning attunement. But it took place some distance away, far outside the city. Would Hekla accompany her? It was a long way to go and she didn't want to make the drive alone.

"Not really my thing," said Hekla.

"I'll pay your way," said her sister. "You'll share my room and I'll cover the workshop fee. It's in a place called Verglas lodge, out in the middle of nowhere: birds, cows, trees, probably. Come on, it'll be fun."

Initially Hekla resisted. She didn't have a believing bone in her body. But when her sister continued to pester her, she began to think *Why not?* It would be a vacation, a chance to get out of the city. The workshop would do nothing for her—none of the events her sister convinced her to attend ever did—but she'd tune it out, just as she always did, and enjoy spending time with her sister.

❋

When the day came and she arrived at her sister's place with her bag, she found her hunched over the toilet, vomiting. *I can't go,* her sister said between bouts. *Too sick. Something I ate.*

"We'll skip it then," said Hekla. "Or go late."

Her sister groaned. "We can't go late. It isn't done. But you go."

"I'd rather skip. I was only going for you."

"It's non-refundable," said her exhausted sister. "Take my car. I need you to go so I won't feel like I lost all my money."

Hekla, as much to avoid seeing her sister vomit again as anything else, reluctantly assented.

She arrived at Verglas lodge quite late, hours after the other participants. She had no excuse. Her sister's car had not broken down, nor had she been unavoidably detained. It was simply that, outside the confines of the city for the first time in a decade, she had allowed herself to meander. She had stopped in a gravel pull-out beside a river and watched the eddy and flow of the water below, finally picking her way down the slope. She waded in up to her knees, and then, instead of climbing back straightaway, wandered along the bank. Only once she saw the sun setting did she realize how much time she had lost and how far she still had to go.

She arrived at an hour that, in the city, would have been considered merely uncomfortably late, still within the range of acceptability. Apparently, country etiquette was different. The chest-high gate at the bottom of the property was chained closed.

She parked the car on the road's shoulder, heaved her bag over the gate, then clambered over as well. The gravel of the drive was coarse enough that her bag's wheels wouldn't turn. She was forced to carry it.

She followed the road up through the trees until it opened into a weedy parking area, Verglas lodge looming above it. Tired from lugging the bag, she set it down and stretched, taking a moment to catch her breath. Above, the lights of Verglas lodge, both inside and out, had been extinguished.

She picked up her bag and crossed the lot. There was a set of steps cut in the hill at the far end of the lot, hard to make out until she drew close. She climbed them and followed a stone path at the top until she reached the lodge's porch.

The door was massive, stained dark. It had a scene carved on it: she could see a fleeing creature, perhaps a stylized deer, surrounded by a profusion of curves. Flames, maybe?

She looked for a doorbell but saw none. She rapped on the head of the deer, if it was in fact a deer, but nobody came to the door.

Leaving her bag on the porch, she followed the wrap-around porch to the back. There were no lights on there either, and the only door she found, a battered metal one out of character with the rest of the lodge, proved firmly locked.

She returned to the front door and rapped again. "Hello?" she called, then listened. Still no answer.

She tried to call her sister for advice on what to do, but her phone had no signal. She spent some minutes knocking before she thought to try the handle. It was unlocked.

Had it always been unlocked? Perhaps she had simply foolishly forgotten to try the door when she first arrived, had begun by knocking. After all, the gate had been chained closed, the lights off: was there any reason to think the lodge door would be open? True, she was a meticulous person, the kind of person who almost certainly would have thought to check the door when she first arrived. But she found it preferable to think she had forgotten to check it than that someone had unlocked it while she was behind the lodge, and yet hadn't turned on any lights.

She pushed her way in, then stood just inside the doorframe, waiting for her eyes to adjust. She could smell something sharp and also the smell of pine—a cleaning product perhaps. She let her hand run along the wall just beside the doorway until it found the blunt stubs of light switches. She flicked up one then the other, but nothing happened.

For a moment she had the distinct impression that she was somewhere other than she was meant to be. That she had taken a wrong turn and was now entering a long-deserted place. Surrounded by darkness, it took her some effort to stop from backing out the door. She closed her eyes and held still, trying to master herself.

✻

After a while she calmed down again. She was not certain how long she had held still. Probably just a minute or two, though it felt much longer. Perhaps it had been.

There are cars in the lot, she told herself, *this must be the right place.* Probably it was just a matter of a broken switch, or perhaps these switches were turning on lights elsewhere, where she couldn't see. Perhaps the power was out, or perhaps the lodge wasn't connected to the grid, was running off a generator that had been shut down for the night. *There are many plausible explanations,* she told herself, *and very little to worry about.*

"Hello?" she called. Her voice vanished into the darkness.

She got out her phone, turned its flashlight on. In the light, it became an ordinary entrance hall: bare wood floors, gleaming where the light struck them; wood-paneled walls; a ponderous hanging light fixture made of a metal painted dull black; the head of a deer, turned slightly, as if surprised. To her left was a reception counter, a bell on it, a rack of hooks on the wall behind.

She approached the counter and rang the bell, waited. After a while, she rang it a second time. She looked for a door, a room the clerk might be sleeping in, but there was nothing, only the rack of hooks, a number burnt into the wood below each one. None of the hooks held anything, save for one at the very bottom, from which a key hung. Number nine.

It was obvious, then. They had left the door unlocked for her and here was the key to her room. It had to be hers: there was only one key.

She went around behind the counter and took the key. Number nine. Carrying her bag so as to make less noise, she made her way down a nearby hallway and deeper into the lodge.

✳

She guided herself using the flashlight on her phone, shining it on each door in turn. As with the hook board, the number of each room had been burned directly into the wood, somewhat crudely. The odd numbers were on the left and the even numbers were on the right, until she reached room number five, where, suddenly, the sides reversed. The numbering ended at room eight. At the very end of the hall was a final, narrower door without a number on it. A supply closet, perhaps.

She backtracked and looked for other hallways leading off the entrance hall. There was one other. It led her to a dining room, where she saw a table laid for breakfast. She found a meeting room, a kitchen, and a storeroom farther down the hallway, but no door marked with a nine.

Puzzled, she returned to the entrance hall. Was there an upstairs? Didn't seem to be: no stairway that she could see. When she turned her phone-light upward, she saw only exposed beams and the slant of the roof.

She could sleep in her car, but that was hardly safe— anyone could come along. Maybe there was a separate cabin somewhere on the property with a nine on its door?

But instead of going outside to see, she returned to the first hallway, counting her way past each room in numerical order. She stared at the unnumbered door at the hall's extreme, then reached out and grasped the knob.

It turned.

She pulled the door open. Beyond was a cramped passageway, walls and floor and ceiling all encased in cedar. She had the vague impression of stepping into a defunct sauna. She moved down the passageway and there, at the end, there it was: a door with a shaky nine burned into it at the level of her forehead.

✳

She dropped her bag beside the bed and tried the light switch. It made a clicking sound, but no lights came on. She set her phone on the dresser with the light shining up at the ceiling. It didn't light the room well, but it was enough.

The bed was unmade, the sheets and blankets folded in a pile on top of it, as if the maid had forgotten to make it. And the bed was a twin—it wouldn't have been big enough for both her and her sister. She made it quickly and sloppily, all the while thinking, absurdly, *You've made your bed, now lie in it.*

There was no bathroom, only a half-wall near the back wall of the room, behind which was a commode. A mirror hung beside it, though it had been turned to face the wall. She turned it around and found it foxed, almost useless. In it, her face seemed covered with flowers of mold. She hesitated, momentarily transfixed, then shook her head and turned the mirror back to face the wall again.

Her phone was almost dead. There seemed no place to plug it in, no outlet. She sighed, then quickly undressed, climbed into bed and turned out the light.

It was very dark—so dark that when she waved her fingers in front of her face she saw nothing at all. She lay in bed, staring up into the darkness. Soon she began to see little vague flashes of light, her eyes misfiring as they attempted to see. Closing her eyes, she turned on her side and tried to sleep.

＊

She dreamt she was in another place, all plastic and steel, far in the future or perhaps simply elsewhere, another world. She was the one in charge, or not quite, not exactly. She was missing her leg and the prosthetic she wore was a living thing, a strange creature that knew how to look just like an artificial leg. Nobody except her knew it was anything other than an artificial leg. Once removed, it could unfurl itself and become more or less human. Less, she would have said, rather than more, but then one day she unstrapped the leg in preparation for sleep and it unfurled and took its customary place beside her bed, conversing with her in its soft, soothing voice as she slowly drifted off to sleep, the voice humming gently in the background. What was this creature? How had it come to be beholden to her? How had it come to take the place of her leg? In the dream she did not know the answer to these questions, but found herself wondering as she slowly drifted off, falling asleep within the dream.

But then the creature's gentle humming changed in pitch and register and became strangely familiar. She was abruptly awake again, listening, her eyes still closed. She looked through the slits of her eyelids and saw that the creature beside the bed was staring intently at her, eyes gleaming. As she watched, its face shifted, then shifted again to suddenly begin to resemble her own face. Another shift and it looked exactly like her, and the voice it now had was exactly her own voice.

＊

She awoke in the darkness, with the distinct impression that something was in the room with her. She thought she heard a snuffling sound, felt something brush her arm. She tried to move, to reach for her phone, but she couldn't. She heard a ragged wheezing, which it took her more than a moment to realize was her own frightened breathing.

Shhh, she heard a voice say, or maybe it was the air hissing through her clenched teeth.

Suddenly it felt as if a heavy blanket had been placed on top of her. She was very afraid. The heavy blanket, if that was what it was, made it impossible for her to breathe. Slowly, painfully, she lost consciousness.

✳

She awoke gasping. She could move again. She felt around beside her in the dim light and found her phone, turned it on. Already 9 a.m. She was late for breakfast.

She opened the curtain and soon had enough light to get dressed by. Hurriedly, she brushed her hair, and, limping slightly, left the room.

The lights were on in the entrance hall, and a man with curly black hair stood behind the reception counter. He nodded to her as she hurried past, and she nodded back, moving past him and toward the other hallway.

"Miss?" he called from behind her. "Miss? Over here?"

She slowed. She'd never checked in: of course he needed to talk to her.

She returned to the counter.

"You must be Miss Rognund." He had an accent she couldn't place. Somewhere in Eastern Europe, maybe.

She nodded.

"And where is the other Miss Rognund?" he asked.

"Sick," he said. "She can't come."

"I see," he said. "No bags?" he said. "Perhaps they are in the car?"

"They're in my room," she said.

He looked mildly affronted. "But I have given you no room."

"I came late. There was only the one key. I figured it must be for me."

He frowned, held up an envelope with her name on it.

"I..." she started to say, then stopped.

"Did you not follow the procedure for late arrival that was emailed to you with your confirmation?" he asked. And then, almost as if to himself. "No, you must not have. Where, might I ask, did you spend last night?"

"In number nine."

A strange look briefly crossed his face, before being quickly mastered and hidden away. He held out a hand. "Give me the key," he said. She fumbled it out of her pocket. He took it. He started to hand over the envelope, then drew it back.

"How did you find it?" he asked.

"It was just behind the small door," she said. "Not exactly hidden."

"No," he said, "you misunderstand. How did you find your stay?"

"My stay?"

"In nine."

"I... it was fine," she said. And then added. "Any reason why it shouldn't have been?"

Instead of answering he now gave her the envelope. "Here is your key," he said. "Room five."

"But my things," she said. "They're in the other room."

"I will move your things from room number nine," he said.

"I need to repack them," she said.

He shook his head firmly. "I will move them. I will note where they are placed and will do my best to replicate their placement in the proper room, the room you should have been in all along."

"But—" she said.

"You must go. You are late for your workshop."

"But—" she said again.

"Go," he said, shooing her with the tips of his fingers. "Go now. They await."

✳

But they did not await, or at least they had not awaited for her. They were already nearly done with breakfast, the dishes on the table in disarray, the food in the chafing dishes all but gone.

There was no plate left for her: someone had taken two. It was a florid-faced man with watery eyes, wheezingly overweight, with a beard that seemed to have spread too far up his cheeks, as if threatening to consume his entire face. When he saw her take in the two dirtied plates before him, he gave a half-shrug of indifference.

She removed two cups from their saucers and then loaded the saucers with the bits and scraps she could find in the chafing dishes—overcooked hunks of scrambled eggs, limp and greasy ends of bacon, hash browns whose lattice-work had become mush, a soggy toast point. She poured a cup of tepid coffee and then juggled the two saucers and the cup over to an unoccupied corner of the table.

"And you are?" said the florid-faced man, once she was seated.

She introduced herself, apologized for being late.

"You missed yesterday evening's session as well," noted the man, apparently the workshop leader. "A critical session. You are already so far behind," he said, shaking his head. "I am not sure you will manage to catch up." And then, shrugging, he added, "But since the workshop fee is non-refundable, you might as well stay."

She felt a dull, irrational rage rising bile-like within her, but swallowed it back down. Instead she slightly inclined her head toward him.

For a long time there was silence, and then the man gave a wheeze and spoke.

"As I was saying before I was interrupted," he began, "the quality most needed is a peculiar attentiveness, an ability to tune the soul to a frequency where its vibrations fall slightly below the surface of appearances. A whole world lies beneath this world, comprised of the unheard, the unseen. With attentiveness, you shall begin to learn to hear this world, to see it."

Hekla glanced around the room. Everyone except her seemed to pay this man rapt attention. There was a woman with limp blond hair, obviously and poorly dyed; a man whose face so resembled that of a bulldog that he must own one; a woman, obviously wealthy, wrapped in the tie-dyed scarves of a seeker (Hekla's sister had an array of similar scarves); and four seemingly interchangeable men wearing red ties and white shirts.

"How does one do so?" the leader asked. "How does one go from seeing merely the surface of things to seeing what lies beneath? It is a long and arduous process, full of missteps. In a workshop like this one, we can only accomplish so much, but still perhaps we can lead you there quicker than you might arrive on your own..."

She stopped listening. This, she suspected, was a sign that she was on the surface of things, but how could she see this gasping fat man who had stolen her plate and her share of breakfast as a spiritual guru? Listening to her sister read to her the vague description of the workshop over the phone, as she sat in her cubicle surrounded by accountants and actuaries and with her awful middle manager lurking nearby, she had felt that the workshop was probably harmless and worth tolerating for her sister's sake, and to get a vacation. But now, sitting among the participants, it felt like the same set of people as in her office, with an even more awful middle manager.

And then, abruptly, people were standing, breaking into groups of two, leaving her on her own. She approached the leader, who had paired up with the scarved seeker.

"Mr…" she said.

"Szabo," the leader said.

"I don't have a group, Mr. Szabo," said Hekla.

The leader sighed. "Just Szabo will do. You'll have to join one of the other groups. One group will have to have three."

"All right," said Helka, and sat down next to the leader.

"One of the *other* groups," said Szabo. "Not ours." He pointed to the two suited men closest to them, who looked startled to be singled out. "That one."

She pulled up a chair beside the two men, who involuntarily drew closer together, as if slightly afraid of her. Eventually they gave her a partial explanation of what they were meant to be doing. *Tuning*, one of them described it as. It involved, so she gathered, exchanging a series of maxims and then, interrogating them and thereby puncturing the surface of the world and catching a glimpse of the other world hidden beneath. What was meant by *interrogating* was initially unclear, and remained so. She sighed. It was, she supposed, one way of passing the morning.

※

By lunch the group had grudgingly accepted her, or at very least the leader had. Though he had claimed his name was Szabo, she suspected he had been christened something like Rupert or Stephen. By *accepted* she meant that he did not steal her lunch plate, though the way he glumly stared at his now empty plate suggested that he probably would if she left the room. Licking his lips, he delivered a lecture, the same sort of meandering obscurantist mysticism as at breakfast. She secretly checked her phone under the table, hoping to text her sister, but she still had no signal.

Attunement, he told them was, in a matter of speaking *At-one-ment*, the state of being at one with the world. *Wouldn't that be atonement?* wondered Hekla. It was a question, Szabo told them, of seeping through the world's surface to permeate its entire being. And then, perhaps because it was clear that she, Hekla, was the one paying the least attention, he turned to face her and looked at her in a different way than before. For the first time, he fixed her in the spotlight of his attention, his *attunement*, and she began to glimpse what it might be that the others found so intriguing about him.

"Hekla," he said. "Curious name. It means 'cloak,' does it not?" And before she could bring herself to respond, "What is it you are cloaking, cloak? What do you hide?" And then his gaze left her and he turned away and her skepticism was free to rise again.

✳

After lunch, Szabo said, "For the afternoon we shall do something different." He stood. "Have you wondered why I hold this workshop here and no place else?" he asked.

He moved toward the door and went out.

For a moment they all sat there, and then with a great scraping of chair legs the four interchangeable men stood and rushed after him. The two other women were close behind, then the man who resembled a bulldog, and finally Hekla. *Does my name really mean cloak?* she wondered. If so, why had her parents named her that? And more importantly, why hadn't her sister, who scrutinized the names of everyone around her searching for meaning, informed her?

She turned it over in her head, half-distracted as she followed the others into the entrance hall. She was still considering her name, what it said about her, when Szabo turned down the other hall. But she stopped thinking about it entirely as soon as she realized where he was going.

He halted at the narrow door at the end of the hall. "When they were modernizing Verglas lodge," Szabo said, "there was one room they left just as it was. Behind this door lies a fragment of the lodge that used to be."

Hekla felt her arms grow suddenly heavy.

"Is it haunted?" asked the bulldog.

"Haunted?" said Szabo. "What does haunted mean? Shall we say rather that this is a special place, a passage back in time?" He turned the handle and entered the narrow passageway behind it, the others filing after him until the narrow space was too full to contain anyone else. Hekla was tempted to turn on her heel and leave, but when Szabo opened the door marked with a nine and entered, and the others trickled in after him, she found herself powerless to do anything but follow.

✳

"What do you see?" asked Szabo, his voice hushed. "What do you feel?" He paused, his gaze sweeping slowly around the circle. "Breathe in the air. It is the air of the past. Be attuned. Something happened in this room that made them leave it as it was when the rest of the house was remodeled. What happened here?"

"Someone killed himself!" said the woman with limp hair excitedly.

"A ceremony took place," said one of the identical men. "A dark one."

A flicker of irritation passed over Szabo's face. "No," he said. He slapped his hands together sharply. "No! Do not guess! Feel!"

The people around Hekla closed their eyes, breathed in deeply. Hekla kept her eyes wide open.

"Reach," Szabo was saying, sonorously. His eyes, she

noticed, were not closed either. He was staring at her, curious. Her effort to make her face reveal nothing made it feel stiff, almost dead. *Does he notice?* she wondered.

"Let the words come to you from the room itself," he said. "Then inhale them, hold them within your lungs, and let them slip through your lips."

He waited, staring at Hekla. She was not going to speak. There was no fucking way she was going to speak.

"No one?" Szabo said. "Then be attuned to me as a start. Watch and learn."

He held his face in one hand, extending the other hand before him, almost brushing the shirts of the interchangeable men.

"A woman came here," he said. "She hoped to escape her life, but she found someone waiting for her—or something, rather. Here in this room. We know from what was pieced together by doctors later that she awoke in the middle of the night, the room deeply dark around her, and felt someone there with her. Or perhaps something. She could not move, she could hardly breathe. She felt as if something heavy had been placed atop her, a great weight, so heavy that she found herself unable to get enough air. Eventually she lost consciousness.

"When she awoke, it was with a start, gasping, as if coming back to life." Szabo lifted his face from his hand. "She went about her day, a perfectly ordinary day, then packed her things and drove back home. Only later did she realize that part of her had been taken by whatever had come in the night. That part of her remained in this very room, and she had no way to get it back."

He was silent, letting his gaze wander from face to face. "Attunement," he said. "I feel the vibrations the events have left. You will too once you are properly attuned."

Perhaps I knew about this woman, thought Hekla. *Perhaps I glimpsed the story years ago in some newspaper or other and subconsciously remembered when I came to the lodge, and then I dreamed it.*

She hoped that was it. She told herself that it was, but didn't completely believe it.

And then a spasm flickered across Szabo's face, as if he were in pain.

"Something else," he said. "Something..." Abruptly he fell silent. His eyes moved frantically, his gaze refusing to settle anywhere. A spasm rippled over his face again.

A good performance, thought Hekla. *An impressive—*

"Strange," Szabo said, and his voice was different now, less theatrical. "My attunement seems to have shifted to a deeper level. I am being told that the woman in question was missing her leg, though I know for a fact that she was *not* missing a leg. And, even stranger, they tell me the prosthetic she wore looked just like an artificial leg but was also something else. Or, rather, *someone* else. What can this mean? Perhaps this is a metaphor for something real, the room telling us what it can tell us with the language it has at its disposal? It is up to us to properly interpret what it means to say...

"And now I see this 'leg'... unfurling? Yes, unfurling, and becoming a being of glass and steel. It stands beside her bed staring down at her. Slowly it takes on her form and her appearance—catch her!"

But nobody was quick enough to stop Hekla's fall before she struck the floor.

※

She woke up lying on the bed. For a moment she panicked, thinking she was still in nine. But no, it was a different room, the furnishings upgraded, with an actual bathroom instead of a commode behind an odd half-wall. Number five, her new room. A glass of water stood on the bedside table in a puddle of condensation. The clerk from reception was stationed a few steps back from the bed, his hands clasped in front of him, like a funeral director. The door of the room had been left ajar.

"Here you are, then," said the clerk. "Back among us."

"What happened?" she asked.

"According to Szabo, you fainted. I took charge of you so the workshop could proceed."

"Thank you," she said. She tried to sit up, found herself dizzy. He moved forward and pushed her shoulders gently back down.

"Perhaps you shouldn't go back to the workshop," he said. "At least not until they are finished with what they are doing in that room."

"Why?"

But the clerk did not respond.

"I don't want to go back," she told him. "I want to leave."

"Leave?" the clerk said. He shook his head. "It is a little late for that."

✳

After a while the clerk left and she was alone. She tried to stand but the dizziness was still strong and one of her legs refused to support her. She fell onto the floor, had to claw her way panting back up onto the bed. She could not leave, not yet. But she would stay here and rest until she could.

She closed her eyes. Even though it was still early afternoon, she soon fell asleep.

✳

Her dreams, the few she had, were at first vague and indistinct, as if being glimpsed from too great a distance. They seemed vaguely familiar and not at the same time: more as if someone was telling her about their dream than that she was experiencing a dream herself. There were bits and pieces of the hotel in it—a version of the clerk with a different accent, the stag's head now topped with a profusion of antlers instead of the two it had, a much longer and more meandering gravel path leading up to the lodge—but all as if seen through a dirty pane of glass.

And then, suddenly, it all came into focus. She imagined herself walking down the hall, a hitch in her step. She came to the door with the number five burned on it, tried the knob, found it unlocked. She opened it and looked inside.

The room was empty. She stayed, hesitating for a long moment, then went out and continued down the hall.

She walked past room six, then seven, then eight, then opened the door at the very end of the hall, then the door beyond that, the one with a nine burned at the level of her forehead.

Inside, lying on the bed, was a woman who looked exactly like her. She approached slowly, careful not to wake her. She bent over the bed and stared down, but no matter how closely she scrutinized the woman she was unable to say which one of them was the real her.

✳

When she awoke, she was in a different place. Someone was shaking her. It took her more time than it should have to realize that that someone was Szabo, and that he was sitting beside the bed, staring at her.

"What are you doing here?" she asked. Szabo ignored this. "Where am I?" she asked, and when Szabo ignored this as well, she suddenly knew she was in number nine.

But how had she gotten here? Had he carried her? Had she, asleep, wandered back here herself? Why would she ever want to come back here?

"I knew you would come," said Szabo. "I suspected when you fainted, and so I kept vigil and now I know for certain. I hardly dared hope for this. I sat and watched the bed and for a long, long while there was nothing, and then I watched you slowly come into existence here. I have been waiting for you, for someone like you, for years!"

"What are you talking about?" she asked.

"Don't you see?" he said. "You have been chosen. You are attuned, not just your mind but your body too. You belong to this room. You belong to *her.*" He groped for her hand, squeezed it too hard. "Together we will accomplish so much!"

✳

She fled. Szabo hurried after her, at first pleading and then, when it became clear that she wasn't going to stop, yelling and threatening. He grabbed her by the arm and she shook him off. When he grabbed her again she shoved him, got him sufficiently off balance that she could yank her arm free.

She rushed to her room—five not nine—and managed to unlock the door, step inside, and shut it again before Szabo could get his foot in.

"Hekla!" he yelled, pounding on the door. "You owe me this! You owe this to everybody!"

She shuddered. Rapidly she thrust her things into her bag and zipped it shut. Szabo was still pounding on the door, desperate now, back to pleading again.

She came close to the door, wondering what to do. Beneath her feet, the floorboards creaked. Szabo stopped shouting, stood silent instead, listening. Hekla listened back.

"Hekla, are you there?" he finally said.

"I'm here," she said.

"Come out, Hekla," he said. "I want to make you famous."

She didn't say anything.

"I will make it worth your while," he said through the

door. "I'll pay. Just to be around you. Later, once you understand, we'll be partners."

"Okay," said Hekla.

"Okay?" he said, surprised, and she realized she should
have resisted more before giving in. "Then open the door."

"I'm going to take a shower," said Hekla. "I need to
gather my thoughts. I'll be out in a minute."

He was saying something else through the door, but she
paid no attention. She moved into the bathroom, turned on
the faucet, switched it over to the shower. As steam began
to fill the bathroom, she walked to the far side of the room,
opened the window, dropped her bag out, and clambered
out after it.

The car was where she had left it, though the gate was open
now and there was a note under the windshield wiper
written on lodge stationery asking her kindly to move it into
the lot. She opened the trunk and placed her bag inside. She
had just unlocked the front door and was climbing in when
she heard a shout and saw Szabo rushing down the drive,
his cheeks puffing desperately for air, his entourage scurrying all around him. Quickly she started the car, drove.

She didn't stop at all on the way back to the city.
The whole trip she kept glancing in the rearview mirror,
expecting Szabo's car. But she didn't know what sort of car
he drove; how would she possibly recognize him?

She arrived only quite late. It was too late to go to her
sister's house and return her car, so instead she drove back
to her apartment. In any case, her sister didn't expect to see
her until the next day. She was exhausted. She left the bag in
the trunk; she could get it out in the morning. She climbed
the four flights of stairs, opened the door to her apartment,
stepped inside, and fell onto the bed. Almost immediately
she was asleep.

Did she dream? Yes, she dreamed. At first it seemed vague and indistinct, but in the dream she warned herself that she should not be fooled by this. And indeed, when everything sprang into focus and she saw herself walking through the paneled entrance hall and past the stag's head, whose antlers now were so vast and ramified they spread like a tree up the wall and into the rafters, she was braced for what she knew would happen next. There she was, walking down a hall that seemed longer than the hall should be, stopping to open a door, looking into the empty room behind it, continuing down the hall to its very end, then past that end and into a room marked with a blackened number nine, and to the side of a bed in which she saw, sleeping, unaware, herself.

When she awoke, she knew something was wrong. She could not hear the noises of the city she usually heard and the light through her eyelids was too dim. She could hear, if she listened closely, the distant sound of a man's voice, excited, triumphant. She felt something brush her arm. Or no, that wasn't quite right: it brushed *through* her arm, leaving it tingling.

Hekla, she heard him say, barely a whisper. *Focus. We begin to glimpse you. You are nearly here.*

She stayed, eyelids clenched close, willing the noises of the city to rise up around her. They wouldn't come. *Don't open your eyes*, she told herself. *Don't open your eyes.*

But, eventually, she did.

Too Lonely, Too Wild

Kay Chronister

> "And once she went to break a bough
>   Of black alder.
> She strayed so far she scarcely heard
>   When he called her—
> And didn't answer—didn't speak—
>   Or return."
> Robert Frost, *'The Hill Wife'*

FOR A WHILE, you could go anywhere and find them. Old Mr. Miellon's movie-star-beautiful wife in her blue plastic halo of curlers, scrubbing her cheeks with lye in the morning and milk at night. Annabelle Leahy flying down the dirt road to meet her steady after school, throat hoarse and knees scraped-up from hurrying. The new Mrs. Donahue, a traveling salesman's city-born daughter, hammering down fence posts and wading through chicken shit.

Grammy would yank me along before I could see much, muttering, "Protect her, Lord, from their coins and their nails." I thought those women must be demons; I didn't know they were in love.

At home, she'd crack open the family Bible and read wise-woman prayers over me, consecrating, building walls. "Let my granddaughter never be a wife in this goddamn town," she'd say, and I was so little that I recognized neither the cursing nor the curse in the words.

When Grammy died I was twelve. I had no mother and

no father but I did have seventeen dollars and my great-grandmother's stiff husk of a wedding dress and the family Bible, which waited ten years in a carpetbag for the day that Mr. Rishner married me.

✳

Some folks said Mr. Rishner once had a crop yield so rich that he still hid sacks of gold beneath his bed. Others said he was a water witch and he'd dowsed for his fortune in the swamp with a forked stick. You could see his house tucked into the hills all the way from town, a hard-glinting white bead inside a yellow-gray wall of wheat.

Our courtship was maybe fifteen words long. He said no more to me than he said to anyone else and I said more than enough for us both, which wasn't much at all. We both knew what we were aiming for. I wanted to climb up into the hills and disappear from the eyes of everyone who knew I didn't inherit Grammy's witching power. And he wanted a wife. What did any man want?

We were as dead silent married as we'd been courting. He left for the fields before sunup. I stayed inside the white house, shucked more beans and salted more pork than we could hope to eat, and when I had done with that, scrubbed everything twice. If he still wasn't home by then, I'd go out to the porch, and smoke a cigarette and shut my eyes and listen to the longspurs sing so I could hear something besides quiet swelling in my head to noise.

After he came home, we'd sit on the stoop and watch the sky arrange and rearrange all its layers of smoke-colored fleece while birds fussed in the dying trees. In November, when the dark came before dinner did, the last longspur flew away, and something collapsed inside me.

"Wish they wouldn't go," I said, and that was the closest I'd gotten to wanting or not wanting anything since the ring went on my finger. "Too quiet up here."

"They don't miss you," he said. "Waste of time, missing them."

I nodded.

"You'd feel better with a baby," he said.

We'd been trying for months already by then. I chewed raspberry leaves and slept underneath a quilt I'd sewn out of old clothes because that's what Grammy used to say a woman should do, but nothing worked for me.

"I know," I said.

He laced his fingers across my stomach so his arms contained me. I used to think in the middle of nowhere you couldn't help but spread yourself out, but now I knew that really walls didn't have to be wood or stone, they could be arms, they could be anything that held the world out and your body in.

∗

They stared when we went to town, and I felt sick thinking what we looked like to them. Wasted witchery in my blood and muddy water in his. We both needed to account for something. He didn't see their eyes or didn't care. At the post office, he shuffled a stack of letters into my lap, then lifted a dappled coon hound into the truck bed and told me its name was Baby.

I couldn't figure out if the dog was a cruelty or a kindness, so I said thank you and kept my stinging eyes on the back of his envelopes. I didn't recognize the names or cities on the return addresses. No one here was accustomed to getting much mail from outside town.

He'd gotten the feed store to order a dress for me from a catalog, gliding silk colored like blood. I was a fountain inside it. I slipped it down over my underwear in the supply room and stepped out to show him. He smiled without showing his teeth, said, "You have to wear it for me," and I heard myself say, "Of course." When I pulled the dress back over my head, I found a broken old Confederate coin sewn into the neckline, stitched so tight I couldn't yank it loose.

"You have to wear it for me," he said again, as we drove home through the nodding foothills darkness. "Make it your every day."

"I can't wash it," I said.

"I don't mind," he said.

When we came home, the white house felt so small inside the hills that I hated to close myself up inside. We'd been gone so many hours; I had the notion some other woman took up living there while I was away. I was trespassing on her property, resting my hand on her husband's knee. She was what I was inside the walls, and if I opened the door she would be there waiting to become me. She pulled aside the curtain in the front window and I saw her: big scared eyes, thin hair yanked back from her forehead, everyday calico drab and heavy.

I knew already that he couldn't see the woman. Mr. Rishner had only one wife.

"I don't wanna go in."

He nodded his head. I had a feeling like he didn't either. He put the key in the lock and turned it fast, getting the worst over with. Then he nudged the door open with the side of his boot. The house shuddered and creaked as the wind passed through. "Sometimes the crows break in," he said. "We'll send Baby."

"No," I said. "Let him stay." I had pictures in my head that I didn't like of what might happen to the hound if he went inside alone.

He shrugged. "Dog's gotta earn his feed sometime."

"He doesn't," I said.

The three of us sat on the stoop for a while, Baby's head resting on his foot.

"I want to see your dress," he said.

"You wanna see it now?" With the door open, I didn't say, when *she* could see? I couldn't see her face in the window anymore. Inside the house was dead dark. We were wasting warmth, holding the door open in the middle of December, but neither of us was going to say so to the other. She was still there; how could we shut the door until she went?

I dropped my coat first, then my shoes, then the rest into a pile in the snow. He held the dress up against me like he was measuring the size, then I bent my neck and he slipped it over my head. When the coin brushed my back, I shivered.

"Let's go inside," he said, so we did.

For a couple years after Grammy died, I saw more of them: the wives who shouldn't have stayed, but did. One was Miss Angie, who received me in Grammy's will at least partwise because she was the only other granny witch in town. Unlike Grammy, she had a husband who she had to hide everything from, making like all her patients were friends come to quilt or bake. She said he wouldn't approve of what she did, but she wouldn't say why. For the years I lived under her roof, she did nothing but ask me to show her our family Bible.

"I think there's something your grammy wanted me to see," Miss Angie would say, and I'd say maybe so, but I never let her see the Bible, because that book wasn't supposed to leave our household even if that household was only made up of me.

Still she held me back from school, sat me down at her table while she mended sickness like I was a special charm that helped the healing. I watched what she did, when the TV wasn't on something good. Folks came for snakebites and nightmares and something called female troubles but most often they came to get a love potion. Miss Angie sold glass vials with ash and ox-blood inside and no one ever came back complaining, but when we were alone she told me that no bottle of dirt ever made anyone fall in love.

"Do you know how to really do it?" I said once, doubtless thinking on my prospects at some junior high school dance.

"I wouldn't do it if I could," she said, looking insulted. "I wouldn't wish that curse on anybody, and I hope you wouldn't neither."

I was fourteen and had no notion of why anybody wouldn't want to fall in love, except I knew Mrs. Miellon was getting so thin and so pale she looked like death with a smile on, and Annabelle Leahy never could come and cheer at football games anymore, and everyone whispered about Mrs. Donahue having some sort of nervous breakdown at the feed store, screaming that she wanted to go home and she did *not* mean to Mr. Donahue's house.

"Your grammy," Miss Angie said, "she knew a way to undo it."

I had stubborn, unreasonable feelings about that Bible, and all Miss Angie's asking only made those feelings stronger. I didn't care what she was looking for and I didn't care what Grammy's witchery could have done for her, because thinking on the things Grammy had done just reminded me of all I couldn't do. "Sorry," I'd say, sure and even, like I didn't know the word was crushing her slowly. "I don't think so."

Around the time I turned fifteen, Miss Angie lost patience with me and said I shouldn't come home anymore if I wasn't going to help her out. I remember she was bruise-faced that day, and I felt sorry and I felt furious but mostly I felt a confused sort of uncomfortable, like I didn't want to see so much of her. I got to feeling glad that Grammy had hid me from so much, and missing the days when anyone thought about what I should or shouldn't see.

✳

The baby sat inside of me for three months, and then died. I didn't tell Mr. Rishner, but I told the other woman some-times, catching her eye in the ice-covered pond or the dirty window to whisper what I couldn't say at the dinner table. She had such mean eyes, and she never felt sorry for me, but she soaked up my words without argument. When he shut the front door and went off with Baby at his heels, she stayed to scrape clean the breakfast plates and mop the floor, her movements tracing mine until we didn't know the ends of each other.

When we got dressed, she fought me tooth and limb to wear the dingy calico. Sometimes I won and we wore the red silk; sometimes I didn't. Fact is, there wasn't room for both of us to get what we wanted. There was hardly room for one. The white house was shrinking, squeezing tight until I was pulp and dead broken seeds. I felt my head bumping the ceiling sometimes, my feet pushing through the floorboards into the foundation. The hallway was a crawlspace; the bedroom was a snake hole. Deep in the folds of my quilt, I wished to hibernate the winter through. I scarcely slept at all.

There was a dream that came whenever my eyes shut too long: her dream, not mine, but I dreamt it still because we shared everything. The bedroom walls were tree trunks, the sheets were wet black earth, my body was a thorn bush. Mr. Rishner would roll across the bed so he was far from me and then a cold damp arm would curl round my neck. If I turned my head I found the window open, a tree reaching inside with its trunk hunched over to wrap needle-covered branches around my shoulders, my waist, my thighs. Shame woke me quicker than fear and kept me awake, still and too hot beneath the covers, until she ran from me laughing and I dropped back into the dream again.

I covered the window with curtains, then a couple of two-by-fours when the curtains started showing up in the dream. Mr. Rishner came home with the dog, traced the boards with his fingertips admiringly, said, "Nothing gets in or out here, does it?" I thought I believed him.

I found a sprig of alder under my pillow one night and snuck out after he fell asleep to bury it beneath the porch. The night after, I found a whole branch dropping needles in the bedsheets. I said to myself: you can let your head get crowded and you can let your house cramp up, but you can't lose control of your marriage bed. So I dug Grammy's carpetbag out of the closet and set the family Bible on the table. Dust flumed out, cigarette smoke, years-old kitchen smells. Grammy wrote the rules of her world in tiny tight-packed cursive across the title pages of the Biblical books. Exodus said that *if you break a coin and sew one half into your beloved's clothes, they will have to love you back.* Ezekiel said *to kill a witch, carve a heart in a tree and hammer a nail in a little further each day for a week.*

✳

She fought me when I put on my boots and opened the front door. We both knew the black alder leaning sideways into the bedroom window. For six days I carved her heart in the bark and hammered my nail inside, then went to the outhouse and emptied my guts. The sicker I got, the less I saw of her and the happier Mr. Rishner was with me. He came home at night whistling, kissed my cheek when I met him at the door. He'd open a Farmer's Almanac on the table and tell me how the stars aligned, and I'd simmer a pot of something I couldn't keep down.

He said one night, "You expecting again?"

And I said, "I think so," because I was, though not a child.

After dinner we shared a cigarette and a bottle of gin and the sharp March air, and I thought I felt her go; in my head I was already hammering my nail into the center of her heart, but she came back when I took off my silk and put on my cotton nightdress. In her dreams, the tree came through the window to pull me out of the bed and out of the house and out of the hills. And I was scared, but I was light, I didn't ever stop. She ran me down the state highway on my bare feet until Hell opened up and swallowed the white-washed house inside it. I knew then you're never a witch until the day you got to be one, and when I came to, I went to the closet to cut the broken coin out of my dress.

The love spell inside the dress fought me. I was weak; I had six days of hammering in my heart. But I fought too and at last the threads gave and the coin hit the floor. I lifted my nightgown over my head and put on the silk. In a fountain of blood I cooked breakfast, in a fountain of blood I went out to cut down the alder tree. When the tree came down, I took the back of a hammer and forced that nail out until my death was a crooked piece of iron with bark stuck in its end. Then I buried the nail deep in the dirt and filled the hole back in.

Inside, Mr. Rishner scraped the dregs of his eggs from his plate, looked me over and said, "You think you're running a fever?"

"Maybe," I said.

"I need you to come out and say something over the fields," he told me. "Gotta earn your feed sometime."

We went, his fingers drumming a rhythm on the truck's steering wheel. I sat with the family Bible in my lap and sang one of Grammy's old songs. Mr. Rishner fussed with the fence line so long, he never saw me climb up into the driver's seat and get the engine running, the tail of my silk dripping blood on the gas pedal beneath me. I took the truck down into the foothills, then stranded it in a pile of thorns and walked. He could look; he'd never find me.

I figured the others might come with me. We'd make a *V* across the hill country as we flew north. Mrs. Miellon with her burns fading into scars, watching the town get smaller and smaller from the smudged window of a Greyhound.

Annabelle Leahy going out at night, cutting her hair short. Mrs. Donahue sitting in a fancy restaurant booth, telling some eager young man how she opened up the chicken coop and ran her husband's livelihood into a woods full of bobcats and lions. My Miss Angie reading tea leaves in a truck stop town under a false name.

You have to keep a leash on that kind of hopefulness. No one goes halfway bewitched. When I left town, only Miss Angie followed me out. She pulled money from a sock to pay our cab fare, then fifty miles down the road said I was a long way from even deserving Grammy's name and left me on the side of the road somewhere in hill country.

In the hills I got comfortable, tilled my own fields of roots and grasses, slept on a bed of leaves with alder branches hanging over my head. At midwinter, I bore a child so dark and damp and forested, she might not have had a drop of her daddy's blood inside her. I hear that's how witches are born; I surely hope so. My child isn't going to be the marrying kind.

Tattletale

Carly Holmes

TATTLETALE, WE SAID. Tattletail. Rattletail tattletale. We pulled her skirt up and pushed her down, sprawled her on the ground. We slapped and pinched her spine, pretending to feel the scaly thrust of tail pushing through the thick cotton of her knickers. We ran and span in a circle around the crimson blur of her screams, clapping hands and skipping over kicking legs. We leapt the reveal of bruises that trellised her thighs ochre and violet, layering dawn and dusk onto her flesh. We never tattletaled on those.

Tattletale, prattletale, nasty lying rattletail. Dirty-faced at the front of the class, arms flaking fleabag scabs, elbows grey and cracked. We followed the lurch of her eyes as they jittered left and right, fingers a squirm of snakes in her lap, grimacing at the teacher. We waited for her to find the spiders in her desk, the bubble gum on her skirt, and then we waited outside when she stayed behind to tattletale on us.

Nobody likes a tattletale, a filthy deformed girl with a tail. We tipped her over the wall and into the ditch so the spiteful sea of nettles would drag her down and drown her. When she crawled out, a splutter of lumps and bumps, a frenzied hop of hives, we used our sticks to poke her straight back in. Hungry for our dinners, we didn't stay to watch but left her flailing, sinking, not waving but drowning. Second helpings all round that night.

Don't touch the tattletale, the twitching, scratching rattletail. Her germs bob and float above her head like a speech bubble, like a balloon filled with pus. If it bursts over you she'll infect you with her bugs. We needed to clean the tattletale. For her own good. We decided to give her a bath in the pond behind the green. We tossed stones onto the thick crust of its surface and nodded as we watched them waver and sink, the weed closing above them as if they never were.

Stupid greedy tattletale, eyes piggy pink with tears but hand held out for the sweets we dangled. We pressed humbugs into her soggy palms, threaded lollies through the lank dribble of her plaits. Trailing wrappers like rainbows, she trotted in our wake, snorting breath through gobbled toffees. We led her along the lane and across the green, sprinkling the way with shiny treats. She only looked around her properly when we stopped, two in front and two behind, pressing close, but she still kept chewing, jaw flapping and clicking as she ricocheted between us.

Tattletale, we said. Stinking, slimy tattletail. That rattletail of yours needs a proper wash. We held our noses and danced around her, waving hands in front of our offended faces. We put on the yellow gloves taken from our mothers' sinks, stroking the stolen squeak of rubber up our arms and snapping the ends like nurses in a drama. Tattletale hissed and hunched, spinning loose and jerking back as we tugged the elastic of her shorts and twirled her, swung her, stripped her down. Then, naked, she crouched at our feet and began to writhe.

Look at the tattletale; that spike, that stab of rattletail. The whip of muscle in its rippled sleeve of skin birthing from her spine, arching over the cobbles of her back and then springing round. A hum, a buzz, a shriek of sound as she pivots to control it, twitching the maraca tip, thrashing it across our faces so they stream scarlet and our marigold hands rush upwards and bloom with poppies.

The tattletale all rattletail, a slither now, a weave and dance. Grin wide enough to swallow us whole, teeth sharp and curved as rusted hooks. We turn to run, a push and shove of skirts and screams, a snap of girls, ankles swept by rattle tail. And suddenly we're rabbit-still, rabbit-fascinated by the rise and wriggle, the looming slink. A huddle beneath her flickering kiss, hearts scurrying in our furry chests.

The Somnambulists

Simon Strantzas

THE LOBBY OF the Hotel Russo was large enough to lose one's self in, despite the enormous golden chandelier covered in crystal that hung at its centre. It hovered so close to the ground that Seymour felt an irresistible urge to duck his balding pale head while passing beneath it. He jotted down a reminder in his pad to ensure it complied with municipal code.

At the front desk, the young woman didn't immediately see him. He had to clear his throat before she looked up, and when she did her confused expression suggested she wasn't certain what to do. She was the only clerk there, dressed in a fine vest and pressed white shirt beneath a burgundy nylon jacket, and eventually it occurred to her to ask if she could be of any help. Seymour looked into her eyes—a pair of dilated pupils surrounded by deep flecked green—and doubted her ability to deliver.

"I'm here for your preliminary inspection," Seymour said, producing a business card with his name and occupation printed squarely upon it. Perhaps the clerk was dressed more like a bellhop, with the sort of round hat he thought only existed in movies. The clerk's eyes grew wide and shifty while her forehead convulsed.

"Do—do you have a badge?"

"No. I have a card."

The bellhop clerk continued to stare at it as small beads of sweat appeared at the edge of her eyebrows. Seymour snatched the card from her hands.

"Just get me the manager," he said, and turned away to make another entry in his notebook.

Nothing about the Hotel Russo appealed to him. It felt impermanent; transient. There had been a gas station on this street corner a few days earlier. What happened to it, and how did the Russo get built so quickly? Seymour did not remember seeing permits or builders, and yet here it was, erected so swiftly it was a blur. Something about the place made his whole body tense. Some sense of familiarity he couldn't put into words.

Across the lobby the clerk spoke with a short dark-haired man. This, presumably, was the manager. The two indiscreetly glanced Seymour's way, but he pretended not to notice. Perhaps his indifference would make him more intimidating.

The manager waved the nervous clerk away and imme-diately strode toward Seymour, hand extended before he arrived.

"There you are," he said. "I'm Goodwin. I was wondering when you'd appear."

The manager smiled and looked so familiar that Seymour was momentarily shaken. As though he were someone Seymour had forgotten from a long time ago.

"I'm here from the Ministry to ensure you're properly equipped to receive guests."

"Of course that's who you are. But this is a dream hotel. Just look around."

"Yes, it's very nice, but you cannot operate without an inspection."

"I don't think you understand—" Goodwin said, but Seymour cut him off.

"Let's not start on the wrong foot. The less you fight me, the faster this will go."

"But I wasn't—"

Seymour held up his hand.

"Take me to the guest rooms. I want to assess the

amenities."

Goodwin hesitated, about to say something, then changed his mind.

"You got it. Follow me."

Goodwin reached behind the front desk and opened a concealed small door no taller than shoulder height. Before Seymour could react, the manager crouched and passed through without a word. The clerk appeared oblivious to Goodwin's exit, as though it hadn't actually happened. A small part of Seymour doubted what he'd seen until Goodwin's voice echoed from beyond, beckoning him through. With hesitation, Seymour crouched and followed.

The two stood in a long carpeted hallway, wooden doors alternating along the length of both walls.

"Are you going to be sick?" Goodwin asked.

"Pardon?"

"You don't look so well."

Seymour looked back at the door they'd come through, and wondered if it had shrunk. How had he and Goodwin fit through? It was barely large enough for a child.

"The door—"

"I told you. This is a dream hotel. You get used to it."

"I don't understand..."

"Here," Goodwin said, opening one of the hallway doors. He was holding a giant key ring, but where had it come from? "Let's go inside and I'll try to explain."

Once past the door, the room did not look like a hotel suite. It looked more like the guest room of a house, with its bland decorations and worn furniture. Seymour had seen this layout, this mix of old and new, time and time again. Even as far back as the spare room in his parents' home. They were all the same. Through the walls he heard the murmurs of an argument he couldn't quite make out. It was no different from anything else there; whatever he tried to focus upon blurred and slid into the periphery of his senses.

"What is this? Is this a suite or some sort of joke?"

"What do you mean? These rooms are fantastic," Goodwin said. He pointed at the notepad. "Make sure you work that into your report somehow."

Seymour was not in the mood. Goodwin's effort at being good-natured slipped briefly, and he sighed.

"Sit down," Goodwin urged him. "You'll need a moment when you hear this."

"Hear what?" Seymour said, taking a seat on the edge of the small bed. The argument through the walls was nominally distracting.

"Where are we? Right now, where are we?"

"In an unusually decorated guest room at the Hotel Russo."

Goodwin looked around, then nodded.

"And how did we get into this guest room?"

Seymour glanced around, then offered: "We walked through a small door."

"But did we?"

Of course they had, Seymour thought, but when he tried to retrieve the chain of events from his memory he found he couldn't. It was gone. Despite how many times he desperately wished he could forget moments from his past, now that it had happened he found the sensation disturbing.

"What's going on?" he asked.

Goodwin stepped closer. His face was covered in tiny creases like a crumpled paper bag. His eyes, a pair of small black buttons.

"I told you. You're in a dream hotel."

"What does that mean?"

"It's..." He threw his arms wide into the air. "It's a dream hotel. That's what it means."

Seymour said nothing. He tried to take his notebook out of his pocket, but his hands were shaking. The Ministry would not approve of this.

"Look, it's very simple," Goodwin said, walking to the tall window near the bed. He ran his hand slowly down its pane. "This hotel wasn't built with bricks. It was built with dreams."

Seymour frowned. He was confused and resented being so.

Goodwin continued.

"Okay, listen, I'm not an expert on this. I'm just a regular guy who lucked into doing a job he loves. But here's what I heard from someone at corporate but don't ask me who because I can't tell you. She said this hotel actually started with a guy named Russo. We are inside his dream."

Seymour coughed. It was his body's unconscious reaction—an overwhelming mixture of incredulity and inevitability.

"Some guy named Russo?"

"Yes. At first, at least. There are about a dozen Somnambulists now. With just Russo the hotel persisted for only a few days at a time. I think he had part of the lobby in place. It was nice, pretty ornate, but so small and so short-lived that nobody could do anything with it. He treated it like a curse, which I guess it was. He never spoke about it, at least. But nevertheless that lobby would materialize at Front and Simcoe whenever he dreamed, and eventually people started going inside and looking around."

Seymour made a note, but the words appeared as gibberish. He rubbed his eyes but it failed to help.

"Then this Russo guy meets Dressler. I'm sure you know Dressler. Big hotel magnate. He probably owns most of the hotels you've inspected. I have no idea how their paths cross—they shouldn't have; they're from two different worlds—but they do and someone mentions Russo's lobby and Dressler decides he needs to see it for himself. So he takes his men and visits Front and Simcoe and finds the gas station there. Figures he's been made a fool. Then, pop, there's a half-lobby. Dressler gets one look at it and dollar signs light up his eyes. His guys round Russo up, bring him to a meeting, and Dressler asks how he can get into the Russo business. Deals are made, hands are shaken, and Russo gives everything up to sleep full time.

"It does not go smoothly. They try different ways to build up the hotel and make it permanent—they feed Russo experimental drugs, they put him in a coma, they move him to different locations and different environments to evoke a reaction. It affects Russo's mind to the point he can barely speak or remember his name, and Dressler doesn't care because it makes Russo's dreams more solid and tangible. But the hotel doesn't get bigger or stay longer, not until—and you'll love this part—Dressler's personal secretary, the one who types up all his letters, sees a story online about a woman in France who dreams up kitchens. Just goes to sleep and, boom, a kitchen appears. A full-sized, restaurant-grade kitchen. The lightbulbs ping in Dressler's head. Before the week's out, his team has found eleven more people with the ability to dream up different hotel rooms and Dressler pays to have them flown here and moved in with Russo. And, wouldn't you know it, it works. Not only do these Somnambulists start dreaming the same dream, adding their pieces to the whole, but the hotel also becomes more stable, and once it is, Dressler decides it's time to recoup his investment. That's where I come in. I get hired to manage the place and make sure it turns a profit. It's pretty damn exciting."

It made no sense. The story was familiar, but felt wrong, as though the events were out of order. Seymour rubbed his bald pate confusedly.

"But who are these Somnambulists?"

"Just a dozen random people Dressler's company found."

"So then where are they?"

Goodwin took a breath, then paused and smiled. The argument from the other room continued.

"They're definitely... somewhere. I'm not really sure where," he said, his smile unsure. "Corporate doesn't tell me everything, but I'm sure they know what they're doing. The hotel has already sold out its first two months."

"And none of the guests are worried about what they're getting into?"

Goodwin looked incredulous.

"Worried? Didn't I just say we're sold out for two whole months?"

He stood up somewhat indignantly and brushed the sheen of his dark blue jacket. Seymour suspected Goodwin was less offended than he let on.

"I suppose you need to write up your report now and let the Ministry know everything is okay. Sorry you had to waste your time coming here, but as you can see nothing needs inspecting. It's a dream, and nothing breaks or wears out in a dream. There are no rats or roaches where people don't see them. Other than a touch of vertigo from time to time, there's nothing to worry about."

"My inspection isn't done, I'm afraid," Seymour said, "I still need to see the lower levels. The mechanical rooms."

Goodwin blanched as he stammered.

"The lower levels? I can take you but there's nothing down there. Wouldn't it be better if I showed you the administration offices? You can get a feel for how we're handling the incoming guests. It's a state of the art system, and it's really pretty exciting. I was just telling my wife last night—"

"Goodwin," Seymour said, snapping shut his notepad. "You'll need to take me through everything. Without a complete report, the Russo won't pass and the Ministry will shut it down immediately. Or would you rather I go through Mr. Dressler's office?"

Seymour remained quiet and waited. The gas station wasn't important yet it bothered him it was gone. He didn't like a building that sprang up from nowhere, changing the landscape of the city, and he didn't like how cavalier Dressler and Goodwin were about their guests' safety.

Goodwin was no longer smiling when he spoke.

"No need. We'll go to the mechanical level. Please follow me."

Goodwin led him down a papered hallway, a gold rococo design traced on the sky-blue walls. They passed beneath an archway made of red brick and too much plaster which Seymour avoided lingering on too long. He did not like this place. Even the floor was uneven, as though the hardwood were warped beneath the carpets. It was strange, though no more than the raised voices that continuously pursued them.

Around the corner waited an ornately trimmed set of elevator doors. Seymour watched the floor numbers flash without being able to make them out; the constant frustration of everything just of out sight beginning to wear on him.

"There's something off about this place. Things seem to be functioning on the surface, but everything feels unstable and wrong."

Goodwin shrugged.

"I'm not sure what you mean. It all looks fine to me."

"Everything is familiar, as though I've been here before."

"That's part of its charm. It's a dream hotel. No two people are going to experience it the same way."

"That makes no sense. You said people had constructed this place together."

"True, but that's all they're doing—dreaming it into existence. It's just a framework. This place is as much a part of the staff and the guests as it is of the Somnambulists. It's never the same from moment to moment, because it's specific to whoever is looking at it."

"I don't follow."

"I noticed you lingered on that archway back there?

Was it familiar to you?"

Seymour glanced back. He'd known immediately it was the archway that held the door to his childhood home. It didn't simply look the same; it *was* the same, down to the crumbling bricks and excess mortar. It was as unnerving as it was impossible.

"Somewhat familiar."

"It means nothing to me. But it's not for me; it's for you. It's like the window back in the suite—it reminds me of my son. I can't explain all the reasons it's so important because they're so personal they wouldn't make sense to you. There's a nuance that only comes from understanding the full context of every little aspect, and unless you've lived my life you couldn't possibly.

"The rest of the hotel is the same. There are no structures here; only meanings. And the Russo is *built* on meanings, on those of the other guests, on those of the Somnambulists, and Dressler believes that rather than falling asleep so people can transverse their personal meanings, they can come to the Russo and experience those meanings filtered through the heightening prism of other people. Who knows? Maybe all those different meanings will intersect and create something new, some grand overlap where we all might finally decipher one another."

"That all sounds fine," Seymour countered.

"Fine? I think it sounds exciting!"

"But if this is such a utopia, then why do I constantly hear people arguing?"

Goodwin started to reply, but was interrupted by the elevator bell and the doors parting.

They didn't reveal an elevator car; instead another room. This one a dim living room with an unfinished wooden floor and a pair of torn couches positioned near a large unwashed window. Seymour knew it immediately; he'd sat invisibly in that room listening to his parents snipe at one another many times as a child. The sight of it evoked a desperate need in Seymour to flee.

"What is it?" Goodwin asked.

"This place... this room..." He couldn't speak, couldn't find the breath. Goodwin peered inside, his brow furrowed quizzically, then looked again at Seymour and put his hand on the inspector's shoulder. Seymour stiffened, but didn't protest.

"Do you still want to go on? We need to pass through here to access the rest of the hotel, but we can always turn back."

Seymour didn't know if Goodwin was being sincere, or if it were a ruse to prevent further inspection. Experience told him it was always better to assume the latter.

"I'll be fine," he said, steeling himself. "Lead on."

Goodwin hesitated.

"I need to come clean first."

Seymour had expected this, but it came at the worst possible time. He was already having trouble holding himself together.

"I told you about Dressler's plan for the Russo. What I didn't mention was the problem with it. Well, maybe not a problem. More of a hiccup, really.

"Remember how Dressler brought in the group of Somnambulists culled from all over the world? Well, it turns out that two of them had already found each other. Don't ask me how. Maybe it was through the classifieds or online. But they did and they started talking. And, as people sometimes do, they hit it off and after a time eventually married. There have been rumors about the sort of places they were dreaming up when they were together. Some people said it was the beginnings of a modest home. Other people said it was actually the makings of a palace. A few of the crazier ones said they were dreaming up a child. No one really knows and the couple couldn't tell because neither ever saw their labors. They were asleep, after all. But that was fine, because they didn't really care about houses or children. They were in love. For a while, anyway. Eventually, things went sideways, or so the story goes. Their compatibility didn't translate to the waking world—their dreams for themselves, for their lives, never meshed—and soon the arguments and the stress became too much. The young couple called it quits.

"Unfortunately for everyone, Dressler knew none of this when he found and individually recruited them to his convoy of Somnambulists, and it wasn't discovered until after they were hooked into the system and started dreaming their pieces of the Russo. By then it was too late.

"Here's the problem: even though they haven't seen each other since before Dressler took them in, somehow each knows the other is there. Maybe it's instinct, maybe it's something else, but when they get going..." Goodwin paused. Shook his head.

"Well, I don't want to say more than I have to. Let's just go to the mechanical rooms and see how things are. I'm sure they're going to be fine. I just wanted you to be careful."

"What do you mean be careful? What's wrong down there?"

"Probably nothing. But you know how mechanical rooms are. Always a weird buzz or clang coming from someplace."

Goodwin scuttled off before Seymour could ask more questions.

The door at the other end of the room led to a dark set of stairs that Seymour and Goodwin descended. A light shone continuously from an undetected source above, throwing the steps into inky shadow in either direction. Seymour's coat grew heavy and stifling, but there was no railing for support and nowhere to rest, so he was forced to push through his discomfort.

Once they reached the ground, Seymour heard the droning buzz Goodwin had mentioned even though

Goodwin, himself, could not.

"I'm probably numb to it," he said. "I've heard it so much it doesn't even register anymore."

But for Seymour the machinery's buzz shook him from inside out, triggering a cascade of sickening ripples along his back. Yet, despite the drone, that incessant arguing remained, except the voices had become more familiar. And more enraged.

"Where are you taking me," he asked. Goodwin didn't stop or slow down.

"Don't you want to see everything?"

"Yes," he said. "But why are you suddenly willing to show me?"

"Because you asked. Because even though Dressler told me to keep any problems quiet until they're resolved there's no way I can do that. Hiding them only makes them seem worse. I'm showing you so maybe you'll understand the Russo better and what we might accomplish if you give us the chance."

They reached a large square door with a giant wheel in the middle. Goodwin turned to Seymour with an uncomfortable look on his face.

"Obviously, guests aren't allowed down here, so this part of the hotel might appear... unfinished. It's not a restful place, but between you and me it's getting better. Dressler's team sent in a variety of specialists to help the Somnambulists find a harmonious balance. I'm not sure how it all works: brain waves, I think, but I'm no scientist. All I know is things are better than they used to be. Today's the first day in a while we've had any issues. I don't know," he laughed uncomfortably. "Maybe it's because you're here."

Seymour was unamused.

"Let's get this over with," he said.

Goodwin nodded and put his hands on the wheel. With each turn, the ground twisted by a nearly imperceptible degree, forcing everything slightly askew. Seymour didn't know if it were real or a figment of the dark. When the metal door swung open, it revealed the small kitchen from Seymour's childhood. Cabinet doors were cracked and hung partially open from their broken hinges, and the stovetop was caked with hardened spill-over around each of the elements. The refrigerator, too, was browned by old finger-prints, and the floor was carved with long grooves from shifted appliances. The memory of the last time he stood there floated just beneath the surface of his psyche—him banging his teenaged fists on the countertop, demanding attention he would never get. Things in the Russo were becoming too personal.

"The machine room is just up here."

Beyond the kitchen lay a dim grey room, sparse and clinical. In its middle, arranged in a circle around a tower of black machines and blinking lights, were nine hospital beds, each occupied by a sleeper connected to an intra-venous drip and sensors. No one else was in the room but Seymour and Goodwin, and yet the intense shouting now seemed to surround them.

"These are the Somnambulists," Goodwin said, his voice raised to nearly a yell. "Dressler's team moved them here to try and stabilize the hotel."

"Stabilize it from what?"

As if on cue, a tremor rippled up Seymour's legs. He glanced down for an instant, long enough for his surround-ings to transform from his parents' kitchen into their attic. Yet the occupied beds and machinery remained.

"Things shift more the closer we are to the Somnambu-lists," Goodwin shouted. "Their individual dreams haven't had enough time to synch with one another. It's stranger down here than anywhere else."

"How can you possibly think the Ministry would allow this? What kind of hotel are you running here?"

Goodwin appeared both embarrassed and worried.

"It's—well, like I said, today's been a bad day."

Seymour looked at the beds, at each sleeping face in turn. The Somnambulists appeared untroubled, but what did that mean? He might be able to make sense of it were the disembodied screaming to stop. But it wouldn't. He felt as though he were a child again, lying on the dusty floor of that attic, trying to both hear his parents and yet stifle their sniping voices. Lying in that same musty attic the Somnambulists had occupied now. And as Seymour realized this, the screaming voices became his parents'. He shook his head to dispel the hallucination, then paused.

"Wait. Didn't you say there were twelve Somnambulists?"

"Yeah. We isolated the couple from the group until we know what to do with them. They're here and close by, but like I said they haven't integrated correctly; their dreams aren't fully synched. The seams between them, and between them and the rest, are starting to show. Thankfully, it's only happening here on the lower levels where the guests aren't allowed."

Rumbling returned to Seymour's legs, and the shouting voices so like his parents' filled him with dread. The attic was changing once more, abandoned boxes becoming door frames, dusty lamps becoming framed photographs, different forms melting into another or swapping with an inaudible pop, and after the shift he found the walls had become those from the old house's hallway, the bedroom doors all ominously closed, but warped enough that light creeped out in thin strips around the frame. He followed them down the hallway toward his parents' bedroom, the door of which appeared to be flickering rapidly out of place. If the final two Somnambulists were anywhere, they would be in there.

As he opened the door, Seymour prepared himself to find the last two Somnambulists, that young couple, in his parents' bedroom, dreaming their unique aspects of the hotel into existence, because where else would they be but there? Instead, what he found looked nothing like that bedroom, or the attic, or the kitchen, or living room. What he found looked nothing like these things because it looked like *all* things at once, all at tenuous odds with one another. Pushing and pulling with such force that the earth beneath his feet churned violently—asphalt and concrete and hardwood and porcelain ingested and regurgitated, a never-ending collision of rebirth. At the opposite end of the room flickered a dim red light from a glowing exit sign.

"What's going on in here?" he asked.

Goodwin's voice cracked.

"I tried to tell you. Those two Somnambulists are an issue we're trying to resolve. We just can't figure out how yet."

"Do you know who they are? Do you know their names?" Seymour asked, though he already suspected the answer.

"I don't even think Dressler knows their names. They're just Somnambulists, they're all the same. All except Russo. It's his dream they're all building on."

Seymour looked back into the room they'd come from.

"Which one was Russo?"

Goodwin didn't bother looking.

"I have no idea."

It was getting colder and louder and the red exit light wavered ahead. The walls transformed around Seymour like a kaleidoscope, except instead of colors they were aspects of his life he barely recognized. He pulled his thick coat closer and stepped forward. Underfoot he found a rug from his old home, except soggy and soiled, torn where uneven hardwood surged through. He cursed, and went to take another step, but Goodwin's hand gripped his arm.

"I was wrong. It's not safe."

"Goodwin, you need to help me get to those last two Somnambulists."

"Are you crazy? The dreams here aren't fully meshed.

If we go any closer we might not find our way back."

"I have to see them, Goodwin. I have to know."

"Know what?"

"I have to know who they are. If they're my parents."

"They're too young. And they never had a child. I told you that."

"Are you sure?"

He paused for a moment.

"No," he finally said. "I guess not."

Seymour had trouble returning Goodwin's stare. Everything was too wild, too disconnected, and he couldn't focus on any one point long enough to understand it. Only the flickering exit light was permanent.

"Help me," Seymour said.

So they walked into the inchoate chaos. At times their feet no longer touched anything solid, while around them the world churned and the angry voices grew clearer. With each step Seymour was increasingly convinced his parents' voices rattled across the room's impermanent structures. Bricks slipped away from bricks, mortar dust crumbled, first from one wall, then another. Volley and return, the room shrinking with each word as Seymour dashed toward the red light and into an Escheresque world of upside down stairs and sideways scaffolds in continuous flux. What was once a door became a window became a wall, and more than once Goodwin was the only thing that stopped Seymour from stepping through a collapsing passage. When Seymour's notepad slipped from his pocket it moved straight past his head and spun away as though caught by the wind. But it didn't matter; he no longer needed it.

"Do you know where we're going?" Seymour asked.

"It's just through here," Goodwin said, as if those simple directions weren't disconnected from space.

But in the structureless void Goodwin's hand remained locked on Seymour's arm. There was a tug like a fish on a line and Seymour found himself overwhelmed by a tumultuous current, and then spit out into a small bedroom lit by a corona of sunlight around drawn orange drapes. It was his parents' bedroom. But Seymour was interested only in the two bodies lying beside one another in matching hospital beds, a second tower of black machinery and blinking lights between them.

"Here they are," Goodwin said, but Seymour didn't need to be told. He could feel them. He'd always been able to feel them. Waves emanated outward, lapping against his body like ripples in the sea. He raised his hand and the waves broke against his palms, slipped between his fingers.

The two bodies were underneath thin grey blankets, chests rising and lowering slowing. They faced away from him, so Seymour saw only the tops of their heads, but the color and style of their hair looked right.

"Is this what you expected?"

Seymour didn't know what he expected. When he tried to remember last seeing his parents together, he couldn't. It was as though it had been witnessed by someone else, some other Seymour with whom he shared only the faintest memories. *That* Seymour must have understood more than this one, because faced with the two sleeping figures he had no idea what he thought would happen. Were they supposed to spring up and hug him, then each other? Were they supposed to remain asleep forever, fading at once from his memory? Was this a moment of hello or goodbye?

"I don't know," he admitted.

Goodwin nodded, put his hand on Seymour's shoulder. "Some of us in the hotel argue about the Somnambulists, about why they'd agree to spend their short lives dreaming for other people. They don't get to experience things like the rest of us, don't get to visit far off places or try new things, fall in or out of love. Sure, they could do these things in a dream, but is it really the same? I spoke to one of Dressler's men once and he told me that according to their research the Somnambulists have always been like this, even in the waking world. Their dreams so consumed them that eventually the only way they could perceive the outside world was through their dreams. Always one step removed from the immediate, from the here and now. I don't know. It doesn't sound like much of a life to me. No wonder they agreed to withdraw into the one place they felt real."

But that's not why his parents withdrew. It wasn't to feel real, because they were real. What they wanted was escape—not from the world, but from him.

His parents abandoned him. They sank into the depths of anger and spite and sneers, slowly wearing away any happiness that lingered, until it was only a memory. Until it was less than a memory. When Seymour tried, he couldn't recall it ever being different. The memories were nothing, burning flash paper floating on air, consumed instantly and utterly.

Seymour approached the beds, taking care not to touch the humming equipment, the wires and lights. He realized his parents' arguing voices, so loud before, were now gone, leaving a still emptiness for the hotel's hum to occupy. Before him were the two sleeping Somnambulists, their faces buried in their pillows. They looked strange, like discarded string puppets waiting for life to be poured into them. The unbearable sadness of seeing them so mortal overtook him; he was witnessing the ineffable transformed into flesh and blood, into the everyday. He reached out to touch his sleeping mother's cheek, to take his father's inanimate hand, and as he did so he realized neither of them had any features. Their faces were blank.

Seymour stood disoriented in a lightless room. It was the size of a shed, walled in by glass and surrounded by counters faced with candy. Pine tree air fresheners hung over his head and gave the enclosure a sickening stench that nevertheless could not disguise the gasoline fumes. He spun around but there was no trace of the hotel, no indication he'd been anywhere else. Even Goodwin was gone, leaving Seymour alone in the shuttered gas station, lit only by the head and tail lights moving along Front Street. He felt tired, as though he'd just woken from a fitful sleep; grimy slickness coated his fingers and crept into his bleary eyes. He didn't understand what happened; it made less sense the longer he thought about it.

In his pocket he found his notepad, not lost at all, and was surprised to discover it was filled with scribbles and half-formed scrawls he had no memory of writing. His phone was there, too, but he could not remember the Ministry's number.

Seymour tested the lock on the gas station door, then searched frantically for the key. He found it eventually in a small dish behind the cashier's plexiglass shield, which filled him with relief. He'd escaped whatever insanity he'd been suffering, the terrible somnambulistic dream that had led him unbelievably to a gas station on the other end of the city. Already, the dream was fading, and he was anxious to return home to the warm safety of his own bed. He slid the key into the lock, felt the tumblers click into place, and turned the bolt. The glass door's lock clapped open and swung aside.

And the dark that met him was fathomlessness and unbroken.

"What the hell?" Seymour said, then turned and found the gas station gone as well. The void stretched over everything, leaving nothing but a single red light, flickering in the distance.

"What's going on in here?" he asked.

Goodwin's voice cracked.

"I tried to tell you. Those two Somnambulists are an issue we're trying to resolve. We just can't figure out how yet."

"Do you know who they are? Do you know their names?" Seymour asked, though he already suspected the answer.

"I don't even think Dressler knows their names. They're just Somnambulists, they're all the same. All except Russo. It's his dream they're all building on."

Seymour looked back into the room they'd come from.

"Which one was Russo?"

Goodwin didn't bother looking.

"I have no idea."

But didn't he? Because Seymour had been here before, in this spot, watching the ground beneath him in constant flux, listening to the voices arguing, and he didn't see how it was possible to not know who Russo was. If he was the primary Somnambulist, the one onto whose dream all others adhered, then what sense did it make to not protect him? Why even bring him to the hotel at all, to the centre of his own dream? And how could he exist in a place he was creating? If he woke and the hotel disappeared where would he go?

"The dreamer inside the dream," Goodwin said from beneath the red light, dressed in a matching black winter coat with grey fur trim around the collar, and when Seymour looked at him, baffled, Goodwin laughed. Everything was so much colder, so much darker and drabber, that Seymour thought nothing of the snow that dusted the upturned ground and uneven bricks. Goodwin flickered in and out of sight under the unstable glow of the red exit sign. It was as though he might not even be there at all.

And then he wasn't.

Seymour stood alone in a crumbling room with a small red light in the far corner, illuminating nothing but a twin pair of hospital beds in the middle, the machinery between them inactive. Seymour made his way across the broken chunks of concrete and rock that buckled and sagged toward the beds, toward the two shapes lying there beneath a pair of thin snow-dusted blankets. Seymour's breath clouded before him but those two shapes did not stir, and he felt out of scale with the world, as though he'd diminished in their presence. Seymour could see only shadows of their hair in the red light, and when he reached forward to peel back the blankets he wondered what he would say if they woke. If he would ask them what happened, how they got there. Seymour took a corner of each blanket and drew them back to reveal the Somnambulists' faces, only those faces were blank.

He grew more confused the longer he stood next to Goodwin.

"What's going on in here," he asked.

Goodwin's voice cracked.

"I tried to tell you. Those two Somnambulists are an issue we're trying to resolve. We just can't figure out how yet."

"Do you know who they are? Do you know their names?" Seymour asked, though he already knew the answer.

"I don't even think Dressler knows their names. They're just Somnambulists, they're all the same. All except Russo. It's his dream they're all building on."

Seymour looked back through the long series of rooms they'd come from.

"Which one was Russo?"

Goodwin didn't bother looking.

"How many times do I have to tell you?"

Seymour looked at him, baffled, and Goodwin laughed from beneath the red light, dressed in a matching black winter coat with grey fur trim around the collar. Everything was so frigid that Seymour thought nothing of the inches of snow that blanketed the upturned ground and uneven bricks. Goodwin flickered in and out of sight under the unstable glow of the red exit sign. It was as though he might not even be there at all.

And then he wasn't.

Seymour stood alone in a crumbling snow-filled room

with a small red light in the far corner, faintly illuminating nothing but a single occupied bed in the middle, the machinery beside it inactive.

The air held no warmth as Seymour attempted to cross the broken ground. He'd been here before. He'd been here many times before. Over and over again, a nightmare of continuous waking, a dream inside a dream inside a dream, all leading him forward a step at a time toward some inexorable truth, some understanding that he wasn't able to grasp. That he'd never been able to grasp, not when his mother and father refused to see him, not when the Ministry sent him to investigate a hotel he could barely remember. All of it meant something, was a stone in the road leading him here, to this room, in this snow and cold that bit so hard he could no longer feel his hands. At the bottom of the hotel, buried beneath so many dreams, where nothing made sense because a dozen people could not agree on anything. Because even two people could not agree on anything, too distracted by their dreams and their dream's dreams to find that one place where they could mesh together. All they did was fight and bicker and make snide comments until Seymour felt four-foot tall. Until he shrank even further than that. And their faces became as large as moons and as red as dusk, and he shouted and stomped and cried in hopes they'd see him, that they'd listen to his frail little voice, that they'd acknowledge he was there, that he was real. Because he was. He was real. Real as anyone. Made of flesh and blood and bone. He was real and present and demanded to be seen. Demanded to be heard.

But there was no one to listen. There was only the single hospital bed. There was only the tiny red light. And it read "exit" over and over again as he stood beneath it, the only light left. And under its nascent glow he saw the bed and the twisted lump of blankets upon it. He searched for some sign of who it was hidden in the folds, dreaming and dreaming and dreaming, but there was nothing. Just the rise and fall of someone breathing. The machinery around the bed hummed and lit up, little colored lights flickering on and off and Seymour reached forward to take a corner of the blanket—to do what he had done so many, too many, times before—and slowly peeled it back to reveal the bald pale head beneath. Then pulled further until the sleeper's full face was revealed. He stared at it a long time, trying unsuccessfully to remember where he'd seen it before.

The Sound of the Sea, Too Close
James Everington

THERE WERE KIDS in the abandoned school again, Jack realised as he approached. He always knew. He paused now at the locked door, keys in his hand, then turned away. Not yet. He walked past the sun-faded sign marked *Haffield Primary* and down the side of the building. He was looking for smashed windows or other signs of forced entry, although he knew there'd be none. He rounded the corner to the rear of the school, stepped from shade into sunlight; the day already too hot despite the early hour. He heard the sound of waves; he tasted both salt and smoke in the air. He looked straight ahead rather than towards the cliffs as he hurried along the pathway to get round and out of the heat. It wasn't a big building, as schools went: there were only two classrooms, a central assembly area, a staff room, boiler room, small kitchen. All on one level, pressed down by a low flat roof like a hand pressing down on them from the sky. So Jack thought when he'd been a pupil at Haffield, decades before. There were enough kids in the village then to make it seem a real school.

Having circled the school he reached the main door again, tried not to admit to any nerves—or anger or guilt—before he unlocked it. Maybe he was wrong and the school would be empty. When he put the key in the lock he was surprised to find it was stiff to turn, and his hands flickered with a premonition of arthritis. He'd have to lubricate the lock; the school had only been abandoned a few months but already lack of use meant things were seizing up, falling into disrepair. Which hardly mattered: the building would be knocked down if the sea didn't claim it first. But for now it was still Council property, for now he was still a Council employee, and they paid him to look after the place. No one would know if he didn't, but he *was* responsible, and after all he'd barely leave the house otherwise: his silent mid-terrace house devoid of neighbours either side. And now the kids were appearing, so didn't he have to check the school each day?

"Hello?" he called as he stepped inside the small waiting area by a shuttered-up reception window. "Just me, the caretaker. Hello?"

Of course, I shouldn't think of them as 'kids', he thought. Like with Kevin—no matter the years gone, he and Mary always spoke about him like he was still a child.

He opened the inner doors into the assembly area, an empty and dim space that took his eyes seconds to adjust to. (The school had shutters on the back windows to protect against the salt in the air, and it was too much hassle to open and close them each visit so Jack left them shut.) Red plastic chairs were stacked against the far wall; most hadn't been sat on in years. An old clock made a half tick-tock sound on the wall, the second hand jerking forward then back again, frozen at the same point in time.

"Hello?" he called into the room, in case one of them was hiding there. His hearing wasn't good enough to be certain no one replied. Jack sometimes wondered if his eyes were going the same way, the things he saw.

He did a brief circuit of the room, clenching and unclenching his fists to stop them seizing up. To delay looking round the rest of the school, he fetched his step-ladder from the adjacent boiler room, and climbed up to the clock and took it from the wall, silenced it by removing its battery. The ticking sound was replaced by that of the sea—you'd not been able to hear it in this room before, Jack knew. He'd loved that sound as a kid, used it to tempt Mary to the village; to the terraced house just the right size for a family. Now, like the few others left in Haffield, he wished he could block the noise out.

He'd clenched his fists again without realising; the pain as he unfurled them was like penance. It's not my fault, he thought, didn't I try and stop things? Think what *we* gave up, to stop things! Yet still. It was best not to think about it, for all that fear and guilt were the background to all his thoughts, to his every action no matter how mundane. He sighed, and wondered if in doing so he'd covered up a noise from elsewhere in the building. There was no point in delaying further; he turned and walked towards the first classroom. They were normally drawn to one of the classrooms.

When he entered, his eyes were drawn to the back of the room, to see if the far door was already opened. If they'd already got out to the rear of the building, to the bright sunlight and salt smell, he might be too late. But the door was shut. He'd left the blinds drawn the last time he'd been here; sharp blades of light still intruded through the gaps. He couldn't see anyone present, although the room still gave the impression it might be filled with chattering kids at any moment. Posters and notices still lined the walls; toys and books were stacked neatly on the shelves as if in expectation they'd be taken down and played with again soon. There had been too much leftover stuff in the school for the staff to remove it all on that last day.

Jack moved further into the room, walked around the low tables and short chairs still laid out as if for a lesson. He noticed one chair was overturned; he was certain it hadn't been yesterday. When he tried to call out again, his voice failed him.

He stepped forward, cursed as he stumbled; he'd not noticed the tub of crayons scattered over the floor. He put his hand out to steady himself, touched a wall marred with old Blu-tac and dusty curls of tape. Only one picture remained: a child's drawing of a house, a nuclear family outside, a large sun with stick-like rays reaching down to the people, and around their feet the sea, the sea.

Jack swore again as he righted himself; any tumble now and it sent his heart racing.

"That's a naughty word," a voice said, and giggled. A figure was sitting at one of the tables near the back door, its form broken by the alternating light and shade from the blind. It was far too big for its surroundings; when it stood it did so clumsily, comically pulling its adult body from the small plastic chair. But Jack didn't laugh; he felt sick. For although the person looked full grown its movements seemed child-like, and he remembered small sticky hands pulling at him to be lifted up, the trusting grip around his neck.

It hadn't been until they'd taken Kevin away that they'd told Jack and Mary they wouldn't be getting another chance. That they'd been struck from the list. The whole of Haffield had, in fact. Mary had screamed and thumped his chest when they left. The last of the moors beyond the village had been black with smoke that year, and everyone's eyes had been tearing up all the time.

The person stepped towards him, still giggling at his 'fuck' even as it stumbled in its heeled shoes, as if unused to them. As if playing dress-up. Jack guessed the woman's age to be about thirty-five: her hair was in a tight bun, and she wore a charcoal-grey trouser suit. Around her neck hung a pass for some corporate office no doubt miles from Haffield. One ear still had a wireless earbud in, the other presumably fallen on her journey from there to here.

She stank of piss and shit.

She stared at him with eyes wide with a hectic imitation (if it *was* imitation) of child-like excitement familiar to Jack. As if staying up past their bedtime, a treat verging on misbehaviour.

The woman held something in her hand, which she

raised and rubbed on her lips, then chewed. Her teeth, her mouth, were stained bright red with a mixture of saliva and crayon.

"Look," she said, "look." Her voice pitched high so that it sounded artificial, put on. "Lipstick like Kay-Kay's." Her eyes gleamed in the slatted light, darted back and forth as if seeking approval.

In the resulting silence, they both heard the sound of waves. The woman stiffened then clapped both her hands together, the crayon falling to the floor. She turned her head with exaggerated movements left and right looking for the source of the noise, one hand absently scratching at her arse. Her lips smacked together, and more of the frothy red wax dribbled from her mouth, down her suit.

"Bockit spade!" she shouted, darting with alarming speed through the room to the storage units of toys, which she started rummaging through with great excitement. Plastic swords and toy planes and hair brushes cluttered the floor as she let each drop. Jack saw on the table she'd been sitting at an expensive leather handbag.

If he turned and walked away now, came back in a few hours, Jack knew the woman would be gone; probably some of the toys would be gone too, clutched in her hand even as she went to her death. The bag would most likely still be exactly where she'd left it.

He almost did walk away.

Instead he sighed, flexed his fingers to unstiffen them, picked up the bag and approached her. The smell got worse as he drew near, and his resolution faltered. But she was young, to his old eyes, and so trying not to grimace he gently touched her shoulder.

She looked nervous now, in that way kids had when the excitement of a new place wore off and they wondered where they were and how they'd get back. Jack made soothing nonsense sounds like he'd used to when Kevin woke from another nightmare. His arm drew her into a comforting hug—decades' old muscle memory. ("Huggles," Kevin had called them.) He tried not to grimace, tried not to cry, when the woman relaxed herself into it. Her body was hot, feverish as the planet's terrible summers, and after a few seconds he pulled away slightly, tried to free himself from her infant grip that didn't want to let go. To distract her he gave her the handbag; she made cooing, appreciative noises like she'd never seen it before.

He coaxed her up, led her with his arm round her shoulders towards the door—not the one to the outside area, but the one to the dim and silenced hall, then back towards the main school exit. She was talking to him trustingly. "When I grow up...," she said at one point, and giggled. He wondered if parents still said that to their kids—"when you grow up"—still encouraged it, let them think they definitely would.

It's not my fault, he thought again.

Outside, the sunlight was harsh and unforgiving, any clouds in the sky burnt away. The woman shrank from it; Jack turned and blinked away after-images and tears. His body ached with the effort of getting her this far, contorted as it was to guide a grown woman as if she were a child. She looked at him now, with her arid, trusting eyes and waxy smeared grin.

You could hear the sea from the front of the school, although you'd never been able to before.

Instead, he directed her towards what he still called the moors, although the last of the heather and bracken burnt away seasons ago. The landscape around the village was one of sun-baked rocks and dead soil, a few stubby, stubborn plants, skeletal trees, and a cloudless, birdless sky. The road—the only road out the village—could be seen snaking its way through the moors; while navigable, it was in a state of some disrepair.

"That way," he said gently. "You go that way."

"What that way?" she said in her little girl voice and

remembering he told her it was the beach.

"And Josie and Kay-Kay?" she asked quickly, her red-rimmed eyes so dry and caught between excitement and panic. He told her yes.

He watched her set off along the road through the moors; the next village was seven miles inland. Seven miles safer. She was still toddling in her high heels like they were too big for her, although they'd presumably fit fine that morning. Or the morning before—he never knew how long it took them to reach him. He watched her figure become smaller and smaller, both with distance and the distorting heat haze rising from the road, so that he could almost believe her the child she thought herself to be. Looking for someone's hand to hold. He was crying although he didn't know if he should be. Had he done the right thing, or should he have let her go where she wanted? Maybe they came back when he wasn't around anyway, drawn by whatever lemming-like instinct drew them here.

Were they even real? Jack thought, as he turned and walked back inside (not wanting to see the moment when she crested the hill and dropped out of sight). Oh he knew they were *physical*; the shit and the sweat and piss and blood on them proved that. Still, were they *real* real? Who were they? No one ever came looking for them, no reports ever came from the villages inland of their arrival. Nor did Jack know how they journeyed to the school or got inside. There were never any cars parked out front. He'd tried calling the police the first few times, but no patrols came out to Haffield anymore; officially it was uninhabited, a non-place. By the time someone phoned him back, the kids had already headed out back anyway.

They're *not* bloody kids, he thought to himself. Why should *they* get out of it?

His moods, in his old-age, were sometimes unpredictable, flipping with a suddenness like in his youth, and he now found himself irrationally angry. Or maybe it was his lack of anger before that was irrational. Look at what happened to his life, to this place. Just *look*. His fists clenched, but he ignored the pain.

It was then, in the dim silence of the old school he heard a sound, and realised there were more of them inside.

He made a low, stressed sound in his throat, only half-aware he was doing it. What did they *want*, these messed up people? Why come to *him*? There'd been a time he wanted kids, wanted responsibility, but that was—how long ago? He could only work it out by remembering the year Kevin came to them from the agency, and counting forward from there. Holding the nervous young boy's hand and leading him wide-eyed into the "seaside house"—he'd felt like a superhero. As if the fact he'd do anything to protect Kevin and his future gave him the powers to actually do so. That moment was the fixed point in Jack's thoughts, about which all else revolved. They'd hoped for other such moments, but it had remained unique.

When Mary died she was still bitter, her love for Jack still eroded and crumbling from his insistence they live in his childhood home close enough to hear the sea, and what followed was her reluctant agreement. He'd vowed he wouldn't die like that, trussed up and powerless in a hospital bed, given too much chance to think of the past. The past was too painful with missed chances, lost time, and the future was too awful and blighted a thing to contemplate. He wanted to live only in the present moment, even at the moment of his death. At least now he knew how it would happen.

It was only after Mary died that the kids started appearing in the school.

Now he heard, from the other classroom, the sound of someone clumsily moving around, as if unused to their size. He thought, as he always did when given warning (when they stumbled out of the hot dusty light towards him, lips gummy, eyes wide and arid, arms out wanting a hug, wanting comfort, wanting an adult to tell them the bad things were gone), of just walking away, not letting himself see them. Of walking out the school and locking it behind, confronting the blackened space of the moors; of closing his eyes, and hearing the loud calling of the sea, tasting the salt in the air.... . But he never did. Responsibility was responsibility, whether you'd asked for it or not. And so he walked, fingers flexing, joints raging, towards the sound of the kids.

There were two of them, this time. Two men, all dressed up for the fairway: slacks, pastel polo shirts, spiked golf shoes. One of them had what looked like chocolate sauce smeared over his clothes, his hands, his mouth. He wore a pink permed wig from the dressing up box; his companion wore a feathered Robin Hood hat. They were sitting on the floor, pretending to pour tea from a plastic teapot into plastic teacups, with that seriousness of purpose some kids had when playing. They were so absorbed in it Jack watched them unnoticed. He saw they were actually pouring something from the teapot; as he stepped further into the dim classroom he realised the carpet was wet, and what he took to be the sound of the sea was in fact a tap running. He walked quickly to the low enamel sink and saw it was blocked with wads of green and brown tissue paper. The water was unpleasantly warm when he reached down to remove the blockage.

"Someone else always cleans it up eh?" he said loudly to the two men, and they started with the nervous, sudden guilt of children surprised to find themselves in the wrong. The teacup and teapot fell from their oversized hands, splashed to the ground. These people, they never broke character once. It was ridiculous, Jack thought: these guys were, what, early sixties? Why did *they* get to play dress-up and pretend to be someone else, somewhere else? God, but his hands hurt as they squeezed at nothing; his head ached and his vision blurred, and he still heard the sound of water.

"C'mon, stand up!" he yelled, as if he held some authority, moral or otherwise, over the two men. Quickly they scrambled up, their tanned skin, their beer guts becoming more obvious as they did so. They were similar to Jack's age but their bodies betrayed none of the stiffness and wear his did; these men had obviously lived easy, glutinous lives, Jack thought. As if that were the decider, when in truth he'd already decided before he'd even entered the room…

"Sorry," one said in a small falsetto voice.

"'orry," the other echoed, shuffling his feet.

Jack stood clenching and unclenching his fists. He wondered how far the woman had got, crossing the bleak and soot-scarred moors, tripping over her feet.

The sound of the sea could be heard, as if it were lapping at the perimeter of the building. The two kids looked towards the sound, then back at him. Two men used to getting what they wanted, Jack thought, used to just taking without consequence to themselves.

"Want to play outside?" he said, nodding towards the back of the classroom.

"Yay!" one of them shouted, his feet squelching on the water-logged carpet as he jigged excitedly. The other joined in, the curls of his wig slipping to reveal white hair beneath; he stopped and solemnly straightened it.

"Go on then," Jack said. (You spoil him, Mary said, you just give in when he wants… but she had been smiling when she said it.) The kids looked at him cautiously, as if they might still be denied. Jack gestured towards the door at the back of the classroom, although there was really no need; the same instinct which drew the kids to the school drew them out back, if left long enough. He'd disconnected the electricity, so that the door no longer set off the alarm when opened. Not that there was anyone to hear it ringing, anymore.

It was already scorching outside, the sky clear, and Jack shuddered. One of the things, nowadays, was that you could no longer simply enjoy nice weather. Yet the two men seemed to, running onto the straw-dry yellowed grass, arms outstretched like planes, glancing at Jack from the corners of their red-rimmed eyes to see if he was still angry with them.

He gestured them forwards.

Not only did the heat feel wrong, but the outside *looked* wrong too. Jack had been at this spot thousands of times, both as an adult and child. The grass had once been green and spotted with dandelions and daisies; a large chestnut had provided shade in the summer, conkers in the autumn. Jack still saw a plastic slide, swings, a seesaw; remembered all his classmates charging to play on them at break-time. And beyond them—quite a way beyond—tall, sturdy metal railings, protecting the children from the cliff drop the other side.

Now, it was like something had eaten away half of what he remembered as true, for the edge of the cliffs was much closer, and the only inadequate protection was some fluorescent tape staked in the ground, snapped strands of it fluttering in the air, like it was marking an old crime scene.

What happened to Haffield had happened in slow-motion; they'd read reports and seen artist impressions of the inevitable for years. People had stopped being able to get mortgages or home insurance; estate agents stopped listing the properties in the village because no one could buy them. The rising sea levels meant the dwellings in the lower part of the village, down by the small harbour, were already standing in inches of water at high tide. The upper part of the village was still theoretically habitable, but families left every week. And the higher tides didn't just flood the low areas but increased the erosion at the base of the cliffs; gradually they fell away, so that the available land receded year after year...

The agency said they'd taken Kevin away for his own good. That night, Jack and Mary argued about whether they should pack up and leave, for all they couldn't sell the house. To just go. They'd both wept, hot and seething in their bed even though they'd rolled away from each other to avoid touch, their weeping as rhythmic and slowly destructive as the sounds of the sea.

The two kids were playing something different now, some chasing game too complicated for him to understand, the shapes they made running from each other too quick for his eyes to follow. In the haze from the heat, he could fancy they looked smaller, their slacks and polo shirts baggier on their bodies. He was dizzy watching them. It was too hot. The sea was too loud. His hands burned as they squeezed and slowly let go something invisible in his grip. Jack closed his eyes.

"Hide and seek!" he shouted in the darkness. "You run and hide and I'll close my eyes and count to ten."

"We shouldn't have children," he'd said to Mary, years ago when things seemed salvageable. "Not our *own*. Another mouth on a hungry planet? What's the point in living like we do…"—the cut-backs, the going-without, the growing-your-own—"…if we have kids? There's plenty of children need looking after already; there will be more soon the way things are headed. We could foster, maybe adopt." And reminded of a childhood secure and carefree, he'd told her he knew just the place to move to in order to do so. When Kevin came into their life it was like he'd been right.

The sound of the waves was so *hungry*.

When Jack opened his eyes, one of the men was gone.

The other one, the one in the pink wig, was cautiously tip-toeing towards the edge of the cliffs. He looked at Jack with those wide arid innocent eyes, and Jack surged with hatred. Why did *they* get to play innocent? They weren't fucking innocent; no one grown up was.

"Flying," the man said in a squeaky voice, making his

airplane arms, looking down the drop to the rocks and sea, then back at Jack.

"I haven't flown in thirty years," Jack said gruffly, deliberately misunderstanding. Had *this* man stopped flying, made sacrifices? He hoped not.

Hands clenched, let go.

"Wanna keep playing with him," the man said, pointing downwards. "Ona beach." Jack noticed the man's hands were clenched around something too. He walked towards the man and everything seemed to intensify: the heat, the salt-taste, the pain in his joints and chest and the noise of the waves. He took the man's hand, which was bigger than his, and gently curled open the fingers.

"Found ladybird!"

"Look a *ladybird!*" Kevin had said that first week, the first sign of excitement, of engagement with his new home. As if he'd never seen one before; maybe he hadn't, even though they'd not been endangered then. Held out his small sheltering hand with the small life inside for Jack and Mary to see. Where was he now, Jack thought, he'd be a grown up himself and...

The air was too scorched with light to follow the flight of the ladybird from the man's open palm; Jack's eyes watered to blindness and he closed them again. He heard a child-like cry of mingled excitement and disappointment, and the hand pulled away from his. He tried to hold on, then remembering, let go. There was smoke in the air, salt on his lips, the crash of the sea on the rocks and hard-packed sand below. There was the sound of someone counting to ten, and he wasn't sure if it was him.

When Jack opened his eyes there was no one to be seen at all.

He shuffled right to the edge of the drop, as he did every time. The tips of his shoes poked over the edge, and he heard the crumbling sound as small pebbles and loose earth fell away. One day it would go, he knew, and so would he. It was only fitting. Deserved.

He peered down. Was what he saw all fallen from the school, or was some of it from places equally crumbling and in the process of being eaten away? He could see plastic cars and star-ships, doll arms, a bike wheel, dead sea birds noosed in plastic, a deflated beach ball, parts of an old see-saw, torn jackets and coats swirling in the water like they still housed things alive. A bright pink princess palace, a kite, suntan lotion bottles, a feathered hat, a severed hand, a smashed face, a pink wig…

He would count to ten as if he were still playing hide and seek, and then walk away, he decided. It was Kevin's favourite game, for those few months they'd had him, and in all those years after he'd been taken from them, Jack had never been able to find any trace of him. He closed his eyes; and something gave way beneath his feet, then more. Would today be the day?

"Coming ready or not," he said.

All he could hear, now the children were gone, was the sound of the sea too close.

Hungry Ghosts

Alison Littlewood

THE OLD QUARTER of Hanoi was a chaos of noise and light and heat and dust, new sights and sounds striking me every moment. It was a puzzle I couldn't solve or begin to understand; I'd done as Mai had said, taken a left out of my hotel, followed the road to the top and turned right by the ATM, or thought I had. It had sounded simple, but the eatery she'd named wasn't here and neither was my friend.

Now I couldn't see any signs and the narrow ways all looked the same, though completely different to how they'd been during the day. Low plastic stools and coloured lights and the smell of *pho* noodles spilled from numerous bars, along with cries of 'You come.' Tiny shop fronts filled every remaining inch, their owners eyeing me as I passed. Mopeds ruled the city, parking across the pavements, edging their way down the narrow road between the evening revellers.

I checked my mobile. Mai still hadn't replied to my texts, hadn't called. Someone wheeled past me, their bicycle turned into a shop laden with conical Vietnamese hats. A farm worker followed, circular panniers yoked over her shoulders, heavy with guava. I stepped over the suds being swilled from a street food vendor, around raw chickens waiting in a bucket of water, a man stropping a carving knife against a lamp-post.

A new sound impinged on the cacophony of moped engines and music and human voices. This was wavering, discordant, strange; but somehow it was more real than anything else, more welcoming than the tinny pop blaring from the t-shirt concession behind me. All around, everyone was intent on their work or their food or their journey, on the contents of tourists' wallets, and I decided that any direction was better than none. I headed towards the sound, telling myself it might even be coming from the Green Farm, the restaurant Mai had chosen. We had worked together on a volunteer project in the south for a while, establishing an organic community garden in Ho Chi Minh City, and she knew that I'd like to sample some of the traditional culture; somewhere with music like this would be an obvious choice.

What I discovered, however, was a tent pitched by the side of a wider street. It was open at the sides and bedecked with ribbons, and held a small stage where musicians sat before unfamiliar instruments.

The seats in front of the stage were almost full and I peered in, trying to see if Mai was there. None of the faces were familiar. They nodded along to the music as if it was some tune they recognised, their eyes gleaming back the light from the stage, none of them smiling, none of them saying a word.

Before I'd known I was going to move, I stepped in front of a young couple walking in the opposite direction. I greeted them in Vietnamese then said, "Is this the Green Farm?"

The man looked surprised, perhaps even offended, and I wondered if he'd understood my words. It was the woman who replied. "Not the Green Farm," she said. "Entertainment, for anyone!"

"Anyone?"

She smiled. "Yes. Even you!"

I smiled back—feeling better at once—and they walked away. After another look around for my absent friend, and a quick check of my mobile phone, I approached the tent. As I did, someone began to sing: a high, almost otherworldly sound that rose above the pressing humidity of the street, like a breath of clearer air.

Suddenly I was tired. I would rest a moment before I tried to call Mai again. I would sit and I would listen. There were a few seats available, but they were right in the middle of the gathering, blocked by stranger's knees and skirts and bags, so I slipped into an empty row right at the front.

I knew at once I'd made a mistake. A loud hissing arose behind me, cutting across the music: the sound of disapproval in any language. Someone rapped the back of my seat, hard and loud, and I started to turn towards them just as a hand grasped my arm and I turned to see Mai.

My smile faded at the sight of her widened eyes. I had done wrong, I saw that. I'd been tricked somehow. *Entertainment, for anyone*—but not for me apparently, not here, not now. Had the woman been having a joke at my expense? I must have gate-crashed a family party, a wedding maybe, or worse, a funeral. I slipped from the seat and Mai pulled me away, not pausing to say hello.

"I'm sorry," I said. "What did I do? I thought it was for everyone."

"It is." Despite her words, she looked unhappy. "It is a—*merry-making*, for the festival. To honour the hungry ghosts. That is why it is so loud, you see? To reach the ears of the spirits."

I didn't see, not at all, and I frowned.

"The seat you took—that row is for the spirits, not for us. You took a seat that belongs to the dead."

※

Later, we laughed about it. We found the restaurant, which turned out to be wide and candle-lit with cosy wooden tables, and ate warming *bun cha* while we talked. She told me about the festival—the way that people would honour their ancestors, but also the hungry ghosts who had no family to remember them; the ones who had died bad deaths or done evil deeds, who wandered, aimless, about the streets.

When the waitress cleared the table and left us, she leaned over and whispered, "Her mother is dead."

"Do you know her?" I asked. They hadn't appeared to be friends.

She tapped her collar. "She wears a white rose. You see, everyone wears flowers. Today is for mothers too. We choose red if she is living, white if she is dead. And we remember."

"But you don't wear a flower?" She had never spoken to me about her family. As her expression hardened, I realised she hadn't wished to.

"I wear nothing for that bitch," she said. "She wanted my money always. But she never cared for me." After a moment she added, "She dead, you wondering."

Mai laughed. After a moment, we both did. She only said one more thing before we rose from our seats: "Look like both of us make the dead angry tonight."

✳

The following evening, Mai insisted I come for dinner at her home. The taxi driver looked surprised when I named her district, and set me down just before a long bridge carried the road across the span of the Red River. He gestured towards some steps leading down from the carriageway and I turned to ask for clearer directions, but he was already driving off.

From where I stood I could see a host of small blocks of flats, one much like the next. Their extent was curtailed by the wide, slow progress of the river, which despite its name flowed muddy and brown.

I remembered that Mai had spoken of a balcony overlooking the river bend and I descended the steps, then took a side street that led in roughly the right direction. There were crumbling concrete walls, thick bundles of wires strung from post to post along the road, graffiti I couldn't read, and indeed balconies, some full of washing, some meshed over to keep the homes within secure.

At the corner I spotted a small shop selling cigarettes, the balcony above it half covered by a placard advertising vaping, one that Mai had laughed about. The building's entrance wasn't locked and I tentatively stepped inside before climbing the bare concrete stairs to the first floor. The passage was airless and humid, heavy with old smells of cooked meat, and I realised the doors weren't marked with any numbers. As I stood there, though, one of them opened. Mai's head appeared in the gap and she grinned, but her smile didn't reach her eyes and when I drew near I saw how tired she looked.

"Are you OK, Mai? Are you sure about this?"

She didn't speak, just nodded and gestured me inside. The lounge was tiny and dimly lit, crammed with a fraying sofa, makeshift furniture, a rack of clothing. An overhead fan stirred the damp air, its humming interspersed with a rhythmic judder as it rocked on its fitting. There was a small kitchen off to one side. Unlike the lounge it was brightly lit, and though the stove was tiny, good smells poured from it. A rice cooker gave forth steam; bubbling sounds emerged from a pot. I opened my mouth to comment on how good it smelled and realised someone was standing in the middle of the room.

I didn't know how I'd failed to see him before. He must have been seated in the half-dark, while the better lit kitchen had attracted my eye. He was about Mai's age and a little taller, slightly built like many of his countrymen and yet more so, bone-thin and wiry. His eyes were narrowed but for a moment they caught the light, shining almost amber like a cat's, but the image that came to me was of something else: coiled and secret and fanged, ready to strike. He put out his hand and I found myself staring at it.

"Linh," Mai said, as if I should have known. "My boyfriend."

I realised I was being rude and grasped his fingers, too hard, forgetting the gentle handshake that was preferred across this part of the world. He didn't comment, only stared with half-closed eyes, making his own judgements. I hastened to find the Vietnamese to say I was glad to meet him, but Mai slipped a drink into my hand and the moment passed. I wanted to ask her about him, but how could I? I hadn't even known she had a boyfriend. She hadn't mentioned it in Ho Chi Minh City, hadn't said anything the previous evening, and I wondered why; but she returned to the kitchen, was clattering pots, her expression more jaded than anyone of her age had a right to be.

When I turned towards the room again I realised there was something else I hadn't at first noticed. In the corner was a small shrine hung with flowers, a tray of sticky rice cakes and paper votives placed in front of it. I had visited a temple earlier and seen such things there too, awaiting the flame that would carry them to the next life: representations of clothing, cooking utensils, houses, even iPhones and televisions and air-conditioning units, all carefully made out of paper. Here too was a stack of hell-money, of a currency no use in any earthly shop; and a cleverly made paper woman, red lips painted onto her paper face and wearing a long paper dress. With a start, I realised that Linh was standing next to it. He had retreated to the corner, once more without my noticing, and was looking down at the offerings with a sudden eagerness in his eyes.

"Is this for your ancestors?" I called to Mai. Her forehead was dampened with steam or heat or illness as she transferred fragrant rice into a serving dish.

"No," she said, her expression closed, and I remembered what she'd said about her mother. I cursed my lack of tact as she explained. "These are for the hungry ghosts. I told you. All through the seventh lunar month, the gates of hell are open. It is the only time they may feast. They can visit who they please, and can cause trouble if they are not given food and other things."

There was something in her voice and I suddenly wondered what it was like for her here, estranged from her mother's memory, distant from her family, and in a place where several generations often lived together. Perhaps she knew what it was like to feel alone—but then she wasn't, was she? Linh was here. As I looked at him, he reached out—fast and unexpected as a snake—and grasped one of the rice cakes from the offering tray. He crammed it into his mouth, pushing it past his small white teeth.

I stared. I thought the food went to the monks, or at least the flame—was it only offered in order to be eaten by whoever desired it? I didn't think so, but his throat pulsed as he forced the last of it down and he licked his fingers, then his lips. There was no guilt on his face at all. Neither was there anything hidden in Mai's voice as she called out to say the meal she had prepared was ready.

We went out onto the balcony to eat, the living space being too small to accommodate the three of us around its little table. The air was warmer than it was inside, though the others didn't seem to feel it. Hanoi was cooler than the south of the country, though more humid, the air close, seeming to press against my face. At least the view was open, looking out across the river to the distant lights beyond.

Along with the rice, Mai had prepared spring rolls, bo kho—a huge beef stew—cha ca fish, a banana flower salad, dipping sauces and pickles. I tried them all and my spirits rose at being in this place where so few tourists came, eating not with waiters and paying visitors but with a friend. I complimented her on her expertise, inwardly marvelling that she had conjured so much from her tiny kitchen.

We reminisced about our work on the city garden and Linh showed no irritation at our speaking of times he hadn't known, people he hadn't met, things he hadn't experienced. His bright gaze shifted between us and although Mai occasionally shifted to Vietnamese, he didn't respond, showing no sign of recognition or interest, and she appeared to expect none. He sat quite still, only his hands busy as he reached for the choicest morsels, for the bottle of Tiger beer in front of him. After a time, he put down his chopsticks and seized pieces of beef from the stew with his fingers. I watched him suck them into his mouth, a sliver of sauce clinging to his lips, and wondered that he could be so thin. He surely wouldn't remain so for long. Or was it only that, in his own home, this wasn't seen as bad manners but a compliment?

But then, he wasn't at home. I reminded myself he was only her boyfriend, not a husband. Shouldn't he be concerned that she would grow tired of him being so taciturn—so greedy for more, as if he hadn't eaten for months?

Finally we sat back, and as darkness drew in Mai lit a candle and set it amid the remains of the meal. Linh, however, pushed his chair away from the table and stood, walking inside without a word. He opened a narrow door set into one side of the living space and disappeared.

I looked at Mai, half expecting her to make some comment—to excuse him, maybe—but she didn't speak. I realised that far from flattering her, the flickering candlelight made her skin appear almost grey, her hair lank.

"When did you two meet?" I forced a smile.

"A week ago." She briefly smiled back, then looked away.

A *week*? And this was how he behaved—in her home, towards her guests? I glanced at the door he'd gone through. There was no sign of his reappearing.

"He is staying here for a while." Mai nodded as if inviting me to nod too, to agree with her, to understand the situation. "He is in some difficulty. I will sleep on the floor, of course."

"*You* will—?" Again, my voice faded away. What could I say? It was her choice, and I had no idea how things stood between them, no idea what combination of circumstance or custom or its opposite could have brought them to such a situation. Then she cried out and I turned in time to see her wafting a dark winged shape away from the candle.

She made a moue of disgust, throwing herself back in her chair as it fluttered towards her.

"It's only a moth," I said, but she shifted again in alarm, avoiding its touch, trying to wave it away, off the balcony. It wouldn't leave, only flying inward once more.

"The spirits can visit in the shape of moths," she said. "And other things. Bad ones."

She pulled another expression of distaste, though her eyes betrayed something else: was it fear? I wanted to tell her it was only attracted to the light, but I saw there would be no persuading her, and so I helped her carry the remnants of our meal inside. When we'd finished, I said I should go. It was still early but she didn't protest and I touched her arm, told her I hoped she would have a restful night.

Her gaze shot towards the closed door and once again, I realised I'd been tactless. I'd somehow forgotten Linh, sleeping within—or awake perhaps, staring towards us with those eyes, narrowed yet bright. The thought was unsettling but I smiled and forced myself to tell her it was nice meeting him, hiding my thoughts behind polite words.

"Oh, but I should go with you," she said. "I must find a tuk-tuk for you."

I had forgotten about the journey back. I glanced towards the balcony, the night that awaited me outside. I had no idea if the neighbourhood was safe or where I should go to find a ride, or if I should instead ask for a number and book a taxi.

"The bridge," she said. "That is the best place."

She swayed as she spoke, her eyes beginning to close before opening wide again. I exclaimed. "You are ill, Mai."

"No—no. Only tired."

I wondered how many nights she slept on the floor. But she'd only met Linh a week ago, hadn't she? I realised I never found out anything about him, where he'd come from, who he was.

It was too late now. I pressed her to get some rest, told her I'd be fine, and stepped out into the corridor. She closed the door behind me.

As I exited the building, I looked up once more at her balcony. It was entirely dark, the light in the living space already extinguished, not even a candle burning there, and I thought of the strange boy I'd met. I pictured him sitting in an empty room, also in darkness, alone in his silence, and realised I couldn't remember him saying a single word all evening.

In the distance the bridge loomed, the constant flow of light spilling from its deck making the night seem darker still. There was no moon that I could see above the tall buildings, no stars I could make out. At least there *was* traffic. Telling myself I'd soon flag down a taxi I climbed the steps to the carriageway, pausing to look out across the wide blank surface of the river. As I did so I heard a sound, coming not from the road or the buildings spreading into the distance but somewhere beneath me. I stepped closer to the edge and heard it again, a sliding, rustling noise, distinct but furtive, and something else: a sound I couldn't identify until I looked over the railing and peered into the dark.

Below me was a small patch of wasteland, or perhaps the end of an alleyway, wreathed in shadow and heaped in rubbish. It was dark down there and nothing moved. The smell of rancid garbage was cloying in the damp air; I could taste its sourness on my tongue. Then something *did* move, a shadow shifting, and I thought of cats, or rats; but the shape that suddenly became distinct to my eyes was too large to be either.

My mind couldn't piece it together until it moved again. The man was naked, sprawled amid the dirt, contorting his limbs to reach after something I couldn't make out. He dragged it towards him and pushed it into his mouth. That sound came again, part wet chewing, part choking on something crammed in too deep, gorged upon.

He twisted his head, his neck too thin and flexible, until he was looking straight up at me.

We stared at each other. We stared as if we didn't know what it was we saw. He was fat, I realised. His neck was thin and twisted like rope but his belly was swollen and I realised he wasn't fat at all but starving. He opened his lips as if to speak and I caught a glimpse of some revolting morsel within before it turned to flame. It flared briefly, turning the inside of his mouth a brilliant red as whatever he had scavenged turned to hot coals before he could swallow it.

Another movement off to the side broke our gaze. The man—the *thing*—swivelled his head back again and suddenly I saw them all: more figures writhing amid the detritus and the ruin, all the foul remnants of people's lives. Soft sounds arose as they searched for what they needed, grasping old bones with long fingers, seizing on rotting food, their necks surely so thin they could never eat a thing. And then I made out what they were feeding upon: its gouged and mottled skin, the holes bitten into its flesh, the splayed, wrenched limbs.

I staggered away from the parapet, my hand to my mouth. I couldn't get across the stream of traffic but ran along the walkway, wanting to get as far away as I could. I raised a hand in a signal for help, *anyone*, only then realising that the car pulling over to the side of the road was a taxi.

I got in and the driver turned and raised his eyebrows, as taxi drivers do, wanting to know our destination. I tried to say something about what I'd seen but one word blurred into the next and he scowled.

I tried to calm my thoughts. He wasn't here to help me, not with this, and I didn't want to be thrown out of the cab within reach of those—what *were* they, exactly?

I closed my eyes a moment before saying the name of my hotel. He nodded and pulled away from the curb. I felt the distance opening between the car and the bridge and concentrated on taking deep breaths. Perhaps, now that I could speak clearly, I should try to explain to him what happened. I could ask for his help, get him to call the police. A picture rose: the inside of a cell, being questioned by sharp, lithe men in uniform, ones who didn't care for my accent or my presence in that part of town or my lack of certainty about anything. I knew nothing of the police system here. I knew nothing about what may have left a body lying in an alleyway in the first place. I might have to drag Mai and her boyfriend into it, and that might cause trouble for them in ways I couldn't foresee.

I remained silent until we reached my hotel and I paid the driver and nodded to the doorman as I went inside and pressed the button for the lift and rode it up to my room, where I let myself in and sat on the bed. I stared down at my hands. I'd expected them to be shaking, but they were not. To all outside appearances, nothing had happened. It was only in my mind that those images remained.

I sat and waited to know what to do, but nothing came. I pictured myself calling my parents in England, rousing them from their ordinary day, a pleasant morning in the garden perhaps, to say—what? And what would they say to me in return?

I switched on the television, not looking at it, just letting the anodyne sound of advertising jingles wash over me. I went to the bathroom and splashed cold water on my face, twice brushed my teeth.

Then I sat on the bed again and persuaded myself I

hadn't seen what I thought I'd seen. That it was only the plight of the homeless that so shocked me; the thing they found nothing more than a chicken carcass or a discarded bone; that the after-image of a corpse I carried in my mind was as unreal as any of the things I'd heard that day.

✳

The next morning I wandered aimlessly, discovering some of the sights of Hanoi more by chance than design. I saw Hoan Kiem Lake with its ancient pagoda, Thap Rua Tower, and St Joseph's Cathedral where within, more stories were told, fed upon and believed.

I didn't think about any of it. The image that kept coming to me was Mai's face; the way she had tried to smile as her boyfriend stalked from the room. I didn't know which worried me the most—his sudden presence in her life or her listlessness. And looming over it all were the things I'd seen in the alleyway, so close to where she lived and yet so unreal. It all felt somehow part of a whole, though it surely couldn't be. What I'd imagined could only have been the product of anxiety, combined with the heat and the wine I'd drunk.

The day was passing into evening, the sky darkened and tainted with exhaust fumes and the scent of cooking, when I found myself standing outside a temple once more.

The festival of the hungry ghosts was still happening. I could see it in the faces of the supplicants who filed in and out, men and women wearing grey robes. Once inside, they pressed incense sticks to their foreheads before lighting them and setting them to burn in a huge bowl. Fragrance poured into the evening, not quite masking the smell of the street vendors outside. Further in, open doors revealed the glimpse of a golden Buddha, more offerings set before him: the fruit known as Buddha's fingers, neatly arranged packets of biscuits and dried noodles. One wall was covered with tablets bearing the photographs of ancestors safely delivered to the next life.

In front of it all, right in the courtyard for the hungry ghosts to find, was an open fire. The ground was blackened in that place, the flame fitful, licking greedily here and there as it received fresh bounty. And next to it, bending to present some new offering, was Mai's boyfriend.

He straightened, closing his eyes to savour the clouds of incense, as if its perfume was intended just for him; as if he was relishing all of the things being transferred by fire to the other realm. He took a stack of hell money from the bag slung over his shoulder and began to peel off the notes, one by one, feeding them to the flame.

He was facing towards me, but showed no sign of recognition as I went towards him. There was no one between us, no one else standing so close to the fire, and I remembered something I'd heard: that the offering pyres opened a doorway to the spirit world. Lingering by them could be risky, in case something should escape and possess the careless; but that didn't seem to worry Linh. He felt no danger. The firelight played over his features and he gazed into it with longing, even with greed.

The sight made me shiver. In the fierce light, the planes of his face were too harsh, making me think of bones. He had almost burned all of the money. Soon he would look up and see me, and the thought of what might take the place of his avid expression was discomfiting, but first he reached into his bag and removed another item. I recognised the little woman made of paper.

I somehow didn't like to see it clutched in his hand, though I could not have explained why. I crossed the last few steps towards him as he thrust it into the fire then immediately walked away, straight past me, heading for the way out.

I didn't catch at his arm or call after him. I didn't say his name. I reached out and snatched the offering, brushing off the charred edges of its dress. I held it against me and turned in time to see Linh leaving the temple without glancing back. I had not examined the paper doll in detail before and I did not do so now. I already knew the face drawn onto its blank features was that of my friend.

*

I did not walk far. I could not stop thinking of Mai, of how she might be feeling at this moment. A woman in a too-tight top thrust a drinks menu in front of me and automatically, I smiled back, then let her guide me to a tiny table at the edge of the street. It wasn't what I wanted, not really, but I accepted the drink she placed in front of me and watched as she lit a candle and set it on the table. She looked quizzically at the paper votive I placed next to it before she left.

I sat and sipped, watching the hordes filling the evening street: a constant stream of men, women and children, all intent on going somewhere. Perhaps, I thought, we were all hungry ghosts; empty spirits with no real destination, no purpose, no controlling impulse other than to feast while we could.

A shadow shifted in front of me, something small and speckled, and I realised it was a moth.

The spirits can visit in the shape of moths. And other things. Bad ones.

The insect drew closer once more, drawn to the candle-light, coming within a hair's breadth of being singed. Its wings were already touched with black—and I saw the pattern written there and caught my breath.

The moth had two dark eyes. They flickered so quickly they did not seem to blink; they regarded me, and below them I saw the outline of a mouth, slightly open, ready to strike. I wondered if this was the type of moth that mimicked birds, protecting itself by appearing a predator, but it didn't look like that, not quite. The eyes were too far apart, the mouth too wide. The moth had a blunt, almost triangular form and I realised it didn't look so much like a bird as a snake, seen from low down and in front; the point of view of a mouse in the moment before it is eaten.

I reached out to the votive doll, wrapping my fingers around it. The moth fluttered before the flame, its eyes steadily gazing. I lifted the paper doll and brought it down, trapping the moth inside its hollow body.

The creature's struggles were loud, its wings skittering inside the paper dress. I glanced about me, but no one had seen; no one cared. I peered down at the ragged line where the charred dress met the table. Tiny black legs appeared, retreated, appeared again, almost methodical in their movements, as if the moth was systematically hunting for a way out.

I lifted one side of the dress a fraction. New rustling sounds came from within. Was that a proboscis, tasting its freedom? I raised the doll a little more, grimacing at the dark, squat shape that appeared in the gap.

The moment the moth emerged, I brought down my hand. The creature's body collapsed inward, the touch of it on my fingers soft and grotesquely damp, though the residue it left behind was powdery, like fine dust; like ash. The scent of charcoal rose into the air and I told myself it was coming from the votive's charred dress, but somehow I didn't really believe that was true.

※

Mai turned to me and smiled. It was a good smile, still a little tired perhaps, but her glow had returned; her hair looked glossy and strong. She poured the wine I'd brought for her and handed me a glass. It was the evening after I'd seen Linh and she hadn't mentioned him at all, hadn't even alluded to him. When I asked how he was, she looked blank for a moment.

"It is strange," she said. "He did not come back yesterday. I suppose I will hear from him." She looked sad, though briefly, and I didn't know if it was because she thought she should or if it was something she really felt.

I took a sip of wine—warm, rich—and wondered if she was right, if she would hear from him again. Somehow I didn't think so. The flat seemed bigger without him. Lighter too, despite the dark pressing in from outside.

"Do you feel better now, Mai? I was worried about you."

It took her a little while to answer. "I feel—" she paused, "a little strange inside. But better, yes. I do feel better."

I nodded. I did not think she would miss him. I really thought that she would be all right.

Then she said, "Soon, I have to eat. But first we should go and see the lamps."

I didn't know what she meant, but she gestured towards the balcony. She let me step out in front of her, into the heat and the sound of distant blaring horns, and in front of us, the dark blank of the river. But I realised it wasn't quite blank after all: little lights were floating there, pinpricks in the dark, moving slowly outward from the bank as they were drawn by the tide.

"The festival is over," Mai said. "And so we float lotus lanterns on the river. When they go out, that is when the hungry ghosts find their way back to hell. Unless they can find a way to stay."

I stared at her profile, though she didn't look at me; I couldn't read her expression. I breathed deeply of the damp and heavy air. There were no moths, I realised, not tonight.

We did not speak again. We only sat and watched the lotus lanterns floating away down the river, until they began to wink out; disappearing one by one into the darkness, until it seemed that not a trace of them remained.

A Coastal Quest

Charles Wilkinson

ONE MORNING WHEN Samantha accepts she's sick
of them all—her husband, son and daughter—she goes
on a search, or so it seems, for the place where she will be
happy. It's bright holiday weather: the clouds on the blue
gloss sky, white-plump playthings, bearing only an impos-
sibility of rain. From the top deck of the ferry, she can see
the island, its coast occluded by mist, so that it seems to be
hovering above the sea, ready to take off, spacecraft-smooth
but showing an underbelly of earth, into the unbounded
morning. Now that she's rid of her family, broken all the
sacred connections of blood and relationships, she feels
only euphoria.

"Are you on vacation?"

She hasn't noticed a small man leaning against the
railing, only a yard or two from where she's standing.
Even though there's no edge to the breeze, he's wearing a
dull green jacket the colour of oxidised copper. Her mood
drops slightly. She doesn't want to talk to anyone, let alone
someone whose leathery lack of expression matches his
stout walking boots. But she makes herself reply.

"I suppose you could call it a break—of sorts."

"You're not with the survey?"

"No."

"So you won't even be attending the conference."

There's something odd about his accent, which is
mainly British but with a slight rising tone at the end of the
sentences.

"I am afraid I don't know anything about this conference of yours." She sounds testier than intended. Should
she abandon everyday politeness just because she's free of
them? "What's it about it?"

"The geology of the island. It's more varied that any
comparable area of land in the country."

"Is that so?" She speaks flatly, turning the question's
tone into that of a statement. As she's made a token effort
at conversation, she doesn't want any more involvement. If
she's not careful, he will ask where she's staying.

The ferry's moving with so little resistance across un-
ruffled water it might almost be sliding. Now that they're
closer to the shore, mist is less evident, no more than a
softening of hard lines, a faint suggestion of diluted milk.
When she looks round, the geologist, if that is what he is,
has gone.

Once they've docked and she's hailed a taxi her spirits
revive. The guest house where she's staying is little more
than a minute's ride from the harbour. With only light
luggage, she might as well have walked; embarrassed, she
tips the driver generously. The paint on the façade of the
Regency villa has the uneven texture of clotted cream. There
are two ragged palm trees in the small garden on either
side of the path to the front door. Someone, the proprietor
she assumes, is watching her through a sash window on the
ground floor.

"Miss White?"

She's reverted to her maiden name.

The proprietor has opened the door before she's rung
the bell. A squat, dark man in an open-necked shirt with
the sleeves rolled up. His patchy hair, greasy in spite of
being sparse, has an unusual balding pattern.

"Yes."

The business of signing in accomplished with commend-
able speed, she's soon in a small room overlooking the bay.
The ferry is moving out of the harbour and on its way to the

mainland, the pale cliffs just discernible as a blurred line on the horizon. She opens her suitcase and takes out her copy of Robert Tamar's *Terrain without Time*. An illustrated memoir of the author's visit to an isolated cottage on the island's coast, it describes how his stay becomes not merely a retreat from suburbia but a quest for permanent serenity. When had she first become convinced that if she found the place where Tamar had attained true contentment, she too would be able slough off the skin of an existence inflamed by the dissatisfactions of daily life? She'd read the book shortly after the birth of her second child. Was it that long ago her unhappiness had become evident? Perhaps. But it was only during the last year or so that her fantasy of escape had been translated into actuality. Now the principal problem was the dearth of proper nouns in the text. The area where the events took place was undisclosed. Neither the county nor the names of the nearest town or village were mentioned. Even the house was merely 'a white cottage on a gentle slope overlooking a cove, a hundred yards from the beach.' The author had spent most of time his alone. Those who had impinged on his solitary existence were referred to by their occupation (a sailor, the postman, the farmer's wife who provided him with milk, and so on). Animals were alluded too more frequently than people. But there were some clues and they had led her to the island. Once again, she turned to the frontispiece, Tamar's watercolour of the white cottage, the foam of may on the hawthorn bush, the white shingle, a half moon of yellow sand and then the blue-green sea, a suggestion of small waves idling in from the bay beyond. It is all waiting for her to find it.

As Samantha's about to go out for the evening, she notices there's no key to the lock on the bedroom door. The two on the ring that she's been given are both for the front door.

She finds the proprietor peering into a broom cupboard on the ground floor. To her surprise, there's been no mistake. He's also unmoved by her request for a key.

"You'll get one when it's needed. But they haven't even arrived yet?"

"Who?"

"The kids. Loads of the little buggers. If their teachers say that keys are needed, then you'll get one."

His expression as he turns back to the broom cupboard is impatient and perplexed. Whatever resides amongst the dust pans and derelict carpet sweepers is a riddle resistant to solution.

"I'd like one now—if you don't mind."

This time he doesn't even look at her. Instead, he steps over a bucket and moves further inside the cupboard.

"Do you think I'm going to get one special just for you?"

"That's precisely what I'm hoping for. So yes."

With an impatient sigh, he swings round to face her. The lenses in his glasses are evidently of unequal strength for one eye appears larger and angrier than the other.

"Look, can't you see I'm busy? I'm the only person in residence apart from you."

"If you don't give me a key now, I'll move to another hotel."

"Fine. Suit yourself. But payment's already been taken and there are no refunds at The Mariners Reef."

Her temper, which has been simmering, is about to boil over. But she tells herself its best to delay her decision. There's no way of knowing whether the nearby guest houses are booked up. Traipsing around the town with a suitcase so soon after her arrival is an unappealing prospect. She contents herself with giving him a reproachful glance.

Outside, there's a breeze and a scent of seaside salt on the air. Something about the bay, redolent of childhood, reminds her of her brother, now long dead; how they were

pirates in pedallos, smugglers on the sand dunes. Yachts
tack in the middle distance. For a moment, she imagines
a ship in full sail, a toy galleon flying the Jolly Roger and
breasting tiny waves.

As a move might soon be necessary, she keeps an eye
out for alternative accommodation. Almost every building
along the front is either a guest house or small hotel; none
them have signs for vacancies in the windows. Neither are
there any of the cafés or restaurants she was hoping for. A
line of Regency houses has given way to Victorian villas,
most painted in pastel colours, powder blue and pink; a
few are a shabby vanilla with peeling paintwork. Some
properties have palm trees in the front garden. For the first
time since her arrival, she feels exhausted. Perhaps it would
be best to go back, have a bath and then go into the town,
where there are certain to be places to eat. The guest houses
have nautical names, she notices: Golden Beach, The Sailors'
Rest, The Admiral Hotel and Bar, The Crow's Nest B & B,
Fair Wind, The Final Shore.

Once she's back at The Mariners Reef, the very moment
she comes through the front entrance, she's aware of the
vibrations, the sense that every room in the building is now
occupied. She stops and listens. No voices or footsteps on
the stairs. The reception desk is deserted. On the wall above,
there's a picture in oils of an orchard. It reminds her of the
frontispiece of Robert Tamar's book. Although it's clearly by
another hand, the angle of the boughs and the gentle rise of
the slope beyond suggests that it may be a different view of
the same place. The artist has failed to evoke the strangely
buoyant quality, a sense of light lifting off every surface,
captured in Tamar's work. From where she's standing, the
painting appears unsigned. Is the place popular with local
artists? Perhaps the proprietor will know.

As she climbs the staircase, she can hear the subdued
whispering, the softest tissues of sound, from behind the
closed door. Are the promised party of schoolchildren at

last in residence? If so they are either far from boisterous by nature or afraid of their teachers.

On reaching her room, she finds a key in the lock. The door is slightly ajar. A cleaner? She pushes and walks in. A young boy with a narrow white face is standing in the middle of the carpet with his back to the window. His features seem unnecessarily long yet not too wide for his scrawny body. Unkempt hair with the grey-black sheen of pencil marks spills onto his forehead. The large green eyes are set too far apart, although the nose between them is small. He appears to be about ten.

"What are you doing in here?"

Instead of replying, he brushes the hair back from his forehead to reveal a bright gash, evidently deep, the blood almost congealed, but not set quite as firm as jelly.

"That looks..." She is about to say 'nasty', but that seems too trivial to express the severity of the wound, which is surely in need of immediate treatment. "Shall I see if I can find something for it?"

He nods, only moving his heads very slightly, as if fearful that too violent a motion will break open the injury.

"I'll see what I can find. But someone will have to take you to a doctor... or the hospital. You need to get that looked at properly."

She goes into the bathroom and opens her overnight bag. Somewhere amongst the sponges, toothpaste and make-up she knows there are plasters, but possibly none are likely to prove large enough to be suitable. At least she has some antiseptic cream, but it will have to be applied with great care.

"How did you do it?" she calls out, while continuing to rummage.

In reply there's nothing but a rustling, which could be a weak attempt at articulation, the breath hardly able to move across the tongue. She finds the tube she's been looking for and returns. The boy's vanished, as if he were no more than a temporary shadow, but for a second there's a suggestion of a dark scar in the air, a freakish alteration in the light or a memory of wound that was real.

※

The next morning it takes her a while to work out that the breakfast room is in the basement. As she makes her way down the staircase, she hears a continuous clink of cutlery and echoing conversations in a cavernous space growing louder. At the bottom there's a corridor with pictures on the wall. She stops to look at them, but none of them are of the white cottage, the orchard and the coast; the majority are nothing more than cloudscapes or of rock pools with the sky reflected in them. She gives one more than a fleeting inspection. A portrait of a man, possibly the proprietor, it's clumsily executed. The subject's hands appear either heavily bandaged or clad in oversized white gloves. Then she's aware that while she's been examining the painting something has changed. The sounds from the breakfast room have stopped. She opens the door. Inside, it's much smaller than anticipated: a few tables, no more than four or five, a sideboard with a selection of cereals and a hotplate. There's a window with dark brown earth and gravel pressed against it. Presumably this floor must once have been above ground. What caused it to subside?

After she's helped herself to cereal, she realises that there's a couple in the room. They must have come shortly after her, and yet from the dirty plates in front them they appear to have finished their meal. The man, elderly and with a porridge-pale face, looks at her and she nods at him, but in return she receives nothing but an unblinking stare from cold blue eyes. Once she's seated they resume a conversation that they must have started earlier.

"...fell out of the air. Engine failure, it's believed."

The woman's speaking with a kind of subdued

excitement. Her face is whiter than her husband's.

"So there'll have been flames then?"

"Yes, there were flames. On impact. There always are."

"And burns?"

"We can expect them to have been burnt."

The old man nods, evidently satisfied with this assessment.

As there's no sign of any service, Samantha helps herself to a second coffee then leaves. Once again, there's no one on the desk. This time she decides to walk to the centre of the town. It's another wonderful day, the sky a lucid blue, unsullied by cloud.

Far above, there's a solitary hot air balloon, hanging like an inverted exclamation mark and almost motionless. The centre is further away than it seemed the previous day—or the taxi diver must have taken a short cut. The buildings on both sides are the same type of guest houses and down-at-heel boutique hotels that dominate the bay in the other direction: Fair Breeze, Captain's Cabin, The Galleon, The Haven, The Safe Harbour. There are no private residences. For a moment, she panics. Does the whole town consist of nothing more than sub-standard accommodation for tourists? Then she reaches a crossroads. On the far side there are chip shops, restaurants with garish seaside frontages, an art gallery and in its front window and on an easel a preposterous painting of a mermaid. Then there's an estate agent. Samantha stops to look at the properties for sale. None of them have prices listed, although there are a few with stickers slapped on proclaiming they've been sold. Inconspicuous amongst the four-square country houses and spacious apartments, she spots it: a photograph of the white cottage set in its orchard, a sliver of the shingle just visible below the front garden. No pictures of the interior, but a few bald details: the property is for rent—no figure specified; the usual rooms listed; central heating. Not even the name has been given. A bell rings gently as she enters.

To her surprise, the couple she'd noticed at breakfast are in there. They're sitting in chairs set hard against the wall, as in a dentist's waiting room. Although they both glance at her, neither of them gives a glint of recognition. There's no one behind the counter. She presses a buzzer and looks around the room: pictures of properties, listings, a grey filing cabinet, a table with a kettle on it. The couple are now talking, in low tones that nevertheless carry clearly.

"... there was nothing they could do."

"And head on, you say?"

"The fog played its part."

"You'd have thought the driver would have swerved."

"A cliff face one way—a sheer drop the other."

Instead of looking at each other, the couple stare straight ahead, their voices almost emotionless. In spite of the favourable weather, they are both wearing gull-grey raincoats buttoned up to the chin.

"Can I help?"

She swings round. A man with a head of tight black curls and a flat, block-like face is standing on the other side of the counter.

"Oh... yes. It's about a property in your window. For rent. Unfortunately I... didn't see the name... but it's a white cottage, with an orchard."

"I know the one."

"I'd be interested to learn more about it. It wouldn't, by any chance, have any connections with the writer and painter Robert Tamar?"

"He owns it."

"Owns? But surely he's long dead?"

"It's correct to say Mr Tamar's no longer in residence. And the family who were there have... been moved out."

The man's voice is quietly insistent: a churchwarden's undertone...

"Would it possible for you to take me to the cottage?"

"Not today."

"Is it in good order?"

"That's not easy to ascertain at this distance."

"Perhaps it would be best if you took me over there tomorrow. Will you pick me up? At about 11 o'clock. I'm staying at the Mariners Reef."

The man inclines his head, a movement that almost qualifies as a nod, and mutters what sounds like a syllable of assent.

"So that's settled. I'll be outside the guest house on the hour."

A tremor runs through him, causing his head to droop for an instant. Agreement or the onset of a neurological disorder?

"Well, I'll see you then," she adds.

This time he sits down and logs onto his computer. As she turns to leave, she notices that the elderly couple are no longer there. Somehow they have dispersed without a sound, as though they are less than mist.

✳

Samantha wakes up slightly later than usual. From her bedroom, the street with the palm trees on the far side and the curve of the bay are an enticement to step into the morning.

She does not want to go down to the basement for breakfast. It occurs to her that when searching for cafés she has been looking in the wrong direction. There must be somewhere across the road on the seafront where she can get a cup of coffee.

As she steps out onto the corridor, a door opens at the far end and two boys step out.

One has an arm that dangles uselessly by his side; the other has a head that appears to have been crushed slightly out of shape, although there is no sign of blood. Both have the same pallor as the child she'd found in her room. They look at her with no obvious expression before making off in the direction of the staircase. She's reminded that she hasn't told the proprietor about the previous day's intrusion, but then she hasn't seen him since the day of her arrival. Perhaps there will be someone at the desk. She looks up and down the corridor. If all the rooms apart from hers are occupied by schoolboys, they've been commendably quiet. But then something appears to have happened to them. A misadventure en route that requires them to rest?

Once she's outside and walking along a promenade some distance from the guest house she realises she's forgotten to see if there was someone at the reception desk. She glances at her watch. Enough time for a walk before going back to the Mariners Reef to meet the estate agent.

There are some steps leading down from the sea wall onto the beach. The pale-yellow sand is soft and inviting. It will already be slightly warm, although the sun is still low in the sky. In the distance, a group of people, their sex unidentifiable from so far off, are looking up at a cliff face. Something about the way they are standing suggests they are holding clipboards.

At the bottom, she finds a café built into the wall. More than a mere kiosk, it has a counter and three tables and chairs. A parasol with a semi-circular bench stands just outside. The geologist is there, a cup of coffee and folded paper in front of him. He waves at her to join him.

"How was your conference?"

"Fine. But our departure… has been delayed. Some of my colleagues," he says, gesturing to the figures further up the beach, "are doing a little field work to fill in the time."

Once she's ordered she decides to join him. It's been a while since she's spoken to someone who isn't either hostile or evasive.

"What are they doing?"

"They're looking at the strata exposed in the cliff face over there. Hoping to get some idea if it represents true geological time or is just some kind of trick."

"A trick? Why on earth would it be that?"

"Well, there have always been people who believe that the deity created everything just like that, with a snap of his celestial fingers, but many of these features have the appearance of being created separately, over unimaginable aeons."

Wearing the same green jacket, he hardly seems dressed for the beach. His brown brogues have lost their shine. Now that she is closer to him his skin appears not merely tanned and rough but slightly scorched.

"I see. I remember you said that the geology here is very varied."

"That's correct. But what we're now beginning to wonder is whether it isn't *simply an illustration*."

She allows this observation the reproachful silence she always accords to the incomprehensible. The geologist, now disinclined to elaborate, is gazing across the bay at a ferry on the horizon... She's not sure whether it's sailing towards the mainland or on its way back to the island. She watches, hoping it will either grow larger or diminish, but it appears motionless, fastened to the margin where sky and water meet.

A banner headline on the newspaper piques her interest. Although it's upside down, she's able to read it: COACH PARTY IN CRASH. TWENTY CHILDREN KILLED. Are the boys in the Mariners Reef the survivors of this accident?

"Do you know this coastline well?" she asks, taking Tamar's book out of her bag.

He turns towards her. His expression is strangely remote, as if he's been so absorbed in his contemplation of the ferry that he's having difficulty in adjusting to what's near at hand. He has no eyelashes.

"No, only a little. We went out on a boat yesterday, but we didn't have time to reach the far side of the island."

"You don't happen to recognise this?" She shows him the frontispiece and one other illustration of the white cottage.

"Well, yes. It's on the bay on the far side of the promontory. There are very few houses on that stretch of the coast. I can't think why."

"And so I could walk there?"

"Assuming time's no object when you're holiday." Now he's looking back towards the geologists, who have moved slightly closer to the cliffs. "I wonder if I should join them. They might not welcome it."

"Really?"

"Weeks ago I chartered the plane that brought them here, but they seem to resent the fact that I arrived separately."

"That's very unfair."

"Apparently the flight was a… difficult one. As some sort of payback, they've taken to claiming I'm dead."

"Ridiculous!"

"Someone saw it in a newspaper and then told the others."

"Well, you look in pretty good shape to me."

But does he? There's something about the texture of his skin that suggests it's either burnt or weathered by many months of medical treatment. He's still wrapped up in heavy clothes, although there's no edge to the breeze. She puts the book back in her bag and stands up.

As she's close to the cottage, she might as well go over there. There was something about the estate agent's manner that implied he'd no intention of keeping their appointment.

"Thanks," she says. "You've been most helpful."

He's still absorbed in his contemplation of the ferry, fixed on the skyline; there's no reply.

Once back on the road she wonders whether reaching the white cottage will be easy. The geologist saw it from a boat. It's possible she'll face a steep climb down a track.

Even though it's the season, the hotels and guest houses to her left are so numerous it's scarcely credible that there are sufficient souls to fill them. The names have taken on an aura of inevitability: Cliff House Hotel, The Sea Spray B & B, Eternal Waves, Avalon Island Apartments, The Anchor, The Shoreline Shadow, The Tide's Reach. She must be walking quicker than she'd realised for the ferry is no longer visible. Or perhaps, it has been moving all the time; not vanishing, it has now crossed the horizon to sail under a different light.

Then before she's fully aware of it the guest houses have been superseded by short springy grass on chalk cliff tops. A delirium of sunshine hazes the path ahead, but the sky's so determinedly blue that it seems on the point of solidifying, becoming something that could break. Certainly the light seems to be bouncing back off it in a conspiracy to blur and soften edges.

As soon as she sees the lane down to the white cottage she recalls it. Of course, she's been down here many times. The bend that conceals the last stretch of the track down to the cottage, the lie of the camber beneath her feet, are familiar. And now there it is, straight ahead: the white cottage, the orchards with the apples almost luminous in day's gleam, the shingle that traps the sea-whisper. The front door's open, but then why shouldn't it be? This place is her home.

It's once she steps over the threshold that she notices the alteration. At last she achieves some sense of why she left. Robert Tamar's paintings still hang on the wall. How could she have forgotten that she owned every picture in the book? The furniture is as she left it. No, it is something about the incorrigible depth of the silence. The sense that whatever joy was once in the house has fled. She switches on the radio: *"It is believed that hours after his wife left him, he slit the throats of his two children before turning the gun on himself.*

His wife has not been seen since she caught the ferry at…"
She turns the voice off.

Now she remembers how she boarded the ferry to the mainland. A foul morning, the sea's turbulent green; the spray rising as she walked out onto the deck, even though they'd been told to stay inside, safe on the right side of the rain-streaked windows. So how had she found herself returning to the island, as if it was a place she'd never known? To a day suffused with the innocence of first holidays, beaches with fine warm sands, the salt air heady with adventures? Then she recalls how she walked on the slippery deck to the rails. Below her the waves, the foam webbed like scar tissue. The solution lies in the sea, that was what she'd told herself.

All three of them are in the living-room, where she finds them arrested in the ungainly attitudes of death: her husband with the neat wound in his forehead, its blood shadow not yet browning the wall; the children with their wounds still bleeding, as is the privilege of the freshly dead. At last, she understands that she's looking at a tableau that has been arranged days ago. In the world next to hers, the bodies must have been taken away by now. Perhaps they are awaiting examination in some cool corner of a hospital. And she cannot join them because she is both here, in front of this scene imprinted on eternity, and underneath the water.

You, Girls Without Hands

KL Pereira

I

THEY NEVER SAID your body was yours. Even if you called it by name, they had other names for it, other means of control. The axe, for example. The axe is in the business of cleaving, the slip of the blade unsewing knit flesh, unspooling the ink of your veins. There's no other way to say this. Your father (not really your father) will say that the axe is about love, and love is about obedience, but this is a lie wrapped in a lie. The business of cutting is always the business of control, power. Carnage is the afterthought.

II

Your family tells the story this way: you had your hands cut off (the structure of the story erases blame, but you know who did this to you, every one of you knows exactly who did this to you. How could you ever forget?). Later, when you tell the story it is not about want but about ache, necessity, spell, survival.

III

Fathers who are not fathers, and daughters who are cut, tell different stories.

In this story, the hand is a hand: becomes a pair of hands. Thumbs two. Fingers eight. The hands are power inching up creases of skin. The father-not-father cannot abide force that isn't his. He believes he owns everything that he says he means to love, and here, love means devour, destroy. The devil doesn't threaten him, gods don't force him. You don't step in, tender and white as sacrifice, to save him from ruin. You do not give yourself over to slaughter. What woman does?

IV

Things your father-not-father didn't count on:

1. Once a part of the body is removed, it belongs to itself.

2. The hands have their own agenda, slick sticky lines of nerve and memory etched into skin, tough as tree bark.

3. The duties for which your hands were created have always included murder, or to be more specific, the duties that were born from the cleaving of your hands from your wrists were destined to bring despair to the cleaver, to those who helped erase the cleaver, to enact the wringing of necks with fingers.

4. Spells are sunk deep in the hearts of your palms.

V

You, a girl, a woman, know all the rules of removal and replacement and how they may occasionally be broken. After the cleaving, this knowledge rests, cupped in the creases, the tangles of life and love and money lines etched into the flat of your palms. The disembodied always know what came before, what led to what needs to happen next. Even when packed away in the darkest corners of sewing shops, ready to be reclaimed, body parts can listen. They dream, possess motives and plans. Your hands, once replaced, will do what you tell them.

When you finally find your hands—those twin cradles of bone and sinew, nail and skin—box-sealed in an old sewing shop in a corner of the city that has never before appeared to you, you are finally ready to use them. What you did before you were ready doesn't matter. You survived.

You know exactly how to reattach them: you lick your stumps, which have never stopped weeping blood, and your once boxed hands grow from them, nails sprouting like sharp stalks of razor weed from strong gnarled finger joints, from wide wooly palms. You do not, I repeat, do not, set a sewing needle to flesh, any more than you ever spun gold for that imp of your father-not-father.

VI

Here are the final things you must understand:

1. Your hands do not become birds of forgiveness.

2. Sacrifice is a requirement, yes, but never again of yourself.

3. After the deed is done, you will not remember what his eyes looked like, nor his fingers, toes, ground bones. You will only feel calm.

4. After the deed is done, your nails turn black as plums and shiny as blood. Your limbs are yours now, as your soul is felled and reformed into that which is only your own. You are finally only your own.

The Quiet Forms of Belonging

Kristi DeMeester

FOR YEARS, I have drowned in everything but water. In oil. In petals. In the thick, golden coat of honey. In Helene's coarse, almond-scented hair. In the scattering of her clipped fingernails she left on the bathroom counter as yellowed half-moons. Those shed parts she sloughed off and left for me to find when I cleaned; my hands gathering the dead portions of her body left behind.

I collected her inside a jar. I painted the outside black. It is still not enough to contain the woman who is my sister.

I wondered if she's been bewitched. If the reason her eyes change from brown to gray is because a ghost has stepped into her skin. If her tongue has forgotten the incantations we fed each other as children because she's drunk a potion that has locked the words behind her clenched teeth. If our father came to her in the night, speaking mumbled words over her inert body, before he finally vanished behind the door, meant only for him.

Once, she told me what it was like to be haunted, but her mouth did not move, and I've forgotten the sounds she made. If anything possesses her, it is not in the imprint her fingers leave on my arm when she clutches it during a high wind, or in the cording of her throat when she swallows the water I bring her in the cut-crystal glasses our grandmother willed to us. It is the only glass I haven't broken, my fingers uncontrolled and trembling as I take them down, unable to keep myself from dropping them. Every morning, I cut my feet on the shards, but I cannot find the broom, and my hands are so clumsy. My sister does not move to bandage my wounds, to hunt for peroxide, for a bandage, but her breath rattles out of her, and it is all the sorrow I need.

My memories are small: our father, this house, my own small rebellions. There has never been anything else. Helene never asked what existed beyond these walls, and I followed suit, but my body could not keep itself from its indiscretions. I committed them without thinking. Misplacing our father's shoes; closing doors he told me never to close; eating the meat he carried into the house still raw and bloodied and wiping my mouth on the pale curtains hanging in the front room; scattering his papers, the geometric designs swirling at my feet as I passed smudged fingers over the marks and measurements he left there.

Once, I asked Helene what came before. Before the house. Before us. She stared back at me, her eyes reflecting the moonlight in the darkness of our bedroom and told me it would be better if every question inside of me dropped away. There was never anything else. Nothing else mattered. My questions were banal. Pointless. Worthy of eating and vomiting up like so much waste. There was our father. His two daughters. This house that he commanded. There was nothing else. Even the trees that drowned the house in a dim, green light were like an illusion, and if we ever dared to push past them, we would find only pale mist. A never-ending numbness.

Still, I found myself waking under the sky, the house looming behind me like some sleeping leviathan, the woods sighing around me as the wind pushed me backward. And I would return, too afraid to take more than two-hundred steps beyond the house and our father, too afraid to look for the things I didn't understand. I was not strong enough to face whatever was beyond the house, to peer into any possibilities outside the lives our father had presented to us. Far easier to drift through those ever-shifting walls and pretend I didn't want the meager love my father offered me because I was not Helene.

I pricked myself with needles. Held my hands over candle flames until I could no longer bear it. Pushed a fist in the soft place under my ribs until the bruise was the size of a pear. There was no amount of violence I could enact on my body that would allow my father, allow Helene, to see me as anything more than a mistake covered by skin. For Helene to gather me to her, to press the heat of herself against me, melding and coming together into a body greater than our father. Our mouths and teeth becoming something monstrous.

*

For three months, seven days, thirteen hours, fifteen minutes, seven seconds, Helene has cupped her body into the corner of our father's bedroom. Her forehead has left a dark smear of oil on the wall, and her skin is bruised and bloodied from the friction. I imagine she is trying to press herself into the house, into the walls, to find what our father has vanished into, but she stays silent whenever I ask. Her body or the house—I cannot tell which—has sprouted flowering vines. Jasmine or honeysuckle or roses. She keeps the blooms away from me, and when I go to touch the places where her skin has opened, she bares her teeth in the kind of smile that is dangerous, and I leave her standing, her lips formed around the noise she calls prayer.

On some days, I cannot see the vines, and I wonder if I hallucinated it, or if Helene is conjuring them at will. Our father used to ask her to call things forth. Things he'd left behind. Things that would delight him. A single gardenia bloom. His hunting knife with the pearled handle. The large claw of an unrecognizable beast. And she would blink and tell him where to look. Under a rock outside by the elm tree. Hidden behind my left molar. And he would laugh and pull those items from their hiding places and call

Helene his golden girl.

Now, she is only entropy. A chaos of veins and bone. Discolored flesh. An altar for our father that has not been used in so long.

Four months pass before she speaks. "Give me your mouth," she whispers. Again and again until her voice grows hoarse. "Give me your mouth, and I will lay the spoils before him."

There is blood on my feet, on my hands, and it smears against the glass as I tip the water into her mouth. Her tongue takes in those scarlet, lost parts of me, and she sighs. "I could devour you," she says.

That night, I think about the act of allowance. How there is more surrender than demand in it. How I could allow Helene to gobble up every part of me until there was nothing left. Not even the stain of what I once was. Sometimes I think it would be better. That Helene be the only sister to remain. That she draw the flora, the earth, and damp, and rot into the house, and thrive in it while my corpse bloats, the blood cooled and settled to dribble out of me and feed her.

But every morning, I draw breath. I carry the water. I bleed insubstantial amounts. I suppose I was never a hollow enough vessel for her. For our father. There was always too much of myself, too much of my own will.

The vines reappear but do not flower. They are thorned but do not pierce Helene's skin, and I know they are meant only for me. A defense mechanism against touch. A warning filled with silence.

Around us, the house is growing smaller. At night, it draws breath in small sips. Pretending I can't hear what it's doing. Pretending I don't know it's whispering secrets to Helene.

When we were young, our father winked at us whenever we would waken to new rooms in the house. Doors that opened on darkness or a verdant green so lush it made my mouth water. Floors gone so soft our feet sunk, our muscles aching from the effort to pull them out.

"It does my will," he told us over breakfast. "And one day, it will choose one of you. I wonder which?"

Helene would smirk because she already knew. She was the one born with hair the color of moonlight. The one with the birthmark in the shape of a willow between her breasts. The one whose heart beat like music no human throat should ever sing.

I am not sure I ever believed him. That the house responded to his desires. I think he liked to imagine it did, that when he woke to anything new, anything changed, he told himself he'd dreamed it into existence. I believe the house has always been separate from him, his body a conduit for some greater force he could only pretend to understand.

Since Helene tucked herself away, the house does not move in the day, and it hides itself from me. Like it doesn't know me. Like I haven't grown up here beside Helene, day in and day out, waiting for whatever occupied the liminal spaces to notice there was breath inside of me, too.

The windows are dark, and I cannot bring myself to go outside. To see if the sun has winked out, or if something has moved before it, shrouding us, the world our father created for us, in shadow. Is it possible there are other people, other girls who share blood, moving somewhere that is not this house? Another Helene? Another me? Would they clasp one another and whisper secrets that carried the weight of the entire world? I am not sure if the thought is a comfort or a terror. Even in the light, it's difficult to discern what wears an evil face.

"I have ground you into dust. You are a seed. You are the dry bottom of an evaporated lake. You are the cold, deep of marrow, and I have drawn you out and wet my mouth with your insubstantial, trembling matter." Helene has places on her body that are the color of a moonless night. The color of

a plum. But they are not bruises. My sister is never the one
to stumble. To fall. Once, I saw her floating. Her bare feet
above the ground, her hands slack at her sides, the fingers
twitching as if they could take apart the bones of the house.
Of me. Of our father.

My sister does not sleep. Not since our father found the
final door that swallowed him. The one we had never seen.
The one painted in crimson. When he vanished behind it, I
think he imagined he would finally find whatever reward
he felt the house had promised him.

Whatever passed over us took only our father, and
Helene's heart beat wetly, and if there was a pattern in it, a
melody, I imagine it might be one of despair. Of a longing
for return.

But the house eats portions of what is offered. Our
father taught us that. To be careful of our words. To hold
them within because the walls were listening, holding their
breath, and waiting for a single offering. Our father's body
transubstantiated when he crossed the door's threshold but
without the victorious return. Our father has not become
a god crowned in glory. He's only another thing the house
taken into itself.

If Helene is prostrating herself, if her body has become
holy ground, the house has turned its back. It doesn't matter
that it should belong to her now that our father is gone. My
sister who has my hands, my arms. In these ways, I have
melded myself with her like a vine. Like a root. She will
have to cut me out, and I will follow her as Ruth followed
Naomi.

Her skin loosens around her bones, and she folds into
her own body as if it was something she could eat, something she could eliminate. I do not think our father is dead.
Wherever the door led him, it was not into death.

"I dreamed I slipped you inside out. There was no key
swimming in the loose coils of your body. But I could hear
him. Behind the door." Helene sways on her feet, her body

heavy with this quest she's fashioned for herself, but she cannot move. To move would be a kind of betrayal. She cannot forsake her role. She can only be Helene. The chosen daughter. The heiress to a house that should not exist in the living world.

There is a hole in the plaster where Helene has raked her teeth over the surface. She is taking the house into herself, hoping, I'm certain, that by ingesting what she can the house will see her as sister, as mother, as blood. It settles sourly in her stomach and coats her mouth in a thick, white paste.

"Is it you?" she asks me, and I shake my head, hair flying, insistent that I am a master of nothing in our family, in this house. I do not know how to form the words, how to shape the syllables of what I've begun to believe about our father and his betrayal and of my own resistance to whatever he has set in motion.

Only when Helene seems to sleep do I dare to whisper this new truth I carry. "He never left." I picture him laughing at me. At Helene. Silly to imagine it would be so simple. Silly to imagine his daughters could harness the ghosts of his house.

It was particularly cruel, but there was never any softness in Father. Like the vines, the thorns curl further around us every morning, meant to choke, to prick, to draw blood. Helene watches their progression with the kind of passive energy reserved for saints or martyrs. Those who watch their own bloodletting, knowing their oppressors leach only their own holiness from their bodies. There cannot be any pain in that.

In the night, when Helene lets her eyes drift closed but does not sleep, I hunt for the door. The one our father took. But none of these doors bleed. None of the doors I find in the dark lead to any answers; only more rooms, the furniture draped in thin white cloth like slumbering phantasms. For long moments, I sit in the center of those rooms, waiting for the furniture to shake into life and creep toward me, but nothing moves, and I close the doors and check on Helene and lie beside her, my back pressed firmly against the hardwood until I feel numb—my limbs deadened and tingling.

I sing to her, to the vines, to the door, to our father; my voice shakes, the notes settling over our skins. Halfway through, I realize I have forgotten the words, and the melody dies in my throat. I close my eyes because I have already memorized the bend and shape of this room, of my sister, of the emptiness of this house, and there is no need to see our deaths laid out so simply for us in wood, in fabric, in the sighs that come from the walls.

Our father's bedroom no longer smells of him, of the salt tang of his skin, but of the deep, animal smell of Helene's sweat. "He told me it would be simple. Like drawing breath," Helene whispers to the wall, and I turn my body away from her and wonder if she will pull me apart now. My uselessness laid so bare. I cannot help her. I cannot even find the door. I cannot speak the dead tongues of the house.

The night passes, and my sister does not tear me apart, and the vines twine against my calves, holding me weakly in place. It is easy to break free of them, to keep myself from their thorns, but they've encased Helene's chest, her throat, and she sighs and bends into them as if they are an answer to a question she dare not voice.

I know her question. It is burned into my own lungs. *Where are you? Why haven't you gone? When will it be my turn?*

I close the door and go to get Helene's water. I test her questions with my own tongue, but they fall like dead things at my feet, and there is nothing in the silence to answer. Nothing in my sister's voice belongs to me. I cannot claim any part of her body, not even the pieces of her I have collected in the glass jar. Not even our shared blood, pumping through our veins in thick, reddened surges, cycling again and again through the empty spaces of our hearts.

It rains throughout the day, the pattern beating over our heads as we sit together in the cooled dark of the house and wait for something we cannot name. We can feel it gathering, shimmering somewhere beyond our vision, caught and tangled and choking the damp chlorophyll of the vines. It breathes out when we are breathing in, and Helene tries to hold her breath, tries to catch its slight sounds, but the vines squeeze tighter when she does this, and I was never any good at holding my breath, and even when I try, my heart pounds in my ears, and the rest of the world drops out. Whatever is trying to come through doesn't want us to hear it, to see it's aching, slow movements.

I whip my head around and around, and Helene's eyes are large and liquid, catching in the dim light, but there is nothing reflected there. No doors opening. No large forms stepping through and straightening into a body that reaches and reaches. A body for which there will never be any end. Our father come with his hands crushed into fists. Our father anointed in shadow, wearing the weight of his daughter's like the heaviest of garments.

As if we needed his crumbs. As if we needed the remnants of his shriveled heart.

Inside of that sound, my anger roars into life. "We can't stay here," I tell Helene, and in the distance, there is the dulled crack of lightning, but I do not see it as an omen.

"He's coming through. And he'll take me into the house. He'll show me," she says, and a tendril shoots along her neck, curling against her collarbone as if it could pierce the thin flesh there and flood her sternum with green.

"Look at what he's left us, Helene. This house. Does any part of it tell you he's interested in sharing? We've been left behind. Even if he comes back, he won't see us. We won't matter compared to what he's found. We aren't magic. We never have been."

"If you say another word, I'll tear out your tongue." Helene hisses, bares her teeth at me, and there are thorns against the pale pink of her gums. She tips her head, her hair falling across her face, so I cannot see her eyes. "He should have pinched your nose shut when you were born."

Her arms are wasted. The length of her concaved into itself, the bones stretched against skin, her vertebrae sprouting tight knots up her back. It would be so easy to pluck her up and carry her out of this place, but there are still her teeth. She would not allow anything other than bloodshed.

That night, I try to sleep as I listen to the vines breathe instead of Helene and wonder if it would be better this way. For her to draw the life out of me in one great act of violence rather than waiting for the vines to choke us, or for our father to return and create for me a tomb from hands I no longer recognize. I pull the blankets around me, and they are warm, and I sweat, and I smell the scent of myself, and in the morning, my eyes ache with not sleeping, and my head feels swollen, but I go downstairs. I get Helene her water. I wish for poison.

The deaths available to us would be messy. Painful. I cannot face such a death, and I am shamed by my own cowardice, that even in the bravery of contemplating such an act, I am still tethered to this body by my fear. Helene would laugh to hear it, so I fold this secret tight into the hidden parts of myself and hope instead the vines will kill her so I do not have to. If they are merciful, they will take me next.

Throughout the afternoon, Helene eats the portions of the house she can reach, and I wonder that the walls do not fall into tremors as it tries to throw off my sister's careful, insistent scraping. Whatever heart lies in the center of the house must still be buried too deep. She is no true threat. Her mouth is filled with grit; it amounts to nothing. Helene must understand this, but she doesn't stop, and I watch her craft a hole for herself in the wall, watch as she creeps inside.

That night, Helene falls into a fairy tale sleep. A princess who will not wake no matter what the damsel who has come to save her does. Screaming her name, pulling her hair, kissing the green tint of her mouth, biting at the soft flesh of her upper arm, none of it is worth the energy it siphons from me. She slumbers, and I work quickly, untangling the snarl of vines and thorns from her inert body, ignoring the pricks against my own flesh, the slow trickle of blood.

"Count it as an offering," I say. And for good measure, I lift my voice and hope my father can hear. "Then kindly fuck off."

When I lift Helene's body, she weighs so little that I ache for the woman she used to be. The depth of her. How her presence filled whatever container it found itself in and threatened to swell, to drown, with every breath she drew. I force myself to stand, to step forward, and still, she sleeps against me, her head tipped back so I can see the milk of her throat, the veins so blue as they push to escape. Around us, the house makes no sound.

I pause, waiting for the walls to crash in, for the floors to rise in a great tidal wave and swallow us, for the doors to close, for the windows to rain glass over our heads, but there is nothing except for the slow creak of a door opening from somewhere within the great belly of the house.

"Helene?" the voice calls, and I run.

Through the kitchen, and the great room where we ate breakfasts; the lemon curd our father made the color of a young sun, spread in thick gobs over dense scones, then toward the great oak door that carried the prints of all of us, and over the threshold and out into the glittering night.

Our father put Helene to sleep for him. His Beauty. He would have her sleep for a thousand years in the bower he created, only to return when he wanted and strip away everything that belonged to her. To pare her away until all that remained was a single, burning bone. There was no holiness, no evil in such a diminishing, but we were his daughters, and we were not his alone.

I run with my sister tucked against my chest, my lungs and thighs burning, but I do not drop her. I dare not let her body touch the ground, the arching, needing roots and leaves that thirst for the girl I've stolen away.

Behind me, a voice howls into the wind, and I run faster. There are hours until sunrise. I will run until my feet bleed, until I cannot feel anything except our hearts beating against one another.

Again, our father lifts his voice; it is more distant, and I understand something he didn't think of when he vanished behind that door. He cannot leave the house. His salvation has become his prison. I could laugh, but there is no breath for it.

I will find a hole to curl our bodies into, and we will sleep together, our arms wound round each other, our legs and hands undistinguishable from the other.

And when my sister finally wakes, I will whisper her name in her ear.

"You are Helene," I will tell her. "And you belong with me."

Workday

Kurt Fawver

MEMO
CORIVDAN INCORPORATED

To: All Hourly Employees
From: Human Resources
Subject: Holiday Party Attendance
Date: Nov. 20, 2018

Please RSVP to the holiday party by Friday afternoon. The event will be held the evening of December 21. Our caterers need an exact count of the number of people attending so that we don't run out of food and refreshments. We will have a buffet-style meal and an open bar throughout the night. Please remember also that attendance at the holiday party is mandatory for all employees.

Thank you, and we look forward to seeing you there.

Message scrawled in permanent marker in the unisex restroom on the twelfth floor of the Corivdan Building. Found Nov. 20, 2018. Painted over Nov. 21, 2018.

DO NOT attend the holiday party. You are all in grave danger. By working at Corivdan Inc. you've put yourself in the sights of a monster. Stay away from the party. YOUR LIFE DEPENDS ON IT.

✳

MEMO
CORIVDAN INCORPORATED

To: All Hourly Employees
From: Jonathan Chadwick, Executive V.P.
Subject: Holiday party
Date: Nov. 21, 2018

I want to personally invite you to this year's holiday party. 2018 has been a massive success for the company. We posted our highest earnings EVER in back-to-back quarters and topped Corivdan's best year to date. None of it would have been possible without you and your work. You're the lifeblood of the company and you deserve to be celebrated, which is why we insist you come!

On tap for the party we have a full buffet, an open bar all night, karaoke, special prizes, and some surprise entertainment! It's going to be a blast! I can't wait to see you all there. And, again, thank you for continued excellence in your work.

✳

Fragment of essay found taped to the microwave in the mailing department break room of Corivdan Incorporated. Found Nov. 26, 2018.

The QO Murders: A Conspiracy of Wealth

In December of 1898, a pair of pheasant hunters stumbled upon twenty-five dead bodies in the forests outside the smoke-shrouded limits of Pittsburgh, Pennsylvania. The sheer obscenity of so much unexplained death in one location would have been sufficient to make the discovery notable, but the corpses also exhibited bizarre and unexplained modifications. To wit, each of the bodies had its eyes scooped out and replaced with silver dollar coins; all the fingers of every body had been cut off and rolls of dollar bills had been stuffed into the gaping stumps; and when authorities attempted to move the deceased, they found the task nearly impossible, as the corpses weighed several times more than they should have. Ultimately, it took four stout men to lift each one of the bodies onto the wagons that transported them to the city, where they were examined by doctors and law enforcement officials. Autopsies revealed that the internal organs of the deceased had been entirely removed and their remaining hollow cavities packed full of gleaming, freshly-minted pennies. The back of each penny, despite its newness, bore two machine-cut capital letters—Q and O—that obliterated the "Indian head" design that adorned all pennies at the time. The amount of money stuffed into the bodies totaled exactly the same in every case: 210 dollars and 21 cents—an amount that would equal over 6,000 dollars today.

No one doubted that what happened to these individuals must have been murder, yet an investigation into the crime never began. City police filed a report concerning the incident, but declined to assign any officers or detectives to collect evidence from the crime scene, identify the victims, or interview potential witnesses. Sheriffs in the outlying municipality where the bodies were found also turned a blind eye to the murders, choosing to delegate all responsibility to city officials.

Newspapers, though especially hungry for audacious stories in the late 19th century, barely covered the murders, writing of them in the abstract. Reporters mentioned few of the more remarkable details about the bodies' mutilations and implied that the deaths were potentially self-inflicted or accidental. Editors buried any stories of the murders deep within their rags' pages, well beyond the attention of casual readers. Without media attention, the murders soon became little more than hearsay.

Why police or journalists seemed uninterested in investigation of the murders remains unknown, though there is some evidence that forces working behind the scenes squelched inquiry into the incident. Certain powerful and moneyed industrialists and bankers such as J.P.

[remainder of essay missing, page torn in mid-sentence]

※

MEMO
CORIVDAN INCORPORATED

To: All Hourly Employees
From: Human Resources
Subject: Holiday Party RSVP
Date: Nov. 27, 2018

This is a reminder that Holiday Party RSVPs are now open and can be returned by email or personally dropped off with Jaylen Vernor in HR. We welcome you to invite spouses, partners, and significant others, but make sure to include their names in your RSVP under "Guest." The more, the merrier!

※

Photocopied note left under windshield wipers of cars parked in the Corivdan Building parking garage. Found Nov. 28.

They care about you as a fire cares about its kindling. Their celebration is not for you, but for the act of feeding the insatiable QO. You are neither the gift giver nor the gift receiver, but the gift itself. Resign now. Do not come back tomorrow. You do not have much time.

✻

MEMO
CORIVDAN INCORPORATED

To: All Employees
From: Human Resources
Subject: Holiday Party Prizes
Date: Nov. 28, 2018

After several inquiries into the nature of the holiday party prizes, we've decided to give you a preview of what you could win.
Included among the prize pool will be:
-box seat tickets to this year's Super Bowl
-two additional paid weeks of vacation time
-full personal use of a company BMW or Mercedes-Benz for a year
-cruise tickets to the Bahamas
-personal chef service for three months
-newest gen smartphones and smartpads
-and more exciting prizes yet to be revealed.
This is our biggest employee celebration in company history! Everyone will win! Attendance is mandatory, but believe us when we say you'll definitely want to be at the party!

✻

Email sent to all email accounts ending in the corivdan.com domain.

To: Corivdan Employees

From: s7a7g7e@mailserv.com
Date: November 29, 2018
Subject: 1926 Baltimore Massacre

In August of 1926, a nameless crabber checking his traps in Baltimore's inner harbor discovered that one of the traps had snagged on something in the bay and would barely budge. A poor man, he had no funds to replace the trap, so he worked at hauling it from the depths for hours. When he finally heaved it out of the water, he found it entangled with a length of sparkling gold cable, and that the cable led to an object beneath the surface that he'd partially dredged up—a statue of some sort, he thought, human as it was in shape and reflective as polished metal.

The crabber enlisted the aid of other fishermen in the area and, together, they worked to raise the "statue." Once rescued from the sea floor, the nature of the object became no clearer. It was gold—that much was obvious—but if it was a statue, it was the most poorly executed statue in the history of sculpture, as the figure possessed a vaguely human form but lacked any notable features other than the letters Q and O stamped upon its chest in ornate calligraphy. Further, the gold cable that connected the crab trap to the statue extended back into the murky depths, hinting at further discoveries.

The crabber notified authorities of his find, imagining it might be of historical significance, if not monetary value. When experts from local universities examined the statue, however, they realized it was not a statue at all. Rather, it was an impromptu sarcophagus, a solid gold shell poured over a human body.

The revelation of a corpse within the gold tomb triggered a police response, and soon the area of the bay where the body had been found was scoured by police and Coast Guard divers. What they uncovered beneath the waves was another thirty-five statuesque bodies, all bound together at their ankles like a chain gang, all bearing the QO stamp on their golden prisons. The gilded manacles and metallic shells weighted the bodies to the sea bed and made recovery of the deceased difficult, but, with the help of barges and cranes, authorities managed to lift the petrified dead from their watery repose within a week.

After recovery, coroners and medical examiners determined that the bodies had been in the bay for less than a month, though more accurate dating was impossible. They also found even more gold inside the airways of every corpse, which implied, horribly, that the deceased had been covered in molten metal while alive and had breathed in the scorching ooze. They agreed that the gold overlay—whether by burning or suffocation—was the cause of death for each and every person reclaimed from the bay, and that Baltimore police clearly had, therefore, a mass murder on their hands.

Given that experts in precious metals estimated the total worth of the gold shells and cables to be well over ten million dollars, no one was brave enough to venture a guess as to who could have committed the murders. Only the ultra-wealthy had the means to pull off the crime, and no one in the Baltimore PD wanted to anger the wrong multimillionaire.

Before any sort of serious criminal probe could even be launched, though, agents from the Bureau of Investigation—the FBI's precursor—arrived in Baltimore and asserted jurisdiction over the murders. Agents from the BOI collected all evidence in the possession of the Baltimore police and set it under a high-level security clearance which only BOI investigators could obtain. They squelched the flow of information from the police to the news media, as well, so that the murders received little public recognition. Rumors concerning "the golden dead of the harbor" circulated in bars and shadowed docks, but nowhere else. The massacre slouched into the realm of folklore and urban legend. People, preoccupied by their daily routines and their struggles to make a decent living, soon forgot about the "golden dead" and their mystery.

Questions remain, though. Who committed the murders? Who were the victims? Why did the BOI step in and seal off the case from both local PD and the general public?

The only detail of the incident that may provide a clue is the stamp on every golden casket, the stamp bearing the letters QO.

✳

MEMO
CORIVDAN INCORPORATED

To: All Hourly Employees
From: Tyler Vine, Head, Information Technology
Subject: 1926 email
Date: Nov. 30, 2018

Do not open an email with the subject line 1926 Baltimore Massacre, as it contains malware that will infect your computer and the Corivdan network. If you have already opened it, please contact your supervisor so we can address the issue further and review your computer's software.

I would also like to remind everyone that company email addresses should not be used for non-Corivdan business. Giving Corivdan email addresses to third parties can result in unwanted spam emails such as the "1926" mailing, which often contain threats to the security of our network and information databases.

Continued use of company email for non-company purposes can result in reduced compensation or dismissal.

Thank you for your attention in this matter.

✳

Series of professionally printed and laminated signs placed at intervals along roadway leading to Corivdan Incorporated. First seen December 2, 2018. All signs removed by December 4, 2018.

At any given moment, police and the FBI have over 150,000 active missing persons cases.

Inactive missing persons cases in the U.S. number well over 600,000.

Almost all missing persons come from middle and lower-class backgrounds.

Fewer resources are spent searching for missing persons with lower incomes.

This is the reason serial killers frequently use impoverished and "transitional" neighborhoods as hunting grounds.

Even middle-class missing persons are low priority cases, though.

When's the last time you heard about the brutal murder of a millionaire?

A person without any significant wealth or fame is a no one in this country, and their disappearance merely verifies their status.

The acolytes of QO count on you to be no one. It makes your disappearance so much easier.

Don't satisfy them. Don't let them come for you. Quit Corivdan now.

✳

MEMO
CORIVDAN INCORPORATED

To: All Hourly Employees
From: Marshall Everington, CEO, Corivdan Inc.

Subject: Bonuses
Date: Dec. 3, 2018

Everyone,

I'm pleased to announce that we will be presenting bonus checks at the holiday party.

As many of you know, we broke all our previous earnings highs for the 2018 fiscal year. Revenue streams are up across every division of the company and expenditures are at a record low. Corivdan is flourishing.

Bonuses are a small way to say "thank you" for the part you play in the company's success. Every hourly and salaried non-executive employee will receive their bonus at the party. You are all the real currency of Corivdan, and I want you to know how much you're valued.

I look forward to seeing you at the party.

✳

Text of audio clip left as voicemail for various Corivdan Inc. employees. Voicemails created overnight Dec. 5, 2018. All Corivdan company voicemail reset Dec. 6, 2018.

[Incomprehensible screams]

[Chorus of voices]: Great QO, Exalted Infinite Hunger, Father of Mammon, Mother of Moloch, we call upon you to expand our worth, our reach, and our power. We now give you your due, knowing that these souls are but motes of dust in your limitless vault and that your share of all things is gloriously ever expanding.

[More screams. Sharper, louder.]

[Chorus of voices]: We pay your fair tribute, great QO, so that you might help us prosper and grow deep with your hunger. We thank you for the expanses you carve within ourselves and the hoards you provide us without. Allow us to possess this world as you possess us. In your name, QO, we ask for more. In your image, always more, always more, always more.

[A sound like many coins clinking as they spill from a container.]

[Wet, tearing noises, followed by gasps, sobs, and more screams.]

✳

MEMO
CORIVDAN INCORPORATED

To: All Employees
From: Allison Mendel, Acting Head, Information Technology
Subject: Renovation of voicemail system
Date: Dec. 6, 2018

This message is to let you know that all voicemail was deleted last night as part of a scheduled system upgrade. You can still access your voicemail as usual and should notice no changes other than a quicker retrieval time of messages.

If you need to recover any important voicemails that were purged, please see **me** in the IT department for approval, as Tyler has been relieved of his duties. One of our technicians will be able to restore any necessary messages.

Thank you for your understanding and cooperation in this matter.

✳

Newspaper article found encased in lucite and glued to the concrete facade of the Corivdan Building next to every entrance. First appeared Dec. 10, 2018. Construction crews removed the articles by Dec. 11, 2018.

Over Seventy Workers Missing in Fire
November 11, 1954

Toledo, OH—Overnight, the Owens Manufacturing plant south of downtown burned to the ground. At the time, more than seventy second-shift employees were at work in the building. None have been located or identified yet.

The plant, which produces engine parts for automobile manufacturers including Ford, Chevrolet, Mercury, and Studebaker, exploded in a blazing ball of green flames near midnight. A chemical explosion is suspected as the cause of the blaze, though fire marshals have also suggested the possibility of arson.

According to eyewitnesses, the fire engulfed the plant almost instantly and the flames remained bright green for the duration of the fire. Some bystanders claimed to see gold flecks in the flames, as well. A few also claimed to hear terrified screams and, in a strange turn, raucous laughter as the plant burned. One witness said that, "It almost sounded like a group of people were chanting at one point, but I don't know where it was coming from or I couldn't hear it, as loud as the fire was."

John Lyons, President of Owens Manufacturing said in a statement early this morning that, "Everyone at Owens is devastated by the tragedy. We offer our thoughts and prayers to the families of all our workers in this difficult time. Rest assured that we will do everything in our power to take care of everyone connect with the Owens community."

Owens Manufacturing employs more than two thousand workers. The second-shift employees at Owens who were at the plant last night are largely comprised of non-union laborers without life insurance or pension plans. Names of the missing have not yet been released.

Losses to Owens Manufacturing and its parent

company, the Quentin-Owens Corporation, which owns steel manufacturing plants in Pittsburgh and Baltimore, are estimated to be over ten million dollars. The losses may be recouped through insurance, though.

"The facility was insured for a very significant sum, so we're sure that we will rebuild and be back up and running soon," said Owens Vice-President Paul Boyle. "We won't abandon our workers and the city of Toledo."

✳

MEMO
CORIVDAN INCORPORATED

To: All Employees
From: Carlos Perilla, Head of Security
Subject: Recent Vandalism
Date: Dec. 11, 2018

Good day.

Given the recent vandalism of Corivdan property, I want to make sure all employees are aware of the procedures for reporting suspicious activity.

If you spot anyone attempting to deface or destroy company property, please do not intervene personally. Instead, take a video or picture of the person in question and call security at extension 7810. If safe to do so, remain near the scene until someone from security arrives.

If you see defaced property, please note the location and manner of defacement and report it to security at the same extension.

We want to insure a safe and positive work environment, so please don't hesitate to contact us when you spot a potential act of vandalism.

✳

Messages found printed on toilet paper rolls and paper towels in all restrooms within the Corivdan Building, Dec. 12, 2018. All paper products removed and replaced by Dec. 13, 2018.

Corivdan Inc. began operations in 1976 as Corivdan Holdings.

Corivdan Holdings did not fare well and, by 1983, was on the brink of bankruptcy.

In 1984, three Corivdan mailroom employees were killed by a workplace shooter carrying a gold-plated shotgun using shells filled with diamond buckshot.

The identity of the shooter, who killed himself after the murders, remains unknown.

In 1985, Corivdan acquired SunTrust Bank and Dekker & Dekker Loans, consolidating under the Corivdan Inc. title. The acquisitions made Corivdan over 250 million dollars at the time and led to more than 5 billion in profits in the following thirty years.

In 1991, six Corivdan interns went missing during a team building exercise in the Catskills. All were presumed drowned in a rafting accident, though their bodies were never found.

In 1992, Corivdan Inc. merges with Quentin-Owens Inc., formerly the Quentin-Owens Corporation. By the end of the decade, the merger nets profits of over 7 billion dollars for both entities.

In 2003, Corivdan posts record highs for yearly profits. It opens a branch office in Orlando, Florida.

The following year, the Orlando building collapses due to substandard construction.

Fifteen employees are killed in the collapse.

No one can explain why the deceased show bruising on their wrists and ankles, nor can anyone explain why all the deceased are found wearing finely tailored suits stuffed with stacks of hundred-dollar bills.

Corivdan donates the found money to the families of

the victims. It collects insurance payouts of over 75 million dollars on the building. It sues the construction agency, the city of Orlando, and the state of Florida for damages.

Corivdan wins its suits and collects another 200 million in awards.

The families of the deceased file similar lawsuits and also win. Their payout is less than 10 million, split over all plaintiffs.

In 2004, Corivdan constructs the Corivdan Building outside Cincinnati, Ohio. It is a state-of-the-art business facility. The company again posts record profits for the year.

In 2018, Corivdan breaks a billion dollars in profit for the fiscal year for the first time.

QO must be paid again.

❋

MEMO
CORIVDAN INCORPORATED

To: All Employees
From: Human Resources
Subject: Waste management
Date: Dec. 14, 2018

Please note that trash will not be taken out this weekend as the janitorial staff is experiencing heavy employee turnover. If a waste bin in your office or workspace is overflowing, you may dispose of its contents in the dumpsters outside the east wing exits.

We apologize for the inconvenience.

❋

Skywriting above Corivdan Building and vicinity. Seen Dec. 17, between 5p.m. and 6p.m.

YOU HAVE FOUR DAYS
QO IS COMING
IT WILL TAKE ITS DUE
QUIT NOW
RUN

✳

MEMO
CORIVDAN INCORPORATED

To: All Hourly Employees
From: Human Resources
Subject: Holiday Party
Date: Dec. 18, 2018

A reminder that the mandatory company holiday party will be held from 7p.m. to midnight this Friday in the conference center (3rd floor, west wing).

The response to the party has been tremendous. Over 90% of you have RSVP'd and many others have confirmed attendance verbally or by email. Needless to say, everyone at Corivdan will be at the party for the food, drink, dancing, and prizes!

And don't forget, there will be special entertainment and surprises!

We can't wait to see you there!

✳

Spray painted message found on the walls of the Corivdan Building's parking garage, Dec. 20, 2018. The final line of the message ends in what may be a dark red paint spatter.

Last chance. Their kind has been around since the dawn of time. Their god has been around even longer. You can't win by sitting at their table and playing their game. Do not believe them. They control all the rules. If you stay, you are doomed to [message cuts off here]

MEMO
CORIVDAN INCORPORATED

To: All Employees
From: Carlos Perilla, Head of Security
Subject: Security Incident
Date: Dec. 20, 2018

Early this morning, security reported an incident in the parking garage where an armed individual was caught committing an act of vandalism. Security engaged and subdued the perpetrator with only minor injury to themselves.

Police and medical personnel were called and have dealt with the situation. If you see any additional police presence in Corivdan today, please lend them your full support.

Thank you for your cooperation.

MEMO
CORIVDAN INCORPORATED

To: All Employees
From: Marshall Everington, CEO, Corivdan, Inc.
Subject: Holiday party
Date: Dec. 21, 2018

Remember to arrive by 7 p.m. this evening for the holiday party. Enter through the west wing entrance, as all other entrances and exits will be locked at 6.

Tonight is going to be very special. I can't wait to see all of you there.

Happy holidays!

Camera Obscura

C.M. Muller

HAUGLAND REPOSITIONED THE tripod a few yards downhill, making sure everything was level on the incline before affixing the camera. He took extra care this time, having nearly dropped the century-old contraption during his last setup. A single dry-plate remained, and if it took additional time for the arrangement, then so be it. Unlike the digital camera that had once been his mainstay, there would be no re-dos. There was one opportunity to get this right, and the challenge of doing so was what had drawn him to such an outmoded format in the first place. He had captured a dozen shots of the abandoned farmhouse thus far, and while at this early stage he could only imagine in his mind's-eye the resulting images imprinted upon each plate, he sensed he had accomplished what he set out to do. He supposed part of the reason he spent so much time at this particular location was because today marked the end of the nearly yearlong project he had undertaken to document the abandoned farmsteads of Minnesota. He had chosen to conclude the project in the southeastern corner of the state (bluff country, as it was known), largely because of his genealogical ties to this region, but even more so because of the topography. Since childhood, he had been drawn to this unglaciated wonderland, what with its mysterious back roads, forested hills, and, most importantly, hidden farmsteads.

He had collected as much information about each site

as local history societies would allow, a bounty of material, really, the highlights of which he planned to include alongside each photo. For as many house histories as he was able to uncover, there were, unfortunately, a few lost to the vicissitudes of time and decay, remaining as anonymous and derelict as their crumbling structures. Haugland never let this dissuade him from photographing a site that appealed to him, as was the case in this final arrangement. When he initially surveyed the area, using the camera on his phone to document possible sites, the place that left the greatest impression was this one. He had emailed a local historian, attaching images of various farmsteads he hoped to obtain backstories for, and had been pleasantly surprised by the immediate outpouring of information. His familial connection to the area (which he prefaced at length in the email) proved of great benefit, and his rapport with the elderly genealogist had grown stronger with each exchange; indeed, the woman seemed grateful for his having gotten in touch, and had spent countless hours researching his avalanche of queries. By the time their correspondence came to an end, Haugland perceived an even greater connection to this land of his forebears. The only mystery lay in this final farmstead, the history of which the elder either did not know or was purposefully withholding. All she revealed was a last name and a profession: Kolsrud, bachelor farmer. There had to be something she was not telling him, though Haugland was hard pressed to call her on it, because her help up to that point had proven so beneficial.

Though deflated by this lack of information, Haugland decided he would include images of the farmstead anyway, use them as a visual denouement to the book, with the added coda that not all mysteries need solving, that mystery was essential to the imagination. Still, Haugland could not help but wonder why the old woman had been so tight-lipped. Did she or her family have some connection to certain events (horrific or otherwise) that had occurred there? This seemed a possibility, and if so, Haugland need only dig elsewhere to obtain the information. Certainly, there were others in town who could flesh out the history of the place. But he wasn't really sure he wanted to dismantle the mystery. At least not yet.

For now, in this bittersweet finale to a project that had consumed so much of his time and energy, Haugland's focus remained entirely on capturing the best possible image. The lighting was ideal at this hour, and as Haugland tinkered with the final settings and position of the camera, he felt pleasantly overwhelmed by both the landscape and the fact he was on the cusp of finishing his passion project. The camera was ready to go, and Haugland, taking a deep and steady breath, depressed the switch that activated both shutter and gears. The intricate internal *tick-ticking* was music to his ears, and as the century camera made its slow panoramic rotation, he eased himself to the gentle slope of the hill, flattening the tall grass beneath him. Hands beneath his head, he stared at the cloudless sky and revelled again in his accomplishments. He would spend the weekend obsessively developing the images captured from this final shoot. As hard as it was to admit, he was looking forward to returning to the city after spending so much time in the solitude of the natural world. He put everything he had into the project, and he knew it would take time to re-regulate himself to life in the real world. Mostly, he would miss these calm moments of communing with nature as the camera did its work. The mechanical whirr, strangely enough, seemed to belong to this environment. If he closed his eyes, Haugland could nearly convince himself he was listening to the hidden clockwork of the world.

Haugland plucked a length of tall grass and stuck it between his lips, savoring these final moments. Even now he imagined the details slowly mirroring themselves to the dry-plate: it was a composition of crisp black and white beauty that in many ways was more powerful than the original landscape itself. Film images had the potential of outliving their real-life counterparts, and digital photos were ephemeral. Haugland's work would be preserved long after these farmhouses deteriorated and became dust. He supposed this was part of the reason he afforded the project with so much reverence.

His placid mood was abruptly shattered by an other-worldly and high-pitched scream. It seemed to emanate from the camera itself, and as Haugland sprang to his feet, the sound was replaced by another he knew all too well: the short, sharp shock of cracking glass. The camera continued along its interminably slow rotation, its broken eye already transferring a replica of its jagged wound to the dry-plate. The lens had functioned brilliantly for the entirety of the year, so why it should choose to fail now was beyond comprehension. Haugland voiced his frus-tration, nearly pushing the tripod over in his rage, but he contained himself enough to allow the camera to finish its course. Perhaps the tainted image would prove interesting and not a total loss. When the ticking gears ceased their full rotation, Haugland carefully detached the camera from the tripod to get a better idea of the extent of the damage. He upended the camera and laid it gently on the flattened spot of tall grass where he had been resting, and then twisted the lens from its wooden housing. A deep fissure bisected the glass, and Haugland felt a crack beginning to develop in him as well. He hoped the incident would not taint the project going forward.

After packing his equipment, Haugland glanced a final time at the old Kolsrud place, a structure that continued to bewitch his imagination. He turned his back on it and care-fully made his way down the hill to the dirt road where his Volvo was parked. The vehicle's presence, as he homed in on its bright and boxy hull, made him slightly discombobu-lated, as though he were not perceiving things through his own eyes but rather through some past-century relative who could never have been witness to (or understood) such an advancement.

✳

While Haugland had intended to begin work in the dark room upon his return, he made the mistake of resting for a time on the sofa before lugging his equipment to the basement. His eyes grew heavy and the next thing he knew it was half past noon of the following day. As he descended to his workroom through the stairwell—a narrow shaft covered with framed photos he considered his best work— Haugland was always left with the impression of exiting one reality and entering into another, which he supposed all creative spaces were designed for. The images on the wall were a visual trigger that redirected his frame of mind, and once he was in the depths of this self-made dream factory, Haugland found it difficult to leave when aboveground responsibilities demanded his attention. Ascending the stairs and resurfacing into the current century was always disconcerting, if not downright depressing. Perhaps this was the reason he relied on the photographic techniques used more than a century ago—he was not a man of his own time, never truly had been. There was a period of his creative life when he fully participated in the digital revolution, producing thousands of photos of the cityscape in which he lived, but in the end the images had left him feeling empty. Their sale had provided little else but a stable income, and in time he began obsessing to a greater extent about the past, going beyond the simple genealogical concerns that interested him from an early age. It had taken years of trial and error to feel comfortable with these techniques of the past, but in the end he found the results far superior to any image he ever produced digitally. And he had no intention of yet again allowing the modern to influence and infect him any more than it already had.

The walls of the work room were once covered by a plethora of city images, but Haugland long ago stripped and replaced them with the bulk of his current project. There would, of course, be a limit to how many images he could include in the book, and he was still on the fence about which ones, in the end, would make the cut. Even the images he considered flawed held a special meaning, resurrecting fond memories of a particular shoot. Some impressions were so powerful that for long moments Haugland felt himself literally transported into the landscape, so much so that at times he could almost feel the heat of the sun or the soft prairie breeze.

Haugland proceeded to the supply counter along the far wall, setting his thermos to the side. He fanned through the selection of vinyl records stacked near the turntable. Most were composers of Scandinavian origin, and Haugland wavered between Sibelius and Grieg before finally withdrawing the latter and setting it with utmost care on the turntable. He adjusted the volume and then poured himself his first cup of coffee. "In the Hall of the Mountain King" built gradual momentum in the small space, putting Haugland in the proper mood. After the red lights were lit, his eyes adjusted quickly to the womb-like setting. Such a comparison became even more apt as selected images slowly came to life in the shallow amniotic of the developer. This was magic hour for Haugland, and once he started working, he always had difficulty calling it quits. He had a timer on the counter, but he purposefully avoided tacking up a wall clock. Under the red light, time for the most part ceased, and when all was said and done and the space returned to blinding white, Haugland was often surprised by how many hours had passed. The early mornings transitioned in no time to deep night, but fatigue was never a factor and sleep was the furthest thing from his mind. He figured this was due to having spent so much time in the womb, as it were, dreaming in his own delectable way, that the real shore of night had no pull. Most evenings he'd be cast adrift, cleaning his cameras for the umpteenth time, perusing his catalog of photos, revising detailed impressions of each, and maybe, if he was lucky, catching an hour or two of sleep at midafternoon the following day.

Haugland's first image developed beautifully, light and shadow approximating what he imagined while initially laboring over the shot: a slight rise in the prairie, the sea of tall grass arching toward a dilapidated island home. In many ways the image drew all the important details out of the physical setting, captured the very character of its soul. The black and white composition lent an air of mystery, stripped away reality's harsh glare. Additionally, Haugland could (like an alchemist) manipulate the scene even further if he wished, heightening its emotions through experimentation. This first image seemed to him as close to perfection as he could hope for. Usually he nitpicked images as they went through processing, but as he pulled this one from the fix and clipped it to the drying rack, its beauty overwhelmed him. It was only as he was turning away to begin work on the second exposure that he noticed a small blemish on the print. A shadowy presence, for lack of a better term, stood just beyond the broken porch, and for the life of him he could not help but think he had captured a ghostly resident standing proudly before its domain. No, the only logical explanation was that the blemish was a bit of soil adhered to the lens. It in no way lessened the impact of the image, and in a sense added a bit of intrigue. The "individual" was blurred and ethereal, giving the impression of a ghost caught in a haunted landscape. Haugland would crop and enlarge the image later on, after making initial prints of the other images. He wondered if he would be able to draw out more detail, or if the blemish would simply collapse in upon itself.

All these suppositions were thrown to the wayside when he developed the second, third, and fourth images:

each contained the self-same blemish, though not in the exact position as the first. The shift in the second photograph was hardly discernible, and Haugland carefully compared the new image against the first to realize that, yes, there had been movement, accompanied by what appeared to be a slight raising of one hand, as though the specter were attempting to gain Haugland's attention. In the third shot the willowy defect moved closer still, and, unbelievably, became more defined. When Haugland closed his eyes, his mind's-eye fleshed the ghostly imperfection into a long-haired young woman, her sleek nose and shapely chin suggesting an overall poetic litheness. All was not lost when he opened his eyes, for the fantasy behind his lids seemed to resolve the flaw even further, leaving Haugland slightly embarrassed by a kind of sexual reverie that spoke volumes to his current companionless state. Indeed, if he remembered back to the last fling he'd had—one in which he hoped to achieve a more lasting relationship—the individual in question (Freya had been her name) more than a little resembled this specter. And while his initial reaction to the flaw had been one of dismay, he grew to appreciate the unexpected (and quite beautiful) detail. He thought the series of ghostly photos might be unified into another smaller-scaled project, and he planned to pitch this idea to his editor the next time they met.

While the specter continued to creep closer in subsequent images, it was only when Haugland examined the tenth that a strange new detail emerged. Nothing yet had come into true focus, all the result of the subject's continual movement. This was part of the charm of using the old technique. Exposure time was much slower than modern film, which could capture most movement with crystal clarity. In this instance, the subject's long hair and what appeared to be a flowing white gown were accompanied by a ghostly trail of smoke that seemed to emanate from her lower back and curl downward around her leg, a kind of spectral tail.

Haugland didn't think much of this at first, figuring it was no more than a portion of the prairie grass she was wading through, but when it came into greater focus in subsequent images, he could not escape the impression this wispy appendage was an essential part of the specter herself. And thus the "ghost book" took another route entirely: one along a more folkloric path involving the Norse figure of the *huldra*, that tail-bearing deity of the forest known for duping men with her beauty, first seducing and then luring them to her mountain home. This and numerous other folk tales had first been related to him by his beloved grandfather Ingemon (or "Ing" as he liked to be called), whose powers of description were so keen that for years afterward Haugland's boyhood dreams were haunted by various incarnations of the *huldra*; dreams that started with seduction and ended, after the creature's warm embrace had run its course, in paralysis and regret. Whether he liked to admit it or not, these encounters had had a lasting effect.

As Haugland continued to develop the final images, he focused less and less on the Kolsrud place and more on the mysterious figure as it continued its slow approach. By the third to last image, facial details were finally beginning to emerge, and as the second to last rose from the depths of the developer Haugland's eyes widened. The Kolsrud place was nowhere to be seen, the entirety of the frame having been permeated by the countenance of the so-called specter, a term that proved inadequate to describe the ethereal beauty of the woman's features. The print was incredibly detailed, so much so that Haugland half expected the subject to part her lips in either pleasantry or kiss. All through the development process, Haugland could not remove his gaze from the image, and stared at it long after he clipped it to the drying rack. Hours might have passed for all he knew or cared. It was the most beautiful portrait photo he had ever captured, and it took him an eternity to draw his attention away and realize a final image still needed to be developed.

The resulting photo turned out to be the antipode of the previous. As the picture drew into focus in the developer tray, Haugland recalled the moment the century camera's lens cracked. The shock he'd experienced was replicated now as he gazed in semi-horror at another portrait, this one cracked and blemished beyond all reason, shattering the woman's previous beauty and revealing a kind of bark-like decay just beneath the surface. Haugland wondered if this was merely the result of the cracked lens, or if the transformation occurred within the figure itself. Of all the wondrous images he captured over the course of his last shoot, this alone was the one Haugland felt no compulsion to keep. He halted the process at the developer and tossed the grotesquerie into the trash.

He quickly cleaned up, and by the time he withdrew from the red-light womb and collected the images from the drying rack, he was already well on his way to forgetting about the final portrait. The undeniable beauty of the second to last image made sure of that.

Two days later, Haugland retraced his route to the Kolsrud place. It was an exhausting drive and the passage of time (at least how he normally perceived it) seemed oddly quite distorted. He supposed part of this had to do with his obsessive work schedule, but the overcast sky was as much to blame. After fifty miles he nearly called it quits and returned home, wishing he'd checked the weather forecast before venturing out that morning. Not that he couldn't capture some stunning black and white imagery on such a gloomy day as this, but quite frankly he wasn't in the mood. The thing that pushed him forward now was a new obsession, the uncovering of a mystery.

The impossible portrait of the woman would not leave him. Indeed, he focused on nothing but fashioning hundreds of prints of her in various modes, cropping out her eyes, her lips, her nose, and exposing the image as a whole with various contrasts and shadings. That single image opened up the possibility of an entirely new project, but for the time being he enjoyed swimming timelessly in the depths of each incarnation, capturing not only crisp details but a multitude of abstract variances as well. Had he been able to sink bodily into the development process itself, he would have done so, becoming one with this mysterious Madonna. All fantasies considered, the only realistic option that remained open to him was a return to the source of origin, though even this seemed no more than an impulsive act whose foundation would, in the end, crumble under false reverie. The logic of this inevitable outcome, the surety of it, had not been enough to make Haugland redirect his obsessional thinking.

By the time he pulled to the edge of the country road at the bottom of the long rise that led to the Kolsrud place, Haugland felt worse for wear. He stepped from the Volvo a bit too abruptly, his stiff legs nearly pitching him into the narrow culvert at the side of the road. He withdrew his gear from the back seat, and slowly ascended the sun-dappled rise, grateful the weather seemed to be shifting from its previous gloominess. Whether or not it would last, Haugland sensed he would at least be afforded a clear enough window of time to capture a few more images, his intent being to again lure the mystery out of hiding.

He positioned the tripod in the same spot as his last outing, locating, to his immense pleasure, the deep indentations the steel-tipped implement had previously marked in the soil. He figured the land would have healed over a bit, but the marks seemed as fresh as he had left them, as though the land foresaw his return, retained this sigil upon its skin just for him. While his first impulse was to rush through the process of set-up, Haugland did his level best to put as much care into his efforts as always, and by the time he attached the camera to the base of the tripod, adjusted the new lens, and inserted the first slide of film, he was confident he had replicated the conditions of his previous shoot.

Before exposing the first image, however, Haugland's first order of business was to make a thorough investigation of the house with his digital camera in tow, hoping to document the dilapidation within, and perhaps even inadvertently capture an image or two of its ethereal occupant. Idle curiosity led Haugland to frame his first digital image directly in front of the tripod, merely to ascertain whether or not the newfangled camera was capable of detecting things unseen. After the image was stored to internal memory, Haugland viewed it through the digital display, noticing nothing out of the ordinary. He dove deeper into the image, zooming as far as he could to the area just beyond the porch, to the place where he first glimpsed the ghostly imperfection. The clarity of the image was impeccable, but revealed nothing beyond what was already there. He shifted the image vector, examining various other quadrants of the house, with special focus on the windows, most of which had been stripped of their glass. He lingered on one of the upper windows, trying to determine whether or not the shadow he detected there contained enough detail to suggest the human form or was merely an oddly hanging drape. He sensed his imagination was getting the better of him, so he shouldered his camera and started toward the house. The sky was relatively free of clouds now, and his intuition told him he would have more than enough time to complete his outdoor shoot. He captured a few more images along the way, even going so far, at the midway point, of doing an about face and snapping a photo of the old camera rising in the distance like an ornate periscope in a prairie sea.

When Haugland arrived at the porch he hesitated a moment, trying to locate the spot where the blurred figure first appeared. Again he turned so that he was facing the buoy of his century camera. He stared directly at the lens, as though waiting for its shutter to open and begin its lengthy exposure, but after a time he raised the digital camera to his eye, framed the shot, and took a series of images from this perspective. He then cautiously stepped onto the porch, half expecting it to give way under his weight, but it held, offering up only minimal complaint. He took a series of close-ups of the disintegrating railing, finding in its textures of peeling paint an infinite amount of abstraction. He turned his attention to the single warped window next to the door, capturing in its reflection a brightly lit but distorted prairie. Even the tripod could be seen, though just barely. Its blurred outline resembled an ill-defined interloper. By the time he stepped into the house, Haugland had taken nearly fifty images.

The interior resembled many of the other locations he'd had the opportunity to walk through: stripped of most, but not all, of its possessions, its floors strewn with curling and decayed wallpaper, as well as dirt blown in from its open front door and windows. Layered throughout were bits of ceiling and shards of glass. There was so much here vying for his attention that he had a difficult time deciding where to begin. He knew if he started in this initial space, he would end up nitpicking angles and lose track of time. For now he decided on another course of action: that of allowing himself to wander freely through each room, making mental notes of areas he wished to focus on. He decided to begin on the second floor, even though ascending the stairs caused more than a little trepidation. Not only did the rungs creak horribly, but the rail was so wobbly that after one touch Haugland decided to avoid it altogether. He always considered the construction of past things to be far superior to modern offerings, but time and the elements, could decimate anything.

When Haugland arrived on the second level, the

interior seemed to have darkened by a discernible degree. He walked cautiously to the window overlooking the front of the house, and at first he thought the unbroken pane was so grimy as to allow only a minimal amount of light, but this was not the case at all. Haugland peered into the distant prairie, sighting his tripod. The wind picked up, and whistled through the broken ruin that surrounded him. Tall grass swayed to and fro, and a sudden gust of wind was strong enough to uproot the tripod and toss it to the ground. The prairie resembled a vast undulating maw, bent on removing all evidence of the camera. Haugland scanned the area, and could not even see his vehicle or the road beneath the rise. Without such anchors, a growing sense of dislocation overcame him, as though the landscape were shifting into something wholly ominous and new. A heavy downpour followed, obscuring and further transforming his view. He listened to the wind blasting through the reed-like apertures of the house, and it too seemed to change, altering from intonations evoking terror into something far more pleasing to his ears, something like singing.

Haugland retreated from the window, determined now to get out of the house and retrieve his rain-soaked equipment before the storm got worse. This might prove to be the final force of nature to topple the century-old abode. As he stood at the top of the stairs looking down, fatigue overcame Haugland and it took every effort during the descent not to fall. Thankfully, the handrail proved more stable than he'd previously thought. Without its support, he would not have been able to descend. The wind and the song intensified as he stood at the bottom of the stairs, leaning for a long moment against the wall, waiting for his energy to return. He closed his eyes, trying to revitalize his previous alertness. The singing was much louder now, and he found it comforted him just as much as the Sibelius or Grieg he played in his darkroom. He opened his eyes and shifted along the wall to the opening that led to the main room and the front door beyond. From there he had a direct view outside, though most of the landscape was obscured by a lithe and long-haired figure standing in side profile on the porch. She seemed to be singing to the prairie.

Minutes passed before she decided to move, and when she did Haugland became aware of the bark-like skin of her lower back and the obscene indication of her tail. She made her way nakedly into her domain, her gaze fixed entirely upon him, singing her beautiful, entrancing song all the while. Her tail flicked playfully to either side of her hips, like a whip in the lead-up to a strike, and her seductive lips were parted in a sinister smile. Had Haugland been able he would have walked directly toward her, meeting her halfway, but he was as inert as his century camera, his own lens open and alert, capturing everything upon the dry-plate of his mind. Each step she took afforded an opportunity to expose another image to memory, the only faculty of his that remained.

As the woman strode across the detritus of the floor, her appearance slowly changed. By the time she was midway to him, her arms and abdomen and nearly the entirety of her neck and face had transitioned from pearlescent to a putrid, bark-like flesh. Her song, though, remained as beautiful as ever, and Haugland was left to focus on it alone as the spindly-limbed *huldra* embraced him like some long-lost lover finally returned home. Her transition—like an exposure gone terribly wrong—was so overpowering that Haugland would have given anything to close his eyes, but such a simple act was lost to him. As the final, horrific exposure coalesced in the back of his mind, he fell to his knees and became one with the detritus.

And all the while his obsession continued its ancient and all-consuming song.

The Fascist Has a Party

M. Rickert

IT WAS HIS birthday, and even if it wasn't his birthday it was a day, and he had been born, and no one could argue with that. He wanted a party, and it was a great day for one—so he declared—the rain only landed on the small heads of those who believed lies they were told by the news which was, after all, totally fake because look, there he was, standing in the sun. Well, all right, it was a room but it was a sunny room, everyone could see that, and if it wasn't the sun it was a light and the light shone on him and that had to mean something, it meant something about who he was, the way he was followed by a spotlight like the greatest superstar that ever lived.

He would have invited the children, but the children were missing. This was a terrible thing and the fault of the other party. When the children came back he would have a party for them. A beautiful party full of the beautiful things they loved. In the meantime, there was no point in letting their absence ruin the day. There would be cake. He had promised cake and there it was, the most delicious cake anyone ever tasted, which was not made of children's tears, a horrible despicable thing to say. "Take a piece," he said. "Cake for everyone!" And if not for everyone, at least for some, and if not for some, at least for him, and if not delicious, at least okay, which was a problem, of course. Someone was in a lot of trouble over the cake which tasted only okay, so he convened a meeting right in the middle of the party and said, "Who is responsible for this crappy cake?" and the staff looked at one another for a full half-minute before they all pointed fingers at each other, which he thought was great fun, so he sat back and watched.

Then he said, "What this party needs is an execution! Where is that traitor?" He said it with such good cheer that everyone clapped and smiled and agreed until they realized he was actually serious, but by that point he was already leading them outside to the gallows and nobody wanted to make a scene. Besides, the guy was brilliant! A genius! And if not a genius he was, at least, the boss, and no one would disagree with that.

So he made a game of it with balloons and crepe paper streamers and an elaborate set of rules he shared with no one. He might have whispered them to his daughter, but no one else. Not even his other children; and you have to give him credit for that though some people say even he didn't know the rules. It didn't matter! It was his birthday, and it was his party and it went on and on, well into the night when someone lit the gaslights and the gallows faded into the shadows, which was a relief, because he did have a way of forgetting his plans.

So they were dancing to the music he said was playing, and eating the cake he insisted was not made of tears, and when they noticed others missing it was assumed they had just grown tired and gone home to sleep their very beautiful dreams of making their county what it had once been, or maybe never had been, but would become again; a place where bodies hung in the shadows of his great light, and the children weren't missing. After all, if you listened closely, you could hear their distant cries, well into that great American morning.

Child of Shower and Gleam

Rebecca Campbell

SHE TOOK THE main floor apartment in a rickety house on a rough street. A block over some speculator had bought properties and boarded them up, lowering the rents to something she could afford, though it still stretched her uncomfortably. But it had a porch and a backyard that was mostly hers, though technically she shared it with the two kinesiology students upstairs and the Engineering doctoral candidate in the basement. Next summer the little girl would be one, and together they would grow rosemary in pots on the front porch and that made it worth it. Even if the kitchen floor descended rapidly toward the back step, so grapes and cherry tomatoes and lentils all rolled away like they wanted to escape. It was okay because when the sun rose, her bedroom was flooded with light.

Despite economies, each week she was deeper in debt, and not for luxuries, either. Onesies. A secondhand stroller. Often at night she woke to a swollen bladder and thought about what else she could eliminate to pay for diapers or baby Tylenol. She didn't have a landline, a car. She didn't drink or smoke. It didn't matter for her, but she wondered what happened to a kid born to fatherlessness and debt. The lists of things she needed continued to grow. Diapers. Tiny washcloths with pictures of lions and giraffes on them. She made these lists on an air mattress beside the still-boxed bassinette she would eventually have to assemble. Formula if her milk didn't come in. Tiny socks.

She was making one of those lists on a Saturday

afternoon before work when she heard the knock, and though she hesitated to answer, she reminded herself she had nothing to worry about. A girl. Eight? Nine? Small, with pale eyes and dust-coloured hair tangled into a mat at the base of the skull. She stared. She said, "um."

Lynn said nothing

"I was wondering if you wanted to buy a picture for five dollars."

She offered a drawing of a heart with wings and a crown, drawn in marker, with the motto *LUv pEEpUL* above.

"No thank you," Lynn said.

"Okay."

The girl didn't go away.

"I have to go now," Lynn said. "I have to get ready for work."

"Are you pregnant?"

"Yes."

"When are you having the baby?"

"Soon. I really have to get ready for work."

"Is it a boy or a girl?"

"Girl," Lynn said. "I have to get ready for work."

"That means I have to go, right?"

"Yes."

The girl left. Lynn watched her through a gap in the blinds as she dropped her five-dollar drawing in the recycling bin. Then she got on her bike and peddled furiously into the humid afternoon.

✳

Another heat wave hit in the second week of August. Before that she had been pleased with her late summer due date, imagining backyard birthday parties before school started, a last celebration at the beaten-down end of summer. She'd tie ribbons around new shoes for the first day of school while the nights lengthened and tipped into September, the last popsicle of the year, blackberries and late plums.

Her tiny AC didn't do much but churn the dense night air, and she was swamped by her own body, rolling into and out of her air mattress, sweat pooling in every crease. She was working nights at the group home, which was easy but lonely, sitting up while the clients slept, listening for a knock at the door and an unwelcome visitor, her phone full of emergency contacts. During the day, when she couldn't sleep, she spent the afternoons outside, listing the things she could sell. Her laptop might get fifty or a hundred bucks. Nothing she owned, she realized as a glass of tap water bloomed in her hot belly, was even worth pawning. Not even an engagement ring that might bring in a hundred dollars.

The little one kicked her sharply between the ribs.

A kid coasted up to the house and dropped her bike onto the concrete walkway by the front door, like it was something she did every day, like the little girl would do in ten years. Like a cat whose neighbourhood wanderings are finished, and who now drops to her side to scratch her back in the dust of her own front yard.

"Hey, Lynn," the girl said.

"Hey," said Lynn. "I don't know your name."

"Nissa. But people call me Nis." She said it as though she wanted it to be true. As a kid, Lynn had badly wanted a nickname that was cool or unusual; she'd tried to get people to call her Ynna for a while.

"Nissa."

"Nis."

"Okay, Nis."

"Can I have some water? I biked all the way here."

The tap water was the temperature of underground, almost cool to the touch, tasting of pipes. Smelling, Lynn thought, as water ran down the sink in the ochre-tinted afternoon, like her grandmother's kitchen, one of the small, hot houses in the small, hot southern Ontario town where Lynn grew up. Not far from where she stood, but nevertheless distinguished by an irresistible barrier, as though light itself could not penetrate the distance between her current location and that old address and phone number. The smell of water, though, running across a sink, like the smell of potatoes steaming in summer, and the firefly darkness of a deep front porch. That was a rope that tightened around her heart.

The front door opened and she looked down the length of the apartment to see Nis in silhouette. She thought of a long corridor and a mirror at the end, revealing an earlier self—undistorted by pregnancy, or even adolescence—standing in the light.

"Hello?"

"Just a minute," Lynn said, "shut the door or you'll let the cool out. You should be careful biking in this weather, you can get dehydrated quickly."

"What's dehydrated?"

"When you don't have enough water in your system," Lynn said without thinking, and when Nissa nodded, she wondered if this was the future, the questions and unquestioned authority of motherhood. The feeling that she could say anything and it would be true.

The afternoon sky was a blue so deep and still it seemed both limitless and opaque. Unable to get her shoes on her enormous feet, Lynn stood barefoot as the day's sweat trickled down her back and over the cartilaginous lump that had recently emerged between her ribs. She thought of the day and decided that when Nissa visited they would go in the backyard to water the plants, the girl following after, and Lynn would tell her autumn plans: late flowers, vegetables. Asters. Lupins.

Then her phone rang with a number she didn't recognize and she hoped it was about the baby furniture. She had been so excited by the offer she didn't mind they also seemed to want her to attend a meeting that probably involved a Bible and some advice about how babies need fathers.

"Hello?" She didn't even hesitate, didn't have the moment of mouth-drying dread that had accompanied every ringing phone in the last year of their relationship.

"Lynn?"

"Is that—"

But of course it was.

"Don't hang up."

"I'm hanging up." But she didn't and her voice sounded so unsteady she hated herself.

"Don't hang up. If you hang—"

"—I'm hanging up now I'm hanging up now."

"Don't hang up. Don't hang up. Don't fucking hang up."

She said other things, or maybe she just cried, and then she ended the call and the texts started and she panicked when she read them and deleted them, but you were supposed to keep threatening communications. It was on the list of things to do when you left. She'd locked everything down, like it said on the list of things to do, and she hadn't been in touch with her Mom or her sister in two years so how had he got the number how did that happen.

The knock made her jump and screech because that was it, he was here, and the door that separated them was as flimsy as tissue paper. But the knock was also soft and familiar so it couldn't be him and he couldn't have her address he couldn't. Could he. Could he.

"Oh." Nis said. "Oh." Then she seemed to think carefully until she asked, "Do you have time for a visit?"

"No. Thank you." Lynn said mechanically. Her phone lit up in her hand. She dropped it.

Nissa picked it up. Then she was in the house, closing the door behind her, while Lynn thought of what her voice must have sounded like through the door, the whine of fear emanating from her heart, *just leave me alone leave me alone.*

Lynn thought she said, go home, but Nis followed her through to the nearly-cool bedroom with the dribbling AC unit. And Nissa was thirsty again, so they sat together on the floor, drinking water from wet glasses.

She should send Nissa home. It wasn't safe. She should double check that the doors were locked. She should send—

"—Is that your garden?" From the bedroom window the grass was rank and luxuriant, so densely matted that they could see only the tops of the plastic deck chairs some tenant had left behind. "It looks like a place no one lives," Nis said, "like everyone is gone."

"It's wild. I like it because you feel like something could hide there. A deer. Or. I don't know. A fairy ring. Something." The chairs might be from Wal-Mart, but they looked like ruins abandoned to the denizens of the back-alley world: squirrels and cats and starlings.

"We should go outside in the shade."

Together they returned to the kitchen where the broken vinyl flooring gave under their feet, and out the screen door where the air seemed like a physical barrier, a thick amber jelly surrounding them, suspending them in gold. Nissa led her to the black walnut and they sat under the dripline, where the grass was shorter and dappled with gold and dark.

"This is a good place to hide," she said, "no one in the world can see us in here." She began braiding the blades of grass where they stood in the ground, leaving their roots undisturbed.

"You aren't making a crown?"

Nis shook her head, picking another three blades to braid together, then trying a four and six strand, then

French braiding the grasses all around them. There was something hypnotic about the little fingers at work.

"When I was little, my Mom left."

"Where did she go?"

"I don't know. She just *left*. Who would leave a little kid like that?"

"That's sad."

"When you have your baby I could come and help you look after her. I could change diapers, my Mom showed me how."

"I thought your Mom was gone?"

"Yes. She showed me before she left."

"You'll be in school when the baby's here."

"Sometimes I stay home from school. I didn't go for a whole month last year. My Dad said, you stay home if you want to."

✻

Then it was dark and Lynn started, as though she had not realized time passed in their green darkness. "Oh, Nis, your Dad will be wondering where you are."

"I know," she said.

"You better go. He wouldn't like you being out at a stranger's house."

When Lynn went out the next morning, the dewless night now passed, the world not refreshed, the braids disconcerted her until she remembered Nis and her quick, dirty fingers weaving the blades together while they talked of nothing Lynn could remember.

✻

Maybe he was here every night after she left for work. Maybe that was his cigarette on the step. Maybe he kicked over the pot of basil by her front door.

She got the call from the group home saying they didn't need her though she'd planned another three days. She was still recalculating her budget when Nissa came over. It was already too hot to stay outside. Lynn had made popsicles from orange juice and mint tea from the tangled plants she'd found in the backyard. They sat in under the old AC. Nis burped, then giggled and licked orange juice off her wrist, missing the rivulet dripping onto her jean shorts.

Step. Step. Step.

Nis stood up, as though to go to the door, but Lynn held onto her arm and pulled her down, holding her still as the steps went up and down and up and down. Lynn's knuckles were white and her nails bit her palms.

"What are you doing that for?" Nissa asked.

"Don't talk for a bit."

"Why?" The girl asked full voice, then repeated softly, "why?"

"Because I don't want him to know I'm here."

The knob on the kitchen door rattled. Then again. Then a shove against the door frame.

"Once when I was a little kid," Nis whispered, "I was all alone in the house because my mother had left. I was scared, but I didn't even cry, Dad said. I never cried."

Step. Step. Step. Lynn thought of her mint and her dill and the richness of nasturtiums that had sprung up before her arrival.

"Where did your mother go?"

Nis shrugged. "She moved back home, Dad said. Out west. On an island. He said it was Salt Spring. Why do you think she left?"

"I don't know why anyone does anything," Lynn said, still listening for the retreating footsteps. I don't know why people leave kids behind. Or why they take them away."

"You're a grownup," the girl whispered with childish disapproval. "Why don't you *know*?"

For five minutes they heard nothing, and the dull

knife-point in her breast withdrew. It never left. It never would, because what had once seemed like a place of safety, an eggshell world, had been shattered by his voice, and his step. No safety, she thought, not for her or the weird little girl who visited, and not for the new one, either, not even with a back garden and a front porch.

"Are you okay?" Nissa asked.

"I'm okay."

"Are you okay? Are you okay?" As though the answer could change from Lynn's feeble lie to something true.

"Don't worry," she said, "but I think you'd better head home."

"Is the guy gone?"

"I hope so. If you see him here just keep walking. Don't come back. Don't talk to him. It's not safe to come into stranger's houses. You don't know what will happen."

She kept her back to the child, whose steps receded slowly as though she might be called back, and Lynn only knew she'd gone because of warm, damp air that gusted through the room.

That afternoon she found the plastic bag Nis had left behind. At first Lynn thought it was garbage, but when she picked it up she realized it contained a small bottle, some-thing you'd find in the craft section at a dollar store, stopped with a cork and full of some viscous golden liquid. Maybe the slime Nissa loved to make? In it floated flakes of irides-cent plastic. She set it on a shelf where it would be safe until she could return it, and for a moment admired the way the sunlight snuck between the slates of the blinds and struck the glitter. It made her think of collecting stickers with holo-graphic silver unicorns on them. It made her think of being a little girl and loving, beyond all things, iridescence and sunset tints. Glitter and silver paper and purple ribbon.

She tried the cap, but it didn't give and it wasn't hers to try anyway. With the faint tug on the cork, a thin film of viscous golden liquid touched her finger, and because she was tired, she touched her left eye, and a drop of that substance entered her sight.

Knock.

Knock.

Knock.

She froze. The air still, her skin slashed black and gold by the light through the broken blinds. She thought, if I don't believe I'm here, he won't know, and he will go away. And maybe that worked, for a moment, but then she heard his heavy steady step leaving the door. Through the broken blind she saw him pause and look out across the tangled lawn, as though watching for someone, then turn again toward her windows. He stepped close to the window and shaded his eyes to look in. It would be okay, though, because she was deep in the old house's gloom, and she pretended she was nothing, just a ghost or a dust mote.

But think of Cortisol cascading through her system triggering unspecified worry in her daughter's developing brain. Even in the warmth and red of the womb, the child might still feel dread, so she breathed more and more deeply and found she could not tear her eyes away from the window. When his face aligned with hers, she started. He's in the light, she kept telling herself, and I am in the dark, we are so still, we are nothing.

Because it was not a face, but a muddy grey shadow, opaque at its core, trailing dark clouds, the way a cuttle-fish trails black, mucousy ink. No eye, no mouth, just that knot of shadow inclined toward the window. At least, that's what she saw with her left eye. With her right eye she saw a familiar cheekbone and nose, a light blue eye and the collar of a green polo shirt against a tanned throat.

The smeary cloud that was also *him* put on his sunglasses and stepped back. Pressure rose in her belly. He dropped his cigarette. The pain grew. He was gone as she realized what was happening and her first thought was no no I'm not ready I don't have enough money—

—the trickle of fluid. But the breast pump and just-in-case formula—the list in her head rattled on as she breathed against the pain. As it eased, her left eye saw a new, faint glow wriggling over the world. In at the windows, around her geranium, seething and gleaming with a brightness that spilled over the leaves and leapt into the air.

When the contraction eased, she picked up her bag and crept out the back of the house, across the tangled yard, past Nissa's braids which now glowed with a growth she had never seen.

The back gate nearly fell apart in her hands as she stepped through and made her way along the alley, overhung with branches of black walnut and spotted with broken bricks and mud and plugged drains and plastic containers. She crept around the fallen branch of a tree and glanced into the backyard of another old rental house, through the vine-grown chain link, to see a young boy systematically breaking the windows. The boy glanced over. She kept walking and hoped that someone, somewhere, was waiting for him.

At the end of the alley she called a cab as another contraction hit, her left eye closed against the bright, boiling life of the boarded-up street, the tangled threads in the grasses, the flitting gleams in the worn back gardens of August. The world, she thought, as another contraction shoved her to a crouch, is swarming and wild and full of lost children.

Like the house and the garden, the hospital teemed with light and smears of muddy darkness. So much pressure, she thought, that pretty soon her brain itself would spill out, destroy her ocular nerve in the—

—another contraction and the woman now beside her said, *breathe*.

The nurse's face was a tangle of gold and silver, bright and undulating. She saw a little boy watching from the corner of the room. He wore a Calgary Flames t-shirt with Kool-Aid stains down the front, and jeans a size too big.

"What's he doing here?" Lynn asked the nurse who attached electrodes to her belly.

"Who?"

"The boy," she said. The last vowel stretched into a cry.

"There isn't a boy here."

"Your face," she said. "Your face." She reached her hand up into the tangle of green and gold threads that obscured the nurse's features.

"Lynn, tell me what you're seeing, okay?

"It's all light," she said. "It's all light."

✳

They moved her to a recovery room the next evening. That night she slept in snatches and woke often to look at Annie in her clear plastic bassinette, to marvel at her tiny hands and her dark grey eyes, her powerful hunger and her unerring instinct for Lynn, who was home to her. Sometime after the night nurse visited she fell into a deep sleep before struggling up in bed to remember where she was, and what the crying meant.

Nissa was standing over Annie's bed.

"Hello," she said, looking through her right eye because her left eye still sparked and glittered. "Did you come to see the baby?"

"Um," Nissa said. "Yes."

For the first time Lynn wondered why an eight-year-old would be in a hospital in the middle of the night. Through her right eye the girl was familiar—dust-coloured hair, torn jean shorts, bare feet.

But then through her nearly-closed left eye she saw something else. Nissa—girl-shaped, familiar, awkward—and around her a far-ranging creature that existed in the same space, whose translucent wings filled the room in iridescent drifts and flows, so she could not tell what was

Nissa and what was flat hospital light refracted through the substance of her body.

"Nissa, where's your Dad?"

"I want to see the baby. That's all. I said I would help take care of her."

"She's asleep," Lynn said, "and it's not safe for you to be in the hospital by yourself. Where's your Dad?"

"I just wanted to see the baby."

Nissa now stood over the clear plastic bassinette, the girl-body a knot, a cluster at the heart of something much larger, comprised in diaphanous layers and smokes, long tenuous wings and streamers that shrouded the light and the doorway, that wrapped—Lynn now saw—around the baby.

"She's very little so you have to be careful. You look so different."

"Nothing's wrong," she said, and the tendrils coalesced in Lynn's left eye, tighter around the child. "Do you know that when I was a little girl I was all alone, all alone and I was only a little baby and my Mom left?" Nissa's voice was fretful. Again her drifting wings obscured Annie from Lynn's sight.

"You've missed her forever," Lynn said, "and she shouldn't have left you like that. Now don't lift her up, she's too small."

"I know. I'm very careful with babies."

Nis had wrapped Annie in her human-shaped arms and in the other ones, the translucent ones, so Lynn swung her tipsy legs over the side of the bed. "You need to be careful with her head, Nis. Let me help you, okay?"

"I know. I've held lots of babies. But how can you see me?"

"I can always see you."

"Yes. Before. When I wanted you too."

With one limping step, Lynn was beside the bassinette. She picked the baby up and felt her warm, silky little head under her chin, and turned her to face Nis, who reached out with a warm, feathery current that ruffled Annie's hair. They stood together for a moment, then the girl's large, pale eyes swiveled and looked up into Lynn's face.

"I'm sorry," she said, "you shouldn't be able to see." Nis reached toward Lynn's left eye with a finger extended, growing long and sharp, the nail like a claw, like the proboscis of a mosquito, like the long, unfurling tongue of the butterfly.

The last thing Lynn saw with her left eye hung permanently in her mind was Nis and Annie together, wrapped in the diaphanous substance that glowed with a life so vigorous it defied gravity and sense. That terminal brightness overcame her eyes and her mind and she said, "Annie! Annie!" But darkness registered before pain, and then she screamed, burying her face in her baby's arms.

Though her functional right eye could no longer see Nissa, she heard the girl's voice close beside her ear. "I didn't like that man, the grey man. I didn't like him at all. Did you like him?"

Lynn could not speak.

When the night nurse arrived the scream was a whimper, and after that she didn't remember much. There was a fever, and pain shattered the left side of her head, so her skull seemed to bubble under the cold cloth they draped across her eyes as they took her somewhere down the flickering white corridors. They said the headache was a spinal leak from the epidural. They said something about blood pressure and her optical nerve. When she could understand them she knew it was neither of those things, it was, rather, that sharp proboscis, that unfurling tooth that hung in her mind where her eye should be.

When she could open both her eyes again, her left side remained empty. Not darkness, but absence.

Her first night without pain she leaned over Annie's bassinette and realized for the first time she was not afraid of his sudden arrival, he had blurred in her mind, like a dream instead of a man. She said to Annie, we'll be okay, won't we? You'll be a girl without a father, but we can manage that, can't we?

Annie woke without crying and opened her eyes, a blue so pale that they might be silver. Lynn thought, I'm sure her eyes were dark. Dark navy, steely and stormy. Not like his eyes at all. I'm sure of it.

But no. Pale and silver-blue, and staring old-wise from such a small and pointed face.

Sleepwalking with Angels

Steve Rasnic Tem

THIS IS THE way you leave the world.

"Dad, I've filled your refrigerator. I got that soft cheese you like. They were all out of fresh peaches, but the produce guy said he'll have more next week. I've sorted out your pills. Are you sure you don't want me to stay and read to you? Is there anything else I can do? We all love you very much—don't we kids? Say goodbye to Grandpa. Say goodbye."

A memory stands somewhere in the room waiting for your acknowledgement. For the longest time you've resisted looking, but this effort costs you more than you can say. Closing your eyes doesn't help. That's when the recollection burns the brightest.

You value your solitude. It's impossible to be yourself around other people; you always find some role to play. You crave those moments when you're missing, when no one is watching, where nothing you do is a mistake.

But you clench your teeth every time you go to bed alone. Falling asleep is like a dive into the abyss. Your adult children say they are worried about you. You could take care of things yourself if they would only give you time. For now, you sleep with your back to that side of the bed.

"We can buy you a whole new bedroom suite, paint the walls a different color. Whatever you want. At least let the cleaners in here, open the windows and air things out, dust and polish and pick up all these clothes and towels and sheets, run the vacuum over these rugs. How long has it been, Dad? How long?"

But you won't let anyone else inside. This difficult life is still yours to handle. You wonder if you should change the sheets. You suspect things may be getting out of hand. You're so tired of everyone's advice you have to stop yourself from screaming.

You haven't told them how the bed creaks at night, how the mattress shifts, and the covers pull away. How every mysterious draft comes with a whisper attached. How someone on that other side has grown cold and needs your warmth.

Once a day a man in a white suit delivers a hot meal to your door. You have no idea how much this costs them. You're a grown man, and you're ashamed to say you've never learned how to cook. You keep busy with nothing. Your hair is usually disappointing. You try to ignore these inexplicable swings in light and shadow, these unfamiliar odors, these unexpected swells of emotion. You don't need to see everything, nor do you want to.

"I know you don't believe, but wouldn't it be wonderful to see her again? We miss her too, and that's what we hope for, that some day we'll all be together again."

Both the walls and your skin resemble old newspaper. But in every lustrous surface: a piece of silhouette, a hint of eye, the suggestion of a moving form. Some of these reflections are not yours. Walking through this house has become an exercise in disintegration. You grow weary of the flies and stink.

"For a long time, I wanted nothing to do with you. I regret all the time we missed. Why do we go through that with our parents when there is so little time left?"

A long-lost cat glides in as if it might finally stay. You caress it, knowing its life to be short and brutal. You try to look out the window for the time of day, but those panes are full of confusion.

Thick tassels of dust hang from doorways and the

corners of ceilings. You never learned how to manage such visible neglect. You swing at them with a broom but have no idea if it does any good. You intend to take more showers. Cleanliness will keep you healthy and hopeful. You believe these perceptions may not be your own.

"Dad? Please pick up. Are you okay? I'll try to drive down next weekend. We'll go to the movies. You loved taking me to movies. Remember how you said they were almost as good as dreams? I'll always remember that. I hope you're doing okay."

The phone rings many times a day, but it is always someone pretending to be someone they are not. Sometimes you can barely hear them. They act as if they know you when they don't know you at all. Sometimes when you answer no one is there but everyone is listening.

You are now old enough to understand there is a line which can be crossed, a balance which can be upended. You should not be here, and yet there seems to be no good solution for it. Everything you have done up until now has been improvised.

"Are you sure you want to give all this stuff away? How are you going to remember the life you two had together?"

※

"Dad? Please pick up the phone. I've been trying to reach you for two days. I'm going to have to drive down and check on you. We had a deal, remember? I may have to call the police for a welfare check, and I know that may embarrass you, but I don't have a choice. I'm hanging up now. Someone will be there soon."

You haven't been outside in ages and you have no desire to go, but something compels you to open the door. You search your closets for some magical suit you can wear but travelling unprotected seems your only choice.

You are surprised how dark the world has become. You

had no idea the hour was so late. But at least all the tiny cracks are obscured. You start to go back inside, afraid to walk the city at night. Still you are driven to take another step, and then more.

The neighborhood has changed but you can't quite pin down the details. Your sense of balance is compromised and you're not sure how to land your feet. Someone calls to you with a name which although familiar isn't quite your own. You pick up the pace even though you have no specific destination in mind. Each time someone speaks to you it comes from a further distance away.

"When you first taught me how to drive, I thought I'd want to drive all the time, remember? I asked you to send me on errands. I took my friends anywhere they wanted to go. Now I dread it. People drive like they're at war."

Cars are densely parked on both sides of the narrow street, people jammed into their shadowed interiors. You wonder what they are waiting for. You stopped driving years ago. You could no longer trust yourself not to kill someone.

Something moves among the trees along the parkway. A dark figure stands in the shadows between two buildings, whispering advice you can't quite hear. You would step closer and challenge them if you were sufficiently brave. Everyone here has a great deal to answer for.

"You forgot to eat dinner again? Dad, how can you just forget to eat?"

On the next corner a once favorite restaurant is shuttered. You press your face against the window. The space appears to be completely empty, occupied by successive layers of dark. The black silhouette reflected isn't yours, but you may have seen him somewhere before. You cannot remember the last time you looked at a photograph of yourself. The family pictures were stored in cardboard boxes at the back of a closet. You don't know what happened to them all. They might have been burned or donated to thrift stores.

You worry that someone else might be passing them off as their own. In any case these images no longer resemble you. Your history isn't yours any more.

"Have you made any friends? We worry that you're so isolated. All these old men sitting around the rec center—maybe some of them can be your friends."

You are aware of other people walking these streets, conversing and conducting business, but they're always so far away. No matter how far you walk you never appear any closer. You can't account for the many discrepancies in time or distance. You can't explain the general scarcity of pedestrians. You stopped paying attention to news reports a long time ago. Perhaps this is the consequence of choosing to be the last one to know.

"Did you see it, Dad? They showed the whole thing on TV. All those poor people dead. The media could use better judgement—it only encourages the terrorists when they see their names everywhere. Do you think it really happened? We all saw it on TV, but today they can fake anything, did you know that? You never know what to believe. You can't trust your own eyes anymore."

More than once you perceive a witness staring from some distant window. You are pretty sure they know something you do not. As you get closer you search for an opportunity to say hello, just so they know you're aware, but every window is empty, and every door closed. Even if you wanted to start a conversation you could not. You may already know some of these people. But you're not sure you can still tell strangers from friends.

The city is consumed by the anticipation of its own decay. You want to let everyone know the first thing you lose is the meaning. Don't make any rash assumptions. Withhold interpretation until you've seen enough. Most of what you believe about other people will prove to be incorrect. Everyone has the right to suffer in silence.

While walking you have a dream in which you meet

several people constructed entirely out of garbage. They follow you home and try to get in. They leave their nasty handprints all over your front door. You hide in the dark pretending you're not there. You're ashamed of your own reluctance to care.

"Why can't we invite them in for dinner, Dad? You always say we should do whatever we can to help. There's so many of them now and they have nowhere else to go."

When you awaken, you're still walking and there is no one left anywhere. Row upon row of architecture recedes into clouds of dust. All around your feet bits of life scurry by. You don't know what they are, if they are even edible, but you snatch and swallow them while you still have the opportunity. This doesn't satisfy you, but then you know nothing will. This is what it's like, you think, to outlive your home.

You burn. You burn.

Tiny insects crawl out of your eyes and down your face like tears. Their overabundant legs mark permanent trails in your cheeks.

You try to remember the last time you spoke to her. You don't know if the failure is in your recollection or with your calendar. This is the life you've always had. Anything important either happens unexpectedly or is ill-prepared for.

You remember other times when walking through the city was like reading a novel or watching a movie, finding yourself in another person's head as you both negotiated an unfamiliar landscape. But not like this. Not for hours, not for days.

Eventually you reach the suburbs of this place. Here all the doors have been left open. All the houses have been emptied; everyone's things gathered into piles by the street. All of humanity is moving. The dead leave their houses for the living and the living are restless because they can be. Still, you see no one. Perhaps they've all gone out to dinner, you think, dinner and a show and the life to come with someone they used to love. You sift through their piles of everything, and yet nothing interests you.

When you reach the bridge, you are terrified of its shuddering construction, so high there is nothing you can see below you but the obscuring fog. This may be the same bridge which brought you here so many years ago, but you really can't remember. You gaze down through the layers of mist, where you imagine the drowning continents lie.

"Have you met your new neighbors? Go out there and introduce yourself. At this point in life you need your friends."

Green Grows the Grief

Steve Toase

BY THE END his bones were like peeling paint on iron.
Sophie had lifted him into bed when they'd eventually
sent him home from the hospital. He weighed less than the
blanket-wrapped urn she carried in her arms.

Behind her, Simon followed; stepping only on the grass
she'd already flattened. Since they were kids she'd always
taken the lead. Always clearing the way for him.

Sophie glanced behind. He was too hot in his suit but
would never admit it.

"It's a sign of respect," he'd said, looking her up and
down in her day clothes which he thought weren't even
suitable for going to the shops in, never mind scattering
their Dad's ashes.

At the back the cousins followed in a snaking trail,
seeds and meadow petals snagging on their t-shirts. Their
children had played together so long and so close for the
past ten years it was hard to tell where one family began
and the other ended.

She rounded the corner of the small copse of trees. The
greenhouses alone, the buildings they were once attached
to long since gone. Somehow the fragile structures of metal
and glass still stood when stone and alabaster had fallen.
Something like grief caught in her throat and she swallowed it before she had a chance to pay it any attention.

Her Dad had worked in the greenhouses as an appren-
tice gardener, and though his working life took him all
over the county, he always returned when he could. Even

when the estate fell into ruin. She wondered what he would think now. Whether he would weep at the chaos of trees and plants, pressing glass out of rotten window putty, or whether he'd rejoice in the vibrancy of life. She didn't care. He wasn't alive to ask. Another question that would go unanswered.

She stopped. Simon stopped behind her, not wanting to face what they had to do shoulder to shoulder. The children had dispersed into the overgrown meadow like so many seeds.

"Am I going to do this on my own?" Sophie asked without turning around. A breeze caught the sky, then caught the branches. They rattled against the remaining glass.

"I'm here, aren't I?" Simon said. She shook her head, partly in disappointment. Partly so her loose hair would hide her grief.

Shifting the urn from one arm to the other she walked to the greenhouse. Roots and grass had long since knotted the door shut. She knelt down, ripping the plants free of rusting metal. When she looked at her hands, her palms were sliced and smeared with blood. The world taking another payment from her. The urn stood cushioned on a pad of meadow flowers. A metal vase of bone and ash. Nothing more. The door finally moved enough for her to enter. She picked up her burden and went inside. Simon did not follow.

She thought the heat would hit her under the magnifying roof. Roll over her skin, snagging it and drawing sweat out of every pore. Enough glass was still above to turn the air humid. Bonsai ponds in the top of book-sized leaves. No, it wasn't the heat that hit her first but the smell. The smell of damp soil. Of leaves browning to smears beneath her boots. Hidden flowers that shook free their scent as she brushed against knots of vegetation. The reek of rotting plants transformed to taste in her mouth. She swallowed and tried not to think of spores and seeds and decay, but instead the urn and her Dad and the pile of ash he now was.

Pine trees rose through the canopy, their branches holding them in place. Vast untended tomato plants blazed with yellow, around their stalks fruit crawling with flies. Across the building, metal troughs full of soil and rotted stems. Each step she took unleashed another eruption of flavours. Plums and apples. Lilac. Under her feet she ground away blackberries, glancing behind at the trail of skins.

✳

Without looking she took off the lid and reached inside, feeling the larger pebbles of bone fall through her fingers. Scooped them up again. When she took out her hand she stared at the grey streak filling the lines of her palm. Staining the calluses at the base of each finger. They would go with the next wash.

There was no perfect place in the greenhouse to scatter his ashes. No matter where she spread the burnt and caramelised bone, her Dad would still be dead.

She took out a fistful of powder and dropped it around some sugar snap peas, then some more into a container of ferns. After each handful she scattered she moved faster. It would never be easy, but it could be quick. The only thing to do was to make the process short. There were no words to say. No words to hear from him any more. Just dust and dirt and silence. Soon she'd forget the sound of his voice. She'd already lost what he sounded like before the choke of cells and the surgeon's blade. Her only memory was the slashed croaking at the end.

As she found paths around root-mats she came closer to the windows and ran her finger down the glass; through the warm smear of algae. Outside, the children ran through the grass, their location visible by the clouds of seeds rising to be carried away on the breeze. Simon stood staring in the opposite direction, as if he couldn't bear to look at the greenhouse in case he caught sight of her.

Another handful of ash. Sophie wondered if she held her Dad's hand or his head. Over the past few months she'd cradled both as he struggled to speak, too weak to use a pen to write when his voice failed. The one time his eyes brightened was showing him pictures of the greenhouse. Seeing the joy on his face she knew what his last wishes were. How important they were to him. Dreams and choices the only thing distinguishing him from the malfunctioning meat he was trapped within.

The tree was in the centre of the greenhouse. She had no memory of the curling path that took her there, as if recollection was rationed and she could not waste it on something as meaningless as paths.

Bark rough and root splayed, the tree had shattered its home, a glitter of splinters upon the ground around her feet. Upending the urn she tipped the remaining burnt bone upon them. There was no breeze to carry them away. She wondered if, when high summer scorched through the dirty glass, the bone would char once more.

Outside she did not speak to Simon, did not call to the children. She walked the path back across the field, knowing the place she arrived at would not be the one she left. That home did not exist.

※

It was July when Sophie returned to the greenhouse, and as she crossed the field the heat lifted blisters from her skin. By the time she stood beside the steel and glass she was ready for the relief of being out of the sky's glare.

There was no relief. No sanctuary from the heat. True, the sun no longer scraped one layer of skin from the other. Now the scent of rotting palm leaves and ferns filled every pore. The stench of lilac as it baked under glass. The sweetness of tomatoes rotting on the vine. It seeped into everything. It had been a mistake to come.

She sat on the floor and crawled under a potting bench, not caring if decades old compost stained her skin. Beetles and aphids crawled over her legs. Caught in her hair. Beside her feet she found fresh falls of broad bean pods.

The urge to feel the cool of the velvet inside was too much and she picked one up, running her nail down the seam as her Dad had shown her many years ago.

The beans were shrunken and withered, velvet absent. Instead the inside of the pod blackened and scored. Rotten. She put it down and opened the next. This one had also succumbed to blight. The third she almost didn't open. Didn't want to see the bloated decay. Swallowing down bile in her throat she opened it anyway. The beans were perfect, plump and pale. She popped one into her mouth and chewed, feeling it turn to paste against her tongue. In that moment she was five again, sitting on the back-step, stealing as many beans as she put into the bowl. The memory was so strong she did not notice the grit until she opened her eyes, breaking the spell.

It tasted of charcoal and dirt. She spat the mess into her hand and stared at the charred bone in the centre and carried on staring until the sun went down.

✳

Back home Sophie spread the remaining beans on a sheet of newspaper then went into the back porch and found the plant pots. Nothing special. Cheap terracotta with a hole in the base for drainage, but her Dad used them every year, never breaking them even when he himself was broken.

She had no soil to plant them, only realising halfway through. When she returned from the garden centre with a bag of potting compost, she walked back into the kitchen, saw the chaos on the table and expected to smell cigarette smoke coming from the open door. It took her two hours before she was in any state to finish the job.

"Funny isn't it," he'd said, before his voice was stolen from him. "Spent all my life looking after plants and a plant is going to kill me. Maybe they're getting their own back for harvesting them with pinching fingers and knives." She'd watched him tip the packet of tobacco into the bin. "Seems a waste, but I can't have anyone else feeling like this."

She remembered the concern. The sadness. Her memory edited out the coughing and the hollowness within him.

＊

The ghosts did not come until the beans sprouted, arriving as the leaves unfurled from the split of skin. Just shadows on the stairs. At the corner of the landing. She never saw enough to know for certain. The scent gave him away. The reek of tobacco and soil and the rich velvet tang of harvest. She carried on planting.

＊

Sophie paused for a moment before opening the door, standing aside to let Simon in. He did not say anything about the seedlings lining the stairs and hallway. Not until they were sat down with a cup of tea.

"We don't mind looking after the boys, but we're worried about you."

So many lies in so few words, she thought.

"I'm fine. I just need some time to get back into a routine."

"He's not here anymore," Simon said. "You can't replace him with this."

After that first time she'd returned to the greenhouse to collect what seeds she could. Tomatoes, courgettes, potatoes. It did not matter. There were traces of him in all of them.

"I need to keep myself busy."

"You could keep yourself busy looking after your children."

Sophie shook her head.

"I don't think I'm the best person for them to be around right now."

"So you expect other people to pick up the slack, while you try to do what? Become Dad and ignore the people who are still alive and need you."

She snapped around to stare at him. What she wanted to say was, "Maybe if you'd helped a little more when he was alive I might have space left for the living." What she said was, "I think you'd better leave."

"This can't go on," he said on the doorstep. "You need help so you can care for your responsibilities."

"Good bye," she said, shutting the door in his face.

Alone in the house, she opened the windows and as the breeze stirred the plants she was sure she heard a tar-coated lung rattle amongst the leaves.

After that the ghosts came often, hidden in the branches and stems. Sometimes Sophie thought she caught words in the dance of leaves. Late at night she woke and heard a trowel digging through loose compost. Draping herself in her dressing gown, she walked along the landing. Sat at the top of the stairs with the carpet scraping her calves. She did not venture down. Just stayed there listening to the sound of secateurs that were not there, smelling tobacco smoke floating up from the kitchen.

Every time a ghost appeared the others did not vacate the house. They accumulated like the plants. Anchored to the spot as if roots of ectoplasm spread under the floorboards. She walked through the living room, past half-potted seed-lings, and charcoal seeds tipped out of pockets onto unread newspapers. There was no shortage of those. She harvested them from the unopened mail beside the door. The house smelt of burnt bone and soil, and she did not want to erase either.

Once a week she listened to Simon knock on the door, ignoring the sound until he went away, then watching him walk down the path, leaving her to the plants.

There was plenty to eat. Tomatoes. Beans. Sugar-snap peas. Sophie did not bother to cook them anymore. Just tore them from the vine and placed them on her tongue. Crushed them and felt the tiny lumps of grit stick in her throat. Mourned once more with each meal.

※

It was his birthday. She almost missed the day, its significance lessened by the date that bookended his life. Only noticed it by the old calendar still hanging in the kitchen. That last birthday, gathered around his bed. Simon put a party hat on him like he was a dress up doll. Held out a cake knowing he couldn't blow out the candles or eat the icing. This is what you could have won. She would never forgive her brother for that. She would celebrate her Dad's birthday for her. For him.

Sophie sat down at the table; soil-covered newspapers all over the stained tablecloth. The salad covered the whole plate, vegetables plump and ripe. Picking up her fork she pinned a tomato in place and cut it in two. The knife was not sharp and the bruised red skin tore. Inside, the finger bones were held in place by damp pith. Taking a piece she chewed while chopping down on the courgette, lifting the knife when the blade scraped against the vertebrae growing inside. She ran her tongue along the tarnished metal, pushing the fine dust against the ridges in the top of her mouth. Still hungry, she bit into the runner beans, stopping only to spit out the half-formed teeth. The noise of them rattling against the plate sounded like rain on glass. She continued to prise and pull the edible from the dead until hunger no longer gnawed at her and the table was covered with too many bones. The ghosts were close. Stood around her as she ate. She continued eating, walking around the house and tearing fruit from plants and forcing them into her mouth. Feeling the bones settle in her bloated stomach. Outside in the yard she scraped away at the potato plants, not bothering to wash off the soil as she chewed, feeling the smooth lengths of ribs stick in her throat. Each plant she stripped, swallowing peas and beans until there was no space left within.

✳

She woke surrounded by bones. Different sizes. Different ages. Some were bare and fresh, the rounded ends not yet fused, others raked and scored by disease. Teeth freshly erupted. Still more yellowed with nicotine.

She arranged them all around her. Grouping them by size and rot. Twenty individual collections. All the same person.

The younger ones smelt of baby powder and sour milk, the older ones, the ones most twisted and damaged by the rot of cancer, those smelt of hospital disinfectant. The ones in-between? The partial skeletons. Fragments of skulls and finger bones. Those reeked of tobacco.

✳

The knocking came as she knew it would, and when it did, the sound was so loud she thought the glass would shatter.

"Open this fucking door, Sophie."

She heard Simon pressing the doorbell over and over. There was no longer any electricity to power it and he started hammering on the door once more.

"I'm coming back tomorrow. With Police. With doctors. We're not looking after the children any more. That's your job."

He didn't know if she was actually in the house. Neither did Sophie. She did not move or respond. Just laid there amongst the ghosts and bones and her own regurgitated food.

The house would not flesh the bones. The carpets and wallpaper, brick and cement. None of these would cord muscle or spin nerves. The house was not the place for these remains.

The bag had carried his tools. Not the bag he took when he was working on other people's gardens. The one he used in his own plot. All the bone just fitted, and only with the zip unfastened. Every femur and finger bone. The newborn and the dying man. Sophie did not question this. It was a time of miracles. A time for magic that was clay-dry and knotted as any root.

The greenhouse was barely standing. The summer growth shattered the remaining panels. Everywhere, plants filled frames where once glass magnified the sun. She rested her head against the door and closed her eyes. Whispered a liturgy, whether for the greenhouse, her Dad, or herself she could not say.

By the time she cleared enough space upon the floor Sophie needed to rest, and when she woke the only light was second-hand, gifted from the sun to the moon.

She laid the bones out around her. Her knowledge of anatomy was less than her knowledge of plants but the bones themselves knew where to be placed. When she finished she lay face down in the dirt, her eyes turned from the light. From the memories she tasted on the air. From what was about to return.

When she woke, Sophie smelt them standing around her. Smelt the reek of unburnt amber leaf. Knew the greenhouse had clothed the bones in skin of leaves and nerves of vines. Knew to look up for her Dad to be returned to her once more. Gaze on him and not lose him again. She opened her eyes.

From where she lay on the floor she saw their legs. Their calves of bone and plant. The decay of heat and humidity rotting the vegetation as it clasped muscle and tendons, and in that moment Sophie knew her Dad would not return to her. The only thing to come back would be decay and the slow sliding apart of memories. Without looking up she crawled across the floor of the greenhouse. Behind her the figures walked in her trail. They did not speak. Did not try to convince her. Just followed. Remained out of sight but present as her Dad always would be now. At the door she crawled through, pushed it closed against the press of plants.

Climbing to her feet she stared across the field. It would be a long way back, but the ghosts would not follow her any more, just the memories she chose to take with her. She opened her hand. In her palm was a single piece of burnt bone. It was enough.

Lacunae

V.H. Leslie

Be not afeard; the isle is full of noises, sounds and
sweet airs
The Tempest

MALCOLM HEARD MENDELSSOHN as the island
came into view. It was hard not to think of his Hebridean
overture amid the rocking of the waves, the dark hollow
of the cave in the distance. It was not quite Fingal's; the
rocky façade lacked the distinctive neat, angular arrangement, though it too had been formed by a volcanic deluge
many millions of years ago. His daughter, Miranda sat at
the prow, dwarfed in her bright orange lifejacket, glancing
back at her parents as the boat sliced through the water,
salt-sprayed and smiling. Dinah shouted something out
to her, something cautionary Malcolm supposed, but the
sound was taken by the wind and silenced by the churn of
the engine. Just along from the cave, Malcolm viewed the
white stone house and he let the coin he held drop into the
water, just as he had always done when crossing the strait,
in payment to the Blue Men—the kelpies that resided in the
deep—for safe passage.

With the engine chugging to a stop, the sounds of the
sea took precedence, the pounding of the waves against
the hull, the screech of gulls overhead. Malcolm had rolled
up his trouser-legs in preparation for stepping from the

boat into the surf, but as he did so, a wave broke and he
felt the shock of cold, an involuntary re-baptism, as the
water seeped through his clothes. He waved away Dinah's
attempts to steady him and she turned her attention instead
to instructing the ferrymen about their luggage. Malcolm
didn't offer to help; it was a job for younger men. Miranda
was already up ahead, running excited lengths along the
beach, stopping occasionally to examine driftage, or to
collect something from the shore that had caught her eye.
She greeted her father as he stepped out of the sea with
palms outstretched, full of limpet and mussel shells, the
coiled remains of periwinkles.

"Look."

But Malcolm was looking past her towards the cave.
It could well have featured in the legends of Ossian, the
supposed fragments of ancient balladry James Macpherson
had discovered and translated in the Romantic era, before
he was discredited as a forger. Whether the stories of Fingal
and his exploits had come from a third century Highland
bard as Macpherson had professed or from Macpherson
himself, had never mattered to Malcolm. He saw the landscape of his youth, the crags and gullies where he played
through Ossian's lens, charged with heroic energy. But he
had been away from home for a long time; like so many of
his forbears, he had settled across the Atlantic, not driven
out as they had been in those bygone times by the greed of
landowners, but lured by bright lights, whilst the brave old
world had persisted and endured. Now the songs of home
would occupy his twilight years. No mere tone poem like
Mendelssohn's would suffice, but a song cycle, a fittingly
epic undertaking in homage to Ossian. It would be his
magnum opus.

Miranda hadn't waited for a reply and was busy
jumping the waves, so he made his way past her, up the
beach beyond the machair, toward the steps of the stone
house. It was just as he remembered it, sand on the flag-

stones, the embroidery sampler on the wall. He made his way through the warren of rooms, nooks providing vistas out toward the grey Atlantic, until he found himself on a familiar threshold. It was simply furnished, as it had always been, the desk arranged against the window, overlooking the expanse of beach, the rocky foreshore at the entrance of the cave just visible. He had composed here every summer for nine years—the duration of his first marriage—where, some would say, he had produced his best work.

He wondered if it was true, that the last four decades had amounted to nothing more than playacting the role of composer. The *Edinburgh Review* critic had certainly thought so, fancifully comparing him to a "shipwrecked Prospero," exiled from the operatic vanguard, because—in words he now knew by rote—"...he had bartered his baton for a magic wand, invoking the Disneyfication of his early oeuvre." He remembered pushing the paper across the kitchen table for Dinah to read, the words too potent to be said out loud. The article ended with the assertion that he had produced nothing of value since *The Silence of Amaterasu*. She had ripped out the page, screwing it into a ball.

"Well, *fuck him!*"

He watched Dinah now, helping the ferrymen carry their bags through the shallows, battling the swell and spray, while Miranda orbited their belongings on the beach, piled high like a haul of treasure, or the mound of a bonfire.

✳

He'd expected to be instantly inspired, the music welling up from a long dormant place inside, just by virtue of being back on the island, but he could hear only the words of the *Edinburgh Review* critic, on a loop like a steady incantation. It struck him as ironic that words he had never voiced could become so resounding in his head. He'd had bad reviews before, especially at the start of his career, when his work

was regarded as experimental, but he'd never really paid
them much heed. Dinah had said that the Scots were just
bitter that he'd been co-opted by the Americans, that they'd
lost a national icon. He didn't see it like that; he'd retained
his dual citizenship and heeded the siren-call of home, his
feet now firmly set on bleached sand, but he did wonder
if he was in fact, lost. Not in the sense Dinah supposed, of
being cloven between two nation states but lost to a different
time and place, akin to the misty void where Fingal and his
warrior-ghosts lingered.

He stared at the blank page, trying to summon a
melody but fixated instead on the sounds of the house, the
animated laughter of cartoons from Miranda's tablet, Dinah
clanging in the kitchen, putting away their groceries. When
the house settled into silence, he found himself gravitating
towards the interior, seeking sound. He found Dinah in the
bedroom unpacking their bags.

"Looking for this," she asked, handing him a grey
dressing gown, threadbare in parts, his charm against
writer's block.

"I didn't think I'd need it," he said, though he put it on
anyway.

An oft-repeated dinner party story, before the *Edinburgh Review* critic had styled him a modern-day sorcerer,
centred on Miranda's childish confusion between the
words *musician* and *magician* and her steadfast conviction
that her father only made music with the aid of potions and
spells. He did, after all, conduct himself in secret, working
from his locked study, and he donned a magician's cape,
albeit a rather old and grey flannel robe. Dinah had found
it too endearing to correct and they kept the pretence
going well into Miranda's first few years of kindergarten,
where the family pictures she drew all featured Malcolm
shrouded in grey, the messy crayon marks making him
appear more animal than human. As her drawing became
more controlled, she would add symbols to his cloak, stars,

a moon, sometimes even adding a magician's hat to the ensemble, so there could be no doubt of his profession. The dinner party guests would laugh imagining the kinder-garten teacher's disappointment when Malcolm declined the offer of putting on a magic show for the class.

"Such a cliché," Dinah said, taking in his appearance, "the creatives in bathrobes while the rest of us have to wear real clothes."

He smiled back, rubbed her shoulders, "What do you think of the house?"

"Quaint. Drafty."

The theme-tune of one of Miranda's cartoons started up again and Dinah sighed. Miranda had clearly exhausted her allocation of screen-time for the day.

"Why don't you have an explore with her?"

"I'm here to work."

She began to fold the garment in front of her with slow, careful creases. Malcolm noted the tightness of her lips, the silence that would ensue.

"Ok, ok."

"And we need to talk about Ayoko," she said as he left the room, though he pretended not to hear.

Miranda skirted the rock pools along the shoreline, testing their depths with a shard of driftwood. She'd beckon to Malcolm to follow but as soon as he caught up, her attention would be diverted elsewhere, and he found himself trailing behind her again. This new world under her feet absorbed her to such an extent that she missed the seals further out in the bay who had come to observe the new arrivals. They seemed to nod at Malcolm but by the time he pointed them out to Miranda they had swum away.

The waves were pitching steadily higher and Malcolm was glad they had arrived in the calm of the morning. He thought of the journeys made in Ossian's time, if Ossian had ever existed. Heroes were meant to undertake epic voyages and crossing rougher seas made for better stories.

Miranda had migrated up the shoreline and Malcolm found her crouched in the marram grass, a small shell pressed to her ear, as if it were a conch.

"Shhh!"

Malcolm stopped moving in obedience, trying to minimise the crunch of his footfall as he repositioned his body weight.

"It's singing."

She held out the shell to him. It was small and speckled, coiled at its peak; a whelk of some description. The habit of listening to seashells had always struck him as strange practice; that the hollowed interior could emit the rushing of the waves was hardly surprising when the shell's cavity amplified the noise of its surroundings. Far more impressive were the shells that created sound, like the Japanese *horagai*, large conch shells of the right shape and composition, that with the addition of a mouthpiece appended to their spired tips could even be played to produce different notes. Miranda's diminutive find could hardly compete with such titans, but he placed it to his ear anyway.

"Can you hear it?"

Her voice was so different to his; she'd been raised an American, her accent clear and unequivocal, lacking the melodic lilt of the islands. He sometimes felt they spoke different languages.

He nodded noncommittally, hoping it would suffice as an answer and though she pocketed the shell, he couldn't tell if she believed him or not.

The rocks were more abundant as they approached the cave. Craggy pillars guarded the entrance, sharpened from where the sea tormented the shore. He remembered that the cave flooded on a spring tide, the surface underfoot rendered smooth and slippery with bladderwrack. As they moved from the light and further into the dark interior, Malcolm was reminded of what an impressive space it was, not unlike a concert hall, the banding on the gneiss reminiscent of the levels of tiered seating. He felt underdressed in his grey dressing gown.

Miranda climbed deeper into the cave and he gravitated towards a rocky obtrusion in the centre, its surface eroded smooth like a crude lectern. The silence swelled as if signalling the commencement of a piece of music.

The wind makes strange noises on the islands, whistling through the ravines and crofts, percussing on the corrugated roofs, strumming the rigging of the boats harnessed at the quayside. But the sound Malcolm heard in the depths of the cave was not devised by the elements, for it was one he recognised all too well. It was raw and unpolished but unmistakably the first few notes of *Amaterasu's Silence*, the aria he had written for his eponymous lead, a divine sun goddess who sought sanctuary in a cave to escape torment from her malevolent brother. 'Silence' was a misnomer of sorts, for Amaterasu's sojourn in the cave constituted her most vocal moments in the opera, the cave amplifying her long-dormant song, her internment in stone giving liberty to her voice.

The sound swelled, pitching towards the familiar melody.

"Miranda?"

Was it here where he'd first heard the legend of Amaterasu? It must have been; the island was so saturated with Amaterasu it was hard to unravel any prior memories. It was certainly here that he'd decided to compose, in alto tones, the world beyond Amaterasu's grotto as a place of chaos and dissonance, informed by his habit of listening to the wind and rain from within the cave. And perhaps it had been here that he'd decided Amaterasu should not sing until she was safely ensconced in the cave, the lack of her mezzo soprano voice extending for the entire first half of the opera, rendering her song, when it finally came, all the more precious.

As well as this, he'd written a series of lacunae—arranged silences—to disrupt the flow of music and signal changes in Amaterasu's emotional state, increasing in length with every tribulation and ordeal suffered, the longest of which marked the moment the boulder was rolled across the entrance of the cave, shutting out a world now plunged into silence and darkness, a total eclipse of Amaterasu's divine light.

The melody in the cave scaled higher but just as suddenly faded into the sound of the surf. Miranda re-appeared, making her way across the rocky terrain, playing stepping stones.

"Miranda, were you singing?"

She didn't seem to hear him, concentrating on balancing across the rocks. But just before she bounded back into the light, he heard her whistling the familiar refrain.

✳

Dinah was at the threshold when they arrived back, the door ajar to the island dusk, like a good fisherman's wife waiting for her husband's return.

"The Museum have been in touch," she said after helping Miranda out of her coat.

He waved away the comment, busied himself with pouring a whisky, trying to ignore the paperwork and laptop spread out on the kitchen counter, regretful that the island's remoteness was now marred with internet access.

"They're becoming impatient, we need to commit to dates."

He had been so flattered at first meeting Dinah, when this attractive woman had approached him at a gala dinner, tongue-tied as she tried to put forward her proposal, coyly admitting she was a little star-struck. She wanted to curate a retrospective of his work to mark the thirtieth anniversary of *The Silence of Amaterasu*. The museum she worked for was on board, especially since *Amaterasu's Silence* had featured in a film, a box-office hit, making his work fleetingly popular with a whole new, younger, audience. She'd given him her business card, adding her personal number and underlining her name, *Dinah*, twice, though the angle made the lines appear more like a caesura //—the pause between music. He had agreed to her suggestion solely to get to know her better, and hardly cared when the project was deferred because of their work schedules and later due to their marriage and Miranda's birth. Now approaching the anniversary of the fortieth year, Malcolm couldn't help feeling that this was Dinah's last-ditch effort to get the show on the road, quite literally, because leaving it any longer would mean him sinking further into inconsequence.

"We never talk about Ayoko," she said, watching him drain his drink.

He used to dream about coming back to the island, the music calling him back across the water. But he hadn't imagined bringing a new wife back with him, or a child. He became conscious of Miranda in the background, sorting shells on the kitchen table. Children were such adept listeners.

"Why would we talk of her?" Malcolm replied, "it's ancient history."

"She's important, to the retrospective."

"It was such a small part of my life—"

"—when you produced your greatest work."

He had taken off his dressing gown when he'd returned from the shore, but now he put it on again, feeling the chill of the house.

"*One* of your greatest works," she corrected, placing her hand on his arm, a condolent gesture.

This was the problem with the retrospective, it implied that everything of worth was in the past, that there was nothing left to come. He knew that in Dinah's eyes he was already washed-up, that it was better to salvage and polish what he had already produced before it was tarnished further by the critics, like treasure salt-worn by the sea.

He watched Miranda move her shells, like counters in a game of her own invention. He thought about the voice in the cave and how unlike Miranda's it was.

"I'd rather not talk about it," he said, and pouring himself another whisky, he withdrew to his study.

✳

It was louder than he remembered living at the sea's edge. The wind blew unrestrained here, rattling through the old house, blustering papers when the windows were opened, bringing gifts of seagrass and kelp to the door like a loyal pet. It was more deafening on the shore; here you could confide anything to the sea, the words swept away almost immediately by the wind. Malcolm had nothing to confess so he pushed on up the beach, keen to prove Dinah and the rest of them wrong, that he was still capable of making music, needing the peace of the cave to hear his own thoughts.

As he entered, he was again struck by the feeling of walking across a cavernous stage, at the head of an orchestra or playacting a character: *Old man in grey bathrobe, enters stage left.* He leant against the rocky lectern, relieved for the silence. Caves were important in the legends of Ossian too and Malcolm had decided to focus on the moment where Fingal's son, slain heroically in battle, appeared as a ghost above the cave where his body is interred, calling for revenge. The ghosts of dead warriors inhabited so much of Ossian's verse, the departed never happy until a bard sings of their exploits.

"Excuse me?"

Malcolm turned, shocked at hearing a voice in such

proximity, though it was faint, no louder than a whisper. The cave appeared empty. He walked further from the light.

"Hello?" he called tentatively, scanning the darkness.

"Excuse me?" the voice rejoined.

He was reminded of the voice the previous day, how unlike Miranda's it had sounded. Cave systems were known to distort and amplify sound, the acoustics of Fingal's Cave for instance harmonised the ebb and flow of the waves as if contriving a lullaby. Though this voice was different still, the sound had to come from somewhere. Malcolm explored the recesses and hollows, unable to discern anyone hiding in the shadows. He moved deeper into the cave, felt the damp surface of the chamber wall, having reached its furthest limits.

"Excuse me," the voice spoke again, "can I have your autograph?"

He had answered many such requests over the years, some not always graciously, but the words and timbre of voice suddenly summoned its bearer into startling clarity in his mind. It was years ago, after a performance of *Amaterasu*. He'd invited her back to the hotel bar and listened to her congratulate him on his success, his singular talent. She'd mentioned something about an audition, whether he could pull some strings. He couldn't even recall her name.

"Excuse me?" the voice persisted, and Malcolm gazed back into the darkness. He tried to move from the sound, but it seemed to follow him, growing more insistent.

"Excuse me!"

It had been just after his divorce when he was seeing a lot of different women. He remembered buying her too many drinks, before leading her into an elevator bound for his hotel suite, making some vague promise of putting in a word with the producer, a quick grope in the confined space the requisite exchange. He hadn't thought of her since.

The voice had lost its civil cadence and Malcolm

realised that it wasn't coming from the cave but from his person. He patted himself down, unsure what he was looking for, feeling inside his pocket a small, chitinous surface. He held it in his palm, one of Miranda's shells, helix shaped, barely significant.

"Excuse me!" the voice said once more, as she had done all those years ago, and he was struck by the memory of her disentangling herself from his embrace as the elevator bell announced its arrival.

The shell dropped to the ground and Malcolm endured the silence of the cave, just as he had done in the elevator cubicle in that interminable moment after his breathing had steadied and the sound of her footsteps had disappeared down the hall.

✳

"This is all a bit staged isn't it?" Malcolm said upon his return, taking in the spectacle of Dinah photographing his study. The room was under siege, books he had never read piled high on his desk, music-stands arranged artfully in shot.

"The Museum want me to document the composer's lair, I hope you don't mind."

He did mind, but with the study lacking a lock, he could hardly keep the world out. He thought about issuing a warning, like the one pinned to Miranda's bedroom door back home, *Diva Den: KEEP OUT*, though for Dinah, such a prohibition would only serve more as an invite. It hardly mattered anyway, the study was and always had been an empty shell, it was the cave where all the music came from.

"I was wondering when you were going to return."

He had walked agitated lengths along the beach for hours, trying to make sense of what he heard in the cave. He couldn't go back there, but he didn't want to be in the house either, the memory too disquieting to bring indoors, where his family dwelt. When he had tired, he sat close to water, watching the seals in the bay, until the spindrift pimpled his skin.

"Something on your mind?"

"Just music," he replied, realising that his lonely meandering would have been plain to see from the study window.

Dinah beckoned him into the room, and he stepped awkwardly over her photography equipment.

"Can you sit in the chair?" she asked from behind her tripod.

He removed his dressing gown and folded it, peeled a red vein of seaweed from the fabric. She instructed him to fold his legs, place his hands together.

"Don't look at me," she said, "pretend I'm not here."

He stared through the series of flashes, shifting under the scrutiny.

"Can you stare out the window and try to look wistful," she smiled, "divinely inspired." His frown became more set and she smiled again before kneeling beside the camera, twisting the dials.

"A quick filmed interview and we're done."

Malcolm shook his head, "Dinah, not now, I don't have the time."

"Well, you've been evading my questions ever since we arrived. I have a job to do too. Besides, it's why we came here."

He wanted to object; he hadn't come here to revisit his past but to write his *magnum opus*.

"I can edit out anything you don't want left in," she assured, "please?"

He looked out of the window, this time without her instruction, saw the waves crest higher, the seals long gone. It was easier to acquiesce.

"So, this is the room where you composed *The Silence of*

Amaterasu? Can you talk to me about the process?"

"Well..."

"Did you have a routine?"

"I, I typically walked in the mornings and came back in the afternoons and evenings to write down what I heard."

"What you heard?"

"The music in my head, it helps being in such a remote place, without traffic and people, where you can hear yourself think."

"And how important was your first wife, Ayoko to that process?"

He fought the urge to look out of the window and glanced toward Dinah instead where she gestured him to continue.

"She was musical too. She could sing."

"Yes, she sang parts of the early overture—there's that beautiful recording. Why didn't she pursue her singing professionally?"

"She wouldn't have made it on the world stage, her voice wasn't quite...right. Besides, my career was just starting up, it was a busy time and we needed someone at home."

He watched Dinah fold her arms, "things were different then," he added.

Dinah pursed her lips but when she spoke again her voice was steady, professional, "Can you describe your time on the island?"

"When we first came, things were good, we were newlyweds."

"And how did you spend your days?"

"We would walk, have picnics on the beach, sometimes take a small boat out. And in the evenings, we would tell each other stories."

"Stories from your respective homes?"

"Yes, fables and legends, there wasn't a lot to do on the island, especially after dark. We had to come up with our own entertainment. When it stormed, we would head to the cave, listen to the strange sounds it made."

"Go on?"

"We liked to explore the coves and crags. Ayoko used to hum this melody, which eventually became Amaterasu's aria."

Dinah looked up from her notebook.

"So, Ayoko came up with the melody?"

"Well, yes," Malcolm replied, "but it's such a small part of the composition."

"And the story, she gave you the story?"

"She *told* me the story, yes."

"So, she co-wrote it?"

"I don't think I would put it like that."

"But the idea was hers?" Dinah pressed. She stopped the recording, lent forward in her chair.

"What else was hers?"

"What do you mean?"

"The silence, the idea for the silence, was that hers too?"

Before he could say anything, Dinah held out her hand to signal an end to the conversation, a gesture normally reserved to reprimand Miranda, and gathering up her paperwork, she quietly left the room.

Malcolm scanned the horizon, sipping coffee, the morning grey and wet. The house had settled into an uneasy silence since the previous evening, interrupted only by Dinah reading Miranda her usual bedtime story, extracts of which he knew by rote: "*The little mermaid sang more sweetly than them all. The whole court applauded her with hands and tails; and for a moment her heart felt quite gay, for she knew she had the loveliest voice of any on earth or in the sea*". Malcolm was relieved for the quiet, for an end to all the questions and talk of the retrospective. But with Dinah's equipment still cluttering his study he was relegated to the corners of the old house, waiting for the rain to relent so he could walk along the beach.

Miranda nursed a bowl of cereal and played with her shells. She was accustomed to the quiet, having been raised by nannies and babysitters, taught that time spent with her parents was to be expended in contemplative pursuits. The beach had allowed her a level of freedom she had never experienced back home, where she could run with the tides and explore the rock pools, her parents blissfully ignorant of her actions or whereabouts. Like Malcolm she gazed out of the window longingly, willing the rain to stop.

"What are you up to, sweetheart?" Dinah asked entering the room, heading for the coffee pot, her voice unusually buoyant, compensating for the strained atmosphere of the night before.

Malcolm made to reply but saw her gaze directed at Miranda.

"Just sorting my shells."

"So, there's a system?"

Malcolm doubted it. The groupings appeared entirely arbitrary, without any consistency in size or shape or colour. Limpet shells and tellins, periwinkles, dog whelks and cockles all crowded the kitchen table. A cursory glance confirmed that this was a taxonomy devised by a child's mind.

"These ones are my pretty shells," Miranda said, handing Dinah a few speckled examples, "and these ones feel nice."

"They do feel nice," Dinah said running her finger along a pearly veneer.

"And these ones," she said, circling a cluster together very delicately, "sing."

"Singing indeed? Malcolm, do you hear this?"

Malcolm had turned his attention back out the window, observing a glimmer of sun streaking between the clouds.

"Well, they don't all sing," she corrected, "some just speak sweetly."

"And how do you find a singing shell?"

Miranda edged closer to her mother, her response almost a whisper.

"You have to listen *very hard.*"

Dinah's phone vibrated from its place on the table, the shells clattering against the surface.

"Sorry sweetheart," she said, scrolling through her messages.

"Did you know that hermit crabs don't have shells of their own, that they find empty shells to live in, like periwinkles and whelks?"

"No, I didn't know that," Dinah replied, looking at her screen. "Malcolm are you listening?" He mumbled a reply, not seeing why he should listen when she was only pretending to.

"The male hermit crabs terrorise the females into vacating their shells," Miranda continued, using two shells to demonstrate their skirmish, "that's called the *moult,* when the crabs lose their shells. When they are between shells, they mate."

Though the shells of the hermit crabs had been cast aside in her underwater scenario, she placed the shells on top of each other in simulation of intercourse, grating the husks against one another.

"Miranda!" Dinah looked up from her phone, "that's not appropriate conversation for the table," and ushering her out of her chair and towards the door, she added, "I think it's time you got out of your bedclothes and brushed your teeth."

The ringtone of Dinah's phone accompanied them down the hall and Malcolm heard Dinah's phone voice as she answered, the conversation diminishing as she moved toward the sitting room to get better reception. He cast a glance over Miranda's shells, picking up a conical specimen, something distinctly sexual about the ventral cavity. He heard the ring of an elevator bell in his mind before *Amaterasu's Silence* began to play softly.

"I put one of the singing shells in your pocket," Miranda said from the doorway, startling him into nearly dropping the one he held, "did you hear it?"

As if pre-empting Dinah's summons, she returned the way she had come, just as Dinah's voice filled the house, calling her back.

✳

A storm was brewing. Malcolm recognised the stillness of the water, a heaviness in the air, the unusual quiet at the sea's edge. Miranda seemed unaware, her eyes cast down, trawling through knots of seaweed. Malcolm followed her closely, watching how she moved back and forth like the tide, harvesting the shore. What was it that she could see and hear that he couldn't? She had found a small red bucket washed up at the strandline—its companion spade still lost at sea—and requisitioned it for her beachcombing, collecting fragments of pottery and sea-glass, redundant egg cases—mermaid's purses—which along with her shells formed a veritable catch.

Watching Miranda at play, listening to her shells, he remembered what she'd said about her collection, that some didn't sing, they spoke sweetly. The woman in the elevator had certainly spoken sweetly, perhaps that was why he remembered her so easily, before the memory had soured. Miranda held one of the shells higher as if to catch a better frequency before casting it aside, whether due to a lack of sound or because it emitted a sound she disliked, he hardly knew. You would have to speak sweetly, he supposed, to gain the ear of a child.

Though the wind was low, he felt a shift in the air, saw Miranda stand as if summoned.

"Listen," she called.

A low plaintive moan filled the air and they both moved towards it, Miranda breaking into a run, her bucket clattering and spilling. Malcolm thought of the ghost of Fingal's son, stationed at the summit of the cave where his body lay entombed, issuing his ardent battle-cry, calling men to action. And at the same time, he wondered if the voices he'd heard in the cave could carry this far, reminded of *Amaterasu's Silence* rising up from the pit.

Miranda came to a stop, took a cautious step back, and when Malcolm edged closer, he saw why. A group of seals had set up camp at the entrance of the cave, basking on beds of kelp, calling to one another in doleful, drawn-out notes, their song sweetly sorrowful when echoed within the hollowed chamber.

He'd seen a lot of different set designs for Amaterasu's grotto over the years. There were always conceptual treatments, the auditorium itself imagined as the interior of the cave, the stage pared down, either minimalist in principle or economy. Then there were those that drew on a Japanese aesthetic; one popular production imagined the space as a concave white screen onto which shadow puppets—the actors of the outside world—danced, while the haloed-boulder obstructing the cave's entrance filled the backdrop like a full moon.

But Malcolm's favourite by far had seen Amaterasu's story transposed to a frozen tundra, the cave appearing to be made of crystal, the imitation stalagmites not unlike the hexagonal columns of Fingal's cave. It reminded him of the Fortress of Solitude in the Superman comics, a place fit for a hero's retreat. He thought of the chitinous surface of Miranda's shells and of the mineral parity of shell and rock; how the pearlized interiors of clams and oysters, their offspring pearls formed by layers of nacre, could rival the lucent beauty of crystal.

Though Dinah's questions had ceased for the time being, the study was still littered with the remnants of the retrospective. He rummaged through Dinah's files, looking at photographs and concert programmes, newspaper cuttings of reviews and articles. Then he replayed the interview on Dinah's camera, listening to his voice and Dinah's in concert, discordant and off-key. Surrounded by the artefacts of his prolific career, it was plain that nothing had really mattered since *Amaterasu*. It was his *magnum opus*, he was the only one who refused to see it, to think so obstinately that there was still more music to make. Maybe it was time for him to take his bow and let Dinah sing his requiem.

"Who are you talking to?" Dinah said, before realising the camera was in playback mode. She let it run and joined him in leafing through the contents of his life. Though Ayoko hardly featured, Dinah paused on a photograph of Malcolm rehearsing with the orchestra. A younger man then, he was hunched over the score, making notes, whilst in the background, barely noticeable stood a slight figure, her eyes closed, her arms raised as if conducting the music.

Veins of light flickered on the horizon, followed a few moments later by the grumble of thunder, the din of the sudden downpour.

"Will you come with me to the cave?" Malcolm asked.

He knew it was asking a lot, to relive traditions that weren't her own, to walk in the wake of his first wife.

She looked out at the rain then back at the photograph.

"No Malcolm."

She had always loved him for *Amaterasu*, just as others had before, but since the interview he'd seen the doubt in her eyes, the dawning suspicion that he was not the sole author. How could he explain that the island had devised an arrangement for two voices, voices that harmonised so well that it was hard to separate their respective parts, though one had always soared slightly higher than the other. But their duet could not continue forever and as those summers had passed, the world outside had become more clamorous, disturbing their peace until they had to arrange silence just to hear their song. It was Ayoko's idea to add lacunae to the score, to make space for Amaterasu's voice. But her own voice wasn't right to carry Amaterasu out of the cave and onto the stage, not at that time; it wasn't white and male, the qualification needed to head an orchestra, to conduct their *opus*, so she was left to command and inhabit the silence instead.

He was soaked to the bone by the time he made it to the cave, his dressing gown sleek like seal fur. He'd thought only of Ayoko as he hurried through the rain, of the times holed-up in the cave, listening to the tempest outside, her voice rising above the dissonance. He made his way to the stone plinth and upended his pockets, arranging Miranda's shells into a loose circle. He'd brought her entire collection, unsure which of her finds was responsible for the voice he heard on that first visit to the cave. Whether he believed in the magic of Miranda's singing shells or not, the hope of hearing Ayoko's voice again outweighed any feelings of irrationality.

It was an impressive collection. In the flashes of light, he recognised the hinged shells of mussels and cockles, delicate cowries and he opened them up in the absurd hope it might encourage them to sing. And there were whelks and periwinkles, their coiled peaks like the tails of mermaids turned in on themselves. Maybe this was all that remained of those fabled creatures, their imprint echoing in the waves and spirals of nature's pattern, and he was reminded of the little mermaid from Miranda's story, willing to give up her voice in exchange for something greater.

Malcolm heard only the storm for a long time but gradually as his ears become more accustomed to the still-ness of the cave, it gave way to a different cacophony. There *were* voices in the shells, voices he recognised for the most part, women that he had hurt or overlooked, loved and spurned. Some spoke, others sang, and some shouted their words vehemently, spitting out their pain in plosive notes, all competing to be heard, their voices, consigned to silence, now liberated within the sanctuary of the cave. Rising above it all was Ayoko's voice, his not-so-silent partner, singing *Amaterasu's Silence* in doleful tones, not just the first few bars this time, but the entire melody, her voice soaring above the din, curating all the pain into a beautiful harmony.

∗

"Malcolm! Malcolm!" he heard his name far off in the distance, was conscious of the reek of seaweed, his cheek wet.

"Malcolm!" came the voice again, calling him from outside the cave. He rose slightly, seeing that he had lain in the pit of the cave, interred overnight, the light streaking through the rock, along with the lapping of the tide restoring him to life.

"My god, are you ok?" He saw Dinah and Miranda run towards him, Dinah kneeling at his side, placing her hand against his head.

"Yes, fine, fine," he replied. She tried to lift him to his feet, but he remained rooted to the spot.

"Let's get you back to the house."

"No. I want to stay here."

Dinah stood over him.

"That's preposterous! You'll catch your death."

"I'm fine," he repeated, leaning against the plinth. "Miranda, fetch me some more of those singing shells," he said and before Dinah could object, she had run back out to the shore to do his bidding. Children were much better listeners than adults, able to perceive possibilities and frequencies adults couldn't even fathom. Untold songs lay undiscovered out there, stoppered like messages in bottles, cast out into a seemingly silent world, just waiting to be found. Malcolm cast a glance about the cave; it was a moult of sorts, an absence in-between, those silenced voices just needed the temptation of a bigger shell to entice them out.

"Malcolm?" Dinah pressed, "we have to leave."

He thought of Amaterasu in her cave, wanting to be left alone, barring the door to the shadows dancing outside.

"I can't," he said, "I have to listen to the music."

"What music?"

He glanced toward the rocky ledge; his chorus of shell already assembled. They all had stories to tell, silences to speak, their pain rendered more beautiful in the depths of the cave. Like Macpherson and his songs of old, he would weave together fragments of forgotten voices and compose a piece of epic proportions, a haunting polyphony, of silence lost and found.

"Malcolm?"

"Wait, they're just warming up. Listen..."

Dinah laughed and the sound reverberated through the cave.

"Malcolm," she entreated, after the laughter had faded and she saw he was in earnest, "please."

But he wasn't listening to her. Instead, he could just make out the shell voices in muted concert, muffled whispers, faint glissandos scaling higher. It didn't matter if Dinah was angry with him because eventually her anger would subside to silence and then there was every chance it would find itself lodged in shell, washed up on the beach for him to find. Then he would add her voice to his choir, where the sound would be so much sweeter.

In the distance he heard footsteps through water, Dinah's voice urgent on her mobile, *I think he's had a fall*, calling for action, but diminishing as she made her way up the shore seeking better reception. He wanted to tell her to get her camera, to come back and document the composer's lair but the music was getting louder, calling for his complete attention. He had a lot of listening to do, to atone for all the silence he had imposed on others, while his music had been free to rise above the cave and into the world. He closed his eyes and inhaled the salt air, pulling the damp fur of his gown about him tighter, listening to the song of salvaged voices, as the seals in the bay wailed at the loss of their pups drowned in the tempest.

Down to the Roots

Neil Williamson

"SO, IS IT all coming back yet?" Ursula Crichton's question snaps Dan back to the here and now. Tires grit on tarmac as she eases the Subaru estate around a corner, a bar of spent sunlight scanning across her face. Outside, brambles and browning gorse overhang moss-scabbed walls. Branches of birch and oak shiver above, clinging on to the last of their leaves, and in the woods' deeper shadows loom spruces and Scots pines. At some point she's rolled the windows down half an inch and the air is cold and sharp with autumnal moulder.

Despite a lifetime of promises there's no doubting where he is. Memories of it, though?

As kids Ursula and Dan were friends but this middle-aged woman in a North Face fleece and no make-up, her scrunched-up hair threaded with wires of silver, is a stranger. She glances over with bark-brown eyes. Dan has been trying to recall since she picked him up at the station, but can only picture a cheeky, stork-legged teen in denim shorts and an Aberdeen football top. He vaguely remembers thinking that he might have fancied her if her hair were cut like Dee Hepburn's instead of Clare Grogan's but not what colour eyes she had. Likewise, he can picture in his mind almost nothing of the village that lies along this winding Argyllshire road. Never had a reason to want to remember it, so it's long gone. Discarded, junked, along with the rest of his childhood.

Dan makes himself smile. "Starting to, yeah," he says.

"It's good to be home."

Ursula grins, the sun sliding off her face again as they enter a cloister of tree shadow and lapse back into the ill-fitting silence that so far has characterised their reunion. Back to the stereo's nineties indie mix, tinny over the road rumble. Dan's recognised few of the tunes. By the time of Britpop, he'd already escaped to Glasgow. Business school and club culture were the scratch and flare to his life, the fizzling touch paper that launched him into the world of banks and security software: the job in the City of London, the Jacob's ladder of promotions, the house in Highbury complete with Home Counties wife and kid, business class travel and expense accounts, living the good life—the *best* life—wherever he happened to be and with whomever he fancied. Strategically calendared vacations in Disneyland Paris and on Barbadian beaches. The condo with the pool that English Sara didn't know about, but Californian Courtney did. It had been a blaze, every second of it.

It was never fucking meant to lead him back here.

It's only when the Subaru passes a pair of gate posts topped with stone pineapples and then swings through a particularly lurching right-hander that anticipation unexpectedly clutches Dan's breath. He thinks *cattle grid* a second before they rattle over one, and *bow-backed bridge* just as they emerge out of the trees and rise over the old stone arch. And that's when memories start to resurface. As they cross the River Afton, he remembers skimming stones in the late summer, defying his mother's warnings for the joy of raising white lips from the brown water. When they pass the sign that reads *Crawfoot*, he remembers pretending to patrol there with Ursula, sharing a borrowed air rifle like sentries in a war movie. And when the car squeezes through the narrow choke that he knows will feed into the bottom end of the Mains, they pass a two-storey building with boarded windows, a rusting roller door and a dilapidated petrol pump, the red and white *ESSO* all but scratched away. The garage's signage has been taken down but Dan remembers the name of the girl who vanished playing near the woods, there and then gone one trick-of-the-light autumn evening. That name, a warning and a prayer around the village for months afterwards: *Christine Hutchison*. Fuck, he's not thought about Christine Hutchison in decades.

They're flooding in now. He remembers standing in the kitchen of the old house, staring at the drab olive Formica while his Mum lectured him about wandering around on his own. The house is a few streets from here, through the Mains and past the school. He remembers the redbrick garden wall and squealing gate. Their living room with polystyrene stonework around a two-bar electric fire, like a cave of modernity. His bedroom wallpaper, aeroplanes among the clouds, pasted up over a horrendous green flock that his curious, picking fingers had disinterred behind his headboard in his early teens. He remembers the unpleasant fuzziness, soft like an over-ripe peach. His Mum had done her nut when she'd found out.

Dan makes himself stop. He blinks, breathes, licks his lips and acknowledges that his childhood hasn't been discarded after all, just buried beneath layers of better memories over the intervening thirty-five years, pasted down determinedly but still there, ready to be revealed in rips and strips. He swallows, feels saliva flood around his parched, beach-wreck of a tongue.

After the garage, the revelations continue at a more sustainable pace. As the Mains opens out like a dusty photograph album, he sees the old church at the low end and the primary school at the high, both exactly as he remembers. The parade of shops strung between them, though, is a sorry sight. The butcher's is still there but the grocer's is now a budget supermarket, its window plastered with dayglow deals. Further along, the baker's has become a knock-off Greggs, and the sign above McKee's Newsagent, where Dan, suddenly, vividly, recalls buying Kwenchy Kups and

Monster Fun on sun-soaked Saturday mornings, just says GIFTS now, barely a step up from a charity shop. He can't remember what used to be where the grubby café is and several of the remaining premises are derelict, giving the impression of an old man's leery grin. It's just after five in the afternoon but this deep into October the street lights are already on. There are few souls about, and they huddle and scurry through the gloaming as if eager to finish their business and get home.

Ursula noses the car towards a parking space. "Just going to pick up a couple of things," she says. "Want to come?" Dan shakes his head. She holds his gaze for a second, the skin around those brown eyes delicate as leaf skeleton. "Right you are." Grabbing her purse from the dashboard, she ducks out of the car and strides off towards the supermarket.

Dan waits until she's inside before he gets his phone out. Just two bars of signal but knowing he's not completely cut off he breathes easier. He opens Facebook and sits for several minutes trying to think of something to say. Fuck's sake. How hard can it be to post a photo of this shit hole and tap out a sarcastic note about how much things have gone downhill? Is he *ashamed* to be here? Is that what it is? Ashamed to leave the car out of fear that someone will recognise him? Ashamed his colleagues will judge him for his crappy beginnings?

Well, fuck that. He's proud of what he's made of himself. *Because* of his crappy beginnings. Angrily, he starts to tap something out but a bubble of emotion wells in his chest. His eyes feel gritty. He blinks, breathes, deletes what he's written.

The truth is…

The *truth*… is that it's not Crawfoot. It's him. Since the promotion and all that came after it he's fallen out of the social media habit. He used to be such a proud man. He doesn't have so much to be proud of any more.

Instead of posting a message of his own, Dan scrolls through his feed. Ursula posted a link to some local produce initiative an hour ago, but nothing about meeting an old friend. Since their unexpected reconnection a few months back—her embarrassingly tentative *I don't know if you remember me*—he's learned that she's not an over sharer. Maybe she doesn't have much to brag about either. That's something they have in common at least.

Of his actual friends, the Americans already feel remote, geographically and socially. It's barely been four months since his step up to European VP. The permanent move back to the UK is supposed to be a reward, a well-earned opportunity to spend time with his family while younger colleagues burn themselves out hitting the targets that'll earn him his bonuses, but it's all gone wrong. Somehow, a tear has appeared through his carefully layered lives and something has seeped through—Sara meet Courtney—and now he's unwelcome in either of them.

He *likes* a picture of one of his colleagues' kids playing with the family dog in the front yard. Goofy pumpkins on the porch in the background. SoCal in the Fall. Movie shot idyllic. He really misses it.

He turns lastly to his English friends. Most of them were Sara's crowd and he feels grubby flicking through the streams of those mutual friends who haven't completely cut him off yet, but he makes himself do it and is rewarded with snaps of Oliver at the nursery Halloween party. The wee fella's done up in a garish costume. Some cartoon character Dan doesn't recognise. He wants to *like* it, to *heart* it, to make *some mark* so that Oliver might know.

He wonders if this is what it feels like to be a ghost.

Dan puts his phone away and gazes out of the window. Ursula is taking an age in the store so he allows his attention to linger on a young mother struggling to drag her child past the coin-operated aeroplane outside the gift shop. There are stern words but the kid—about Oliver's age, the blonde hair shorter and a shade lighter—has dug his heels in so Mum relents and fishes out a pound. The tears turn instantly to laughs as the machine jiggles into motion. Dan realises he doesn't know if his own son would find such joy in something so simple. The mother intermittently checks her phone and glances hostilely around and, when she spots Dan in the car, she stares until he looks away. Next door, they're switching the lights off in the café, the owner, about Dan's age but with a shag of greying curls and a paunch overhanging his jeans, ushering the teenage waitress outside so that he can lock up. She hurries off without even making eye contact, and the owner watches her for several seconds too long before jangling the keys towards the lock.

The aeroplane ride is over and the mother is now talking to Ursula, from whose hand dangles an unbranded carrier bag lumpen with groceries. Dan hopes she's not gone to the trouble of planning something elaborate for dinner. He doesn't want her to try and impress him. It'd be embarrassing. His face flushes as that ugly thought buds and blossoms from the branch of scorn that has burgeoned while he's been sitting here.

Jesus, Danny, he thinks. *Try not to be too much of a dick while you're here.*

The mother and child depart but, before returning to the car, Ursula pauses to look at the aeroplane. No, at something behind it. In the evening gloom Dan has failed to notice it until now. It's like ripping off several layers at once.

The *tumshie tub.*

The old-fashioned hoop-bound barrel is shoved up against the wall, its iron rusting, its wooden struts green and crumbling. Ursula drops a coin into the Baxters soup can dangling from the barrel's rim and then reaches deep inside to pull out a muddy, wizened turnip.

"Fuck's sake," Dan mutters aloud.

Ursula is smiling as she crosses to the car and opens the door. Hands him the shopping bag so she can slip into the driver's seat, and then the turnip too. It's the size of a child's head, a shock of slug-ragged leaves sprouting from the top. Mud crumbles onto Dan's Kühl jacket.

"Remember now?" she says.

∗

Memory, Dan thinks after fake-smiling through a dinner of microwaved *rogan josh* and awkward reminiscences, is a fucked up thing. What it chooses to show you, what it keeps hidden. What peels away easy and what's stuck down hard. He can recall the feel of his old bedroom walls acutely, the fern patterns inlaid in the vegetal green. He must have been to Ursula's family home—hers and her husband's now—dozens of times but it's entirely unfamiliar. They've talked for over an hour and it's been stilted and frustrating. He doesn't remember the things she thinks he ought to. He doesn't want to talk about the things he does.

Especially the Warding, Crawfoot's take on the traditions of the season. Halloween when he was growing up had none of the fun that it has in America: no pumpkins or trick-or-treating, no parties, no cosplaying superheroes or film stars. It was serious business. During the week leading up to All Hallows, the village kids went guising to their neighbours' houses. They'd wear sackcloth masks or ash-blackened faces so that they could pass for the spirits of the dead and carried a joke or a song to prove their humanity and earn an apple and a handful of nuts and sweets. Even so disguised, no child was allowed out without a turnip lantern to ward them. And not just any turnip either. It had to be taken from the tumshie tub and paid for with honest-earned coin. On Halloween night itself, an adult walked the Ward for the 'good of the village'. No-one else. That's the story anyway. It came up several times in the conversation but he didn't pursue it.

It's only now while watching Ursula across the cluttered kitchen table, working determinedly with knife and spoon to hollow the turnip out, that Dan is hit by a memory that punches right through to his soft grey plaster.

He's quite young because the garden wall is as high as his shoulder. A rowan tree dangles overhead, red berries glistening under the streetlight like winter poison. His nose is running from the cold and the air is bitter with bonfire smoke. As he totters after the other kids he can feel the candle inside his lantern rocking, its light guttering with every step, so he's gripping the string tight and trying not swing it for fear that his fierce-grinning protector will snuff out. As he ducks under a branch he feels something touch his hair. He freezes but can't bring himself to turn and see if it's a rowan twig or Herself's *questing fingers.*

Fucking hell.

Dan takes a long gulp of his wine. "I can't believe you still do all this," he says, trying to make his tone light but doesn't think he's quite succeeded. "The modern world still not quite made it to Crawfoot yet?"

Ursula glances up from spooning yellow flesh into a brimming Tupperware. Its sweet, organic smell mixes with the stale spice from the plates that are wedged in between the sheaves of home-printed flyers for farmers markets and Shop Local weekends. "Hardly," she snorts, glaring. Looking away, Dan's eye falls on a stack of adverts for a local business forum. The paper is water-stained, the date some weeks in the past. "A Starbucks here would be a fucking tourist attraction." She resumes scraping, but has something to add. "Actually that's something I wanted to ask you about. Investment, reach, visibility. You know about that stuff, Dan. How do we do it here?"

"Ha!" he exclaims, half out of surprise, half relief, because at last he gets it. Sees all of this for what it is. Thank fuck. Ursula's been fishing, attempting to hook him with nostalgia. Trying to get him invested so that maybe she can persuade him to *invest*. She'd chosen a clumsy way to go about it, picking around the edges, trying to find a corner that'll peel, but without success. Until that unexpected memory of guising just there. He won't deny it shook him, but finding out that there's a mundane, cheap-ass reason for Ursula's invitation to visit makes it almost laughable. This is the sort of duplicity he understands. "I knew it," he laughs. "I *knew* there was an ulterior motive for all this."

Ursula has a thing she does when something perplexes her, a sort of grimace between a frown and a smile. She's doing it now. "Seriously?" she says. "You couldn't just believe I wanted to catch up after all these years? Maybe rekindle a fucking friendship that once meant something? To me at least. Sorry if I've overstepped the mark in asking for a little advice."

Her defensiveness irks Dan. Why is she keeping up the pretence even after he's called her on it? Is it face-saving? The village is dying on its arse because anyone with any sense leaves it as soon as they're old enough to hitch a ride out. They always have. "You're asking for the benefit of my experience?" he says. If it sounds patronising, he doesn't care. "Well, yeah, in my experience there's *always* an ulterior motive."

"Is that so?" Ursula tips out the last of the turnip's innards then examines the exterior, tracing lightly with the point of her sharp little knife. Feeling the natural contours of the rough skin. She's looking, Dan recalls, for *The Face*. Making her choice, she stabs deftly through the skin, then again at an angle to the first cut. After the third incision, a triangular plug pops out, leaving a crude eyehole. That's how it's done, he remembers. Your tumshie gets none of the Instagrammable artistry afforded to the fabled pumpkin. Ursula makes to slice out the second eye but instead she points the wicked blade at him. "All right then, what's yours?"

"My what?" he says, surprised.

"Your *ulterior motive*. Why did you come here?"

"Because you asked me."

"Simple as that?" she scoffs. "You don't know me. We're not friends and whatever history we shared, it is clearly long forgotten. It wasn't even a direct invitation: *You should come back some time and visit,*" she parodies her own voice. "People say that sort of thing all the time. It'd have been easy enough to say you were busy with work or didn't want to leave the family or... politely, say you had no interest in setting foot in this God-forsaken pit ever again, but you didn't. You *jumped* at it. You were practically on the next train up. Why?"

Dan deals her a boardroom stare but she doesn't even blink. He takes another long swig of his wine and swallows slowly. There's a sour edge to it that's starting to curdle his stomach. Of course, she's right. There was no good reason for him to come here. Even when Mum was alive, Home had been that pretty little cottage she'd moved to in Perth and, when she'd ever mentioned Crawfoot, it had been to curse the place. She never mentioned his Dad either, except that one time when he was very small and full of questions. *He went away before you were born, son.* She'd said it matter-of-factly, without rancour. And he'd accepted it because theirs was far from the only Crawfoot family that'd lost a limb somewhere down the line.

Eventually, Dan says: "So, how long did you say your husband was away on business for?"

Ursula's laugh is a howl. "You always were a cheeky fucker," she says, grinning as she goes back to carving the face.

Dan laughs too, or at least pretends to. Thing is, he doesn't even know if he was joking. A random fling? Really? Is that what it'll take to make him feel like he's got some sort of control over his life?

The moment has broken down something between them though. He reaches for the bottle. "Top up?"

Ursula glances up from knifing out a zig-zag grin. "Sure... *ow! Fuck!*" Her blade's been too eager and there's blood beading on her finger. She sucks it off, then shakes the pain away.

Grimacing, Dan upends the bottle over her glass. There's barely a dribble left. "Sorry for distracting you," he says.

"Don't you remember?" she says. "A little blood lends the Warding that wee bit more power." When Ursula turns the turnip around to reveal its ugly face, sure enough there's a tinge of pink on the serrated teeth.

"This is stupid," Dan blurts, and then recoils from the gust of boozy vapour he's just expelled. The stink of it even over-powers the burnt cork Ursula used to paint his face. They'd exited the house looking like commandos, giggling, eyes alight. It's less funny now as they creep past the old garage. He leans against the wall for a moment, silently cursing the speed they'd consumed that second bottle of wine and the eagerness with which they'd then moved on to the whisky. "C'mon, man. Halloween's weeks away yet."

"It's close enough." Ursula's voice shimmers off the bricks from a distance ahead. There's no street lighting, so he can only see her by the light of the turnip's glaring devil grin. "These days we walk the Warding as often as we can. *Herself's* got greedy since you left."

She's just fucking with him again, invoking Crawfoot's own bogeyman: the supposed witch of the woods, blamed over the years for stealing the unwary and for any other general misfortunes that befell the town. A lazy amalgamation of folk tropes. Shit, they couldn't even come up with a decent name for her. Ursula's going to have to try harder than that.

He pushes off the wall and in the darkness almost

walks into the old petrol pump. Below the rotary dials that once counted the gallons, exposed here like teeth in an excavated skull, there's a sticker: "Licenced to H&G Hutchison, 3 Mennie St, Crawfoot, Argyllshire".

Christine Hutchison got took by Herself. *Thanks be to her family.* The phrase echoes unwillingly in his ears. It'd been the village mantra that whole year. He remembers the fruit baskets and fresh loaves, the discreet visits and kind words visited on the family like they'd become holy or something. He remembers...

It's the Halloween night of the year after Christine disappeared. There's a crowd of them, young teens. A nervy knot of giggles and bravado. They're too old for guising, so they're going to walk the Ward. Do their duty, like the adults do, in Christine's name. They'd all known her a bit at school, but their ringleader, Moira Lennox, had been her best friend. Their parents would have forbidden it of course, so they've all sneaked out, using their teenage logic to convince each other that doing it together—doing it for Christine—*means they'll be okay. They all say they're not afraid but Dan can tell they are. He is too, and he doesn't even believe in it. Even, or especially, despite what they've been saying about his Dad recently. They're eejits when they want to be but they're his friends. All the same, there are limits.*

Moira had rummaged through the tumshie tub with such care, scrutinised every ruddy skin until she found the one with the right face. Now, as they follow the lantern single file past the garage, the mood becomes solemn. Dan loiters at the back, not really sure what he's doing here. What any of them are doing, really. Only Moira's motive is clear, the lantern light illuminating her anger. Even without it earlier, her face had been glowing with defiance. The rest of the faces, as they shuffle through the choke, are pensive, each contemplating the real darkness outside of the bounds of the village and what, in their hearts, they either do believe or don't believe or half believe, waits. One by one, they file out into the dark, the cheeks of some of them, Ursula included, glittering. Doing their duty.

But Dan... can't. All of this is stupid, pointless. It's irrational.

And he's sorry, he's sorry. He's so sorry.

Those are his thoughts as he runs home, his skin electric with the anticipation that any second something will reach out for him. To touch his hair, perhaps, or stroke his neck. Or, worst of all, cradle his skull. Sizing it up.

Ursula has reached the town sign by the time he catches her up. "This is *stupid*," he says again, out of breath. It's really cold out here, the sky overcast and the stars hidden, a dampness in the air. It *is* stupid. He shouldn't be here. He should be at home, working out what to do with his life. Trying to patch things up with Sara or calling Courtney and telling her this time he's really going to do it. Jack it all in and emigrate. He needs to be strategizing. Consolidating or moving on. He's not too old to start from scratch again. The Gulf maybe, or Australia.

"It's just a tradition, Dan," Ursula says. "You've come all this way. One short walk around the village is the least you can do."

All right then. Just once round the village, bridge to bridge and then home. A night on the sofa and he can call out an Uber in the morning and be done with this. Nothing will happen.

"So, yeah," he says, following her off the road and along the rabbit path that runs through the pale whin grass towards the river bank, "I can probably sort you out with someone to talk to on the promotional side of things and I know some shit hot fundraisers too. They might have some ideas you can use." He's rambling, he knows, but it's better than thinking.

"Really?" Though she's only a few feet ahead of him her voice sounds distant. There's no breeze, it's just her passage that's making the grass dance in her wake, strobe-like in the lantern glow. "That'd be amazing." The last word is muddied by the trickle and plash of water to their left, the creak of branches. Dan peers but can see nothing beyond the grass. There could be anything out there. To his right he can just about make out the silhouettes of houses. All the lights off, the windows dark like shut eyes.

"No problem," he says, and now his own voice sounds thin out here too, diminished and tenuous. He presses on regardless. "Though to make a significant change, an area like this really needs some proper investment. A draw. Food tourism is big right now. Maybe you could get some development money to open a distillery? Whisky, craft gin. A shop to sell local cheeses and smoked meats?"

Ursula doesn't reply for a moment. Then: "I'm not sure that'd work here. Don't think *She'd* like that."

No, don't say that, he thinks. *Don't bring* Her *into it. Don't give me an edge to pick at.*

They've been walking a good ten minutes now and should be following the river bank up around the western side of the town, but they're still in the long grass. It caresses his legs with every step.

"Ursula?" he says. She says something back but he can't make it out. "Ursula!"

She pauses, raising the lantern as she looks back at him over her shoulder. In the ruddy glow from its impish eyes, her grin looks like a rictus. Her voice is suddenly pin sharp. "We're nearly there."

He wants to believe she means *nearly home*. They're just walking the Ward. Once around the village.

Nothing's going to happen.

He never asked Mum if it was true what his friends said happened to Dad. And all the others from the village who were found wanting. He didn't need to because he doesn't believe in it.

He *doesn't*.

"Here we are."

Yeah, there they are right enough. *Fuck.*

The grass has thinned out, revealing to their meagre

light not the riverbank path but a rectangle of turned mud the size of Ursula's back garden. The little field is coarse and cloddy but isolated clumps of scrawny leaves poke through here and there. Standing before the field is a rusty wheelbarrow with a garden fork balanced against it.

In the centre of the field is a house. Or something like a house. It's a single storey high and in an awful state. Its roof slates are leprous with moss. Its lintels crumbling. Its bricks are in the process of being crushed ever so slowly by a prolific woody vine. There are no windows and just one door, which is too small for a normal person and has peeling green paint... and stands ajar.

"No," he says.

"You can't say no," Ursula replies.

"I don't want to." Like a child.

"You have to. It's why you came here."

"No," he says again and tries to turn away but she shoves him in the shoulder and he stumbles into the wheelbarrow and the fork falls with a scrape and a dull clang that sounds so loud out here in the dark that it almost stops his heart.

"I guess we discovered your ulterior motive, Daniel." She's grinning again, underlit by the rosy flicker and he can tell she won't back down from this.

"Will you wait?" he says.

She lowers the lantern gently to the ground. He can see the scorching around the eyes and manic grin now, and a crack of light around the top indicating that the lid has shrunk from being cooked over the candle flame. The way she folds her arms tells him she's not going to wait until it's burned up completely. "Sooner you go, sooner it'll be over," she says.

What choice does he have?

He nearly has to squat to squeeze through the door but surprisingly there's room to straighten up on the other side. And there's light too. He's not sure where it's coming from, and there's not much, but it's enough to see the short hall that stretches in front of him. The stairs at the end. The hallway smells of turned earth and as he progresses down it he realises that he can touch both walls. In patches they feel soft and fuzzy like over-ripe peaches. Mostly they've been stripped back to the bare brick. Underfoot, twigs and pinecones scatter and snap, or something that feels like those anyway.

The stairs rise into darkness. There can't be many of them in this tiny house but as Dan climbs he quickly loses count. He climbs until his calves complain, and with each heavy upward step the earthy aroma intensifies. He climbs until he forgets why he's climbing, until the smell of soil is so strong it feels like his nostrils are plugged with it.

Then he is at the top, and he's standing in a room whose ceiling is the earth. Skinny roots dangle down. White. Atrophying. Scraps of filthy cloth cling to them, like the last of the leaves.

And Dan stands there, waiting for the touch. The bark-brown fingers cradling a head fat with memories.

Weighing it in judgement.

Dollface

Seán Padraic Birnie

RAYMOND LIVED NEXT door to my wife and I and sometimes he'd come over and we'd drink beers out on the back patio. It didn't matter what the weather was like, we always sat outside. He and I went a way back: we'd been at primary school together, though we'd never been friends, not in those days, and must have crossed paths only once or twice after secondary school. But then a few years ago he and his family happened to move into the house next to ours in Mile Oak and, amused by the coincidence, we got to know one another a little better over beers one night, which became kind of a regular thing. My wife didn't like him. Raymond had a wife too and a young daughter he liked to complain about, and in fact he complained about the both of them a good deal, his combined and ongoing complaint forming our main topic of conversation, which was why my wife didn't like him, because she didn't think it was very sensitive for him to always be complaining about his daughter when we ourselves had lost two babies, one at sixteen weeks and the other the day after the birth. I tried to explain this to him once but he didn't get it, which is why we'd always sit outside on the patio, on old green camping chairs I was always meaning to replace.

On this occasion, Raymond was complaining about his sister-in-law, who so far as I knew my wife and I had never met, because she had bought his daughter a present without asking.

Well, a present's nice, I said. What's the problem?

The problem is the present itself and the fact that it isn't just a present. Not with Mylene. It's a present and it's some kind of a, I don't know. Some kind of a strategy. A device.

Okay, I said, and drank a swig of beer. In the summer I like to drink a nice chilled lager but in the winter I stick to ale. It was winter now. Raymond always sticks to lager, chilled or not, he wasn't particular, being as he was more interested in the ABV than the variety of hop.

What do you think it is she wants?

Oh, said Raymond, waving his hand. The usual. To drive a wedge. Between Mary and me, and between Sophie and me. The thing is, I knew her before I knew Mary, and she's never been, well…

He trailed off, muttering something under his breath. He was always swearing underneath his breath, which was another of my wife's given reasons for disliking him. He swore quite a lot over his breath, too.

Now he was staring at the patio, shaking his head.

So what was it? I asked.

What was what? said Raymond.

The present.

Oh, the present. That fucking thing. It's a doll.

He said the word 'doll' with considerable disgust. I nodded, wondering what could be so bad about a doll.

I hate dolls, said Raymond. Fucking dolls. Fucking Mylene.

Then he swore under his breath again, staring at the cracked patio, shaking his head.

✷

Maybe a week later he told me he might need my help with something.

That was unusual because usually all we did was drink beer together out on the patio, but I said OK.

Thanks, said Raymond. Thanks.

I don't think I'd ever heard him say thank you before.

That bloody doll, he said. Bloody Mylene.

Shaking his head, he studied a crack in the patio.

Just tell me when, I said.

That bloody doll, said Raymond, nodding to himself.

Later that evening, after Raymond had left, my wife said to me: I don't know why you have to have him over all the time.

I nodded, looking up from my phone. We were sat on the sofa, in the glow of the television. Through the wall we could hear the TV in Raymond's living room. On the other side of the wall, he and Mary, or maybe just Mary, were watching the same programme.

Raymond and I go way back, I said. Same primary school and all.

My wife sniffed. Then she zapped the television off with the remote control and went up to bed.

I got up and went to turn it off properly, because the remote just puts it on standby, and when something's turned off I like it to actually be turned off and not just sleeping.

∗

My mobile rang that night. It was three in the morning. It didn't actually ring because I keep it on silent but the screen lit up and filled the room with blue light, and I was awake anyway, as I often am. Tilting the screen down so as not to shine its cold light on my wife, who never has any trouble sleeping, I went out into the hall to answer.

When, said Raymond.

Pardon?

I'd started to wonder if I had been snoozing after all because I was as groggy as if I had just been jolted out of the deepest cycle of sleep. And the landing outside our bedroom had acquired a kind of dreamlike quality. Everything was normal, everything in its proper place, but somehow accentuated. I rubbed my eyes.

When.

Raymond, it's three in the morning.

You said to say when. I'm saying when. When when when. Okay?

I nodded, beginning to understand.

Can't this wait until the morning? I asked.

Nope. Sorry.

Now the banister and the stairwell and the little stained-glass window above the stairs down to the ground floor of the house had lost that odd accentuation. They were themselves again.

I've been drinking, said Raymond. Can you drive?

I counted the units in my head, considered the fact that I'd eaten and had finished X hours ago, and said Yes. Okay.

It was while saying 'Yes. Okay' that I realised that what I should have said was 'Where?'

I went back into the bedroom and got dressed in the darkness. My wife turned over in her sleep.

Outside, Raymond was leaning against the car in our drive, holding a baby, cooing babyishly to it while it burbled back at him. He had a satchel over his shoulder. Backlit by the streetlamp, Raymond and baby and satchel formed a weird silhouette. It was such an odd sight it almost gave me a fright. Maybe the world hadn't quite lost that accentuation. I've always been a funny sleeper, and sometimes when I wake a little of the daft madness of dreams carries over into the day, like the sound of a television or an argument carrying through from the house next door. Not that it was day now, anyway. When I got closer I realised it wasn't a baby Raymond was holding.

Hi, I said.

Evening, said Raymond, though the evening had ended hours ago. Look at this thing.

The orange light of the streetlamp gave the baby face a weird glow, but it was an ordinary doll, so far as I could tell. Nothing unusual about it. It had a slightly stubby nose, if you were to be critical, and maybe its big blue eyes were set a little far apart, but you had to really be looking for something to even think of that.

Well, I said. It's a doll.

Raymond was nodding. I'd often notice him nodding, when I'd not said anything. It was as if he was agreeing with something someone only he could hear had said. Sometimes it coincided with something I had said and I'd never be sure who he was agreeing with, with me or with the someone only he could hear.

It is that, he said. It is that. Let's drive.

Raymond gave directions like a satnav teeming with malware. He took us up the A27 and around the round-abouts where the A27 meets the A23, then back onto the A27 again and out east past the universities, before swinging us back towards town. The roads were mostly empty. It was eerie. I never really drive at that time of night. Who, outside of truckers, has anywhere to be going at that time of night? It made me wonder about the cars that we did pass. Where were they going?

Eventually, after several more circumlocutions, we reached Wild Park, which wasn't even really out of town but which might as well have been for all the time it took to get there.

Fucking Raymond, I thought.

He was clutching the doll in the passenger seat.

All I'd managed to get him to say about it was this:

Present from Mylene. It's a wedge. It's a fucking strategy. I know how that woman thinks. Oh, I know that woman. Mary doesn't know, or doesn't choose to, but I do. Christ, would you look at it?

And he held it up, reaching with one hand to flick on the light in the roof of the car, which for a moment made it hard for me to see the road, but the road was empty.

Do you remember Mylene?

Before I could answer, he said:

We're here. Stop.

I stopped the car.

He took a torch out of the satchel.

Let's walk.

We walked.

Past the toilets, past the football pitches, into the woods.

It was dark in the woods.

＊

Finally satisfied with the spot we'd found, Raymond crouched down. You squat like that, I thought, you'll fuck up your knees. It was a stupid thing to think.

Do you see the problem? said Raymond. He was staring at the doll as if he was hoping it would blink first. Daring it.

It didn't blink.

Not really, I said.

He tossed the doll down in front of him, onto the bracken, and sighed as if he was tired of dealing with people less intellectually capable than himself.

Mylene acts as though she doesn't know that I know what she's up to, but she does, he said.

I nodded, then stopped nodding when I realised it made it look as if I agreed. I didn't know if I agreed or not. Raymond often assumed you agreed with him, whether or not you actually did agree, and sometimes if you weren't careful you could get caught up in that assumption and become complicit in whatever it was he was on about. Mostly I just knew that I was tired.

And it was working, too, said Raymond.

What was working? I asked.

He looked at me sharply, as if I was playing dumb. I blinked first. My eyelids were heavy.

Her plan, he said, looking down into the dirt.

I realised I was nodding again. Maybe it was like shivering: something you do to warm yourself up. I was shivering, too.

Wild Park is just a bit of woodland on the edge of the downs, on the outskirts of Brighton where the downland comes into town, bordered by the A27 to the north and Moulscoomb and Hollingbury to the south. It isn't much, not really, though it is a nature reserve, to give it its due, but at four o'clock in the morning in the winter it can feel like quite a lot more, like a place befitting its name.

It got into my something, said Raymond, who hadn't said 'something.'

It got into what? I asked, looking up. Sorry.

He was nodding again, in that way he did. In the dark in the woods it wasn't so hard to imagine that maybe someone else had said something after all.

My head, he murmured. I've been dreaming about the fucking thing. And every time I walk into a room it's like, I don't know, there it is, looking at me. Leering at me. I go from one room into the next and it's there again as if it's fucking teleported. Except I can't quite remember if I had seen it in the room before, but I feel like I had. And it's only been getting worse. And Sophie, he said, trailing off.

I watched him for a moment. He was breathing weirdly.

What about Sophie? I asked.

Sophie loves it, he said. She loves it. She really does.

I looked down at the doll, at its stubby nose, at its big doll eyes set very slightly too far apart, and tried to see it as he seemed to see it. I couldn't do it.

Mylene knew, said Raymond. She knew.

I watched him. Then I looked at the doll again.

Raymond, I said. Why are we here?

He looked at me suddenly.

I need a witness, he said. To corroborate. The way things

have been going lately, I've started doubting myself.

I realised I was rubbing my temple. I could feel a headache coming on. It was as if my tiredness had transmogrified, become a headache.

A witness for what?

It was beginning to annoy me, drawing him out.

So that I know it is dead, said Raymond.

He removed the satchel from his shoulder, the satchel that I'd forgotten he had with him.

As I watched he opened the satchel and brought out a box of matches, a small trowel, and then a can of deodorant. It was a black Lynx canister of some sort. In the dark I couldn't really see the satchel or the deodorant. In the dark it looked like he had removed the box of matches and the deodorant and the trowel from some secret pocket tucked away in the folds of the dark.

They might have been tucked away in the folds of the past, too: I remembered as kids once, a few of us, Raymond included, at this boy called Joe's house on Kimberley Road when his mother was out, arranging one of Joe's not-inexpensive Action Man figures and a load of toy soldiers in the corner of the patio in his garden. Joe had a load of bangers, which were illegal in England and which he'd brought back from a holiday in France, small little red explosives that looked like sticks of dynamite out of a cartoon. We carefully positioned them throughout the scene, then laid bits of kindling from the fireplace in the living room, bits of scrunched up newspaper, and a whole lot of matches all around. Then one of us— Joe, probably, but maybe Raymond—sprayed the whole tableaux with deodorant. I had been the one holding the bucket of water, which to me meant that if we got into trouble later maybe I'd look like the responsible one. Now Raymond was holding the deodorant again but I didn't have the water.

In the dark the light of the fire when he lit it made my eyes hurt. Oddly accentuated, the doll burned. Its face began to melt. We watched it burn for a while.

We left the doll in the woods in a sad little grave that he dug with the trowel. Then we drove back home.

*

The next day my wife didn't ask where I'd been. She gave the impression that she had no idea I'd even been anywhere, but I was pretty sure that she knew I'd been somewhere. She seemed more annoyed than usual that evening when Raymond came over for a beer.

We sat out on the patio, on the green camping chairs. They were getting tatty and old. I should buy some new ones, I thought.

For the first time ever, Raymond didn't say much. For the first time, I had to spur the conversation along.

Mary's pissed off, he said at last. She suspects something. Sophie's distraught.

I nodded as if I agreed.

They're staying with Mylene tonight.

Do they know?

No, but she suspects something. Mylene's got in her head. I spent all morning pretending to look for the fucking thing. It's surprisingly hard work, looking for something you bloody well know isn't there.

How're you feeling about it now? I asked.

He looked at me suddenly, then smiled. Much better, he said. So much better.

But later that night when he rang he wasn't feeling better anymore.

*

It was 11pm. My wife had gone to bed early for her, at 10, having scarcely said a word all evening, her face buried in the blue light of her phone. I'd found myself sitting in the living room, having another beer. The telly was on but I wasn't really watching it. I'd turned the volume down so low it was hard to tell if the sound was on at all.

I was thinking about the doll, about its eyes, set very slightly too far apart. My phone had dropped from the sofa to the carpet and I hadn't bothered to pick it up again. Then it began to glow suddenly with its own blue light and I saw that Raymond was calling.

Hi, I said.

He whispered something, his voice full of urgency, more a hiss than a whisper.

What? I said.

…come back, repeated Raymond.

They're back from Mylene's? I asked, sitting up, though I knew already that that was not what he had said.

No. The doll. It's back.

For the first time since we'd met I could hear fear in Raymond's voice.

But they're back too, he said. Came back this evening. And Sophie has the doll.

I took a sip of beer and tried to think about this. He had said the doll, not a doll.

Mylene replaced it? I asked.

No, for Christ sake, what I said. The doll is back. The one we—he whispered this—the one we disposed of.

That's impossible, I said. She must have bought a new one. They're hardly unique.

Even as I said this I don't think I really believed it. In the darkness of the living room, a few beers down, the clocks ticking to midnight, it wasn't too hard to believe that what Raymond was saying to me was true.

How do you know? I asked.

I just know.

Sure, I said. Sure. But is there anything particular—I mean, Raymond, you burnt the doll. We watched it melt. Then you buried it. I can corroborate this.

I know, it's impossible, but it's the same doll.

And is it melted?

Not at all.

Not at all, I said, nodding. My voice might have been the echo of Raymond's repeating down the line. For all I knew he was sat in the adjacent room, on the other side of the wall in front of me, but for now our voices were bouncing around through a network of satellites and computers, crossing absurd distances at absurd speeds, entertaining impossible notions.

How do you know? I said again.

The birthmark.

The doll has a birthmark?

Yep. I told you it was weird.

I was trying not to laugh.

Okay, I said. Have you seen any others? Do you know where Mylene bought it?

Mothercare, he said. I went and looked today.

Right, I said.

I was thinking maybe it was just that one and after Sophie reacted so badly I thought maybe I'd replace it. But when I went to the shop I didn't like the look of them. They're smart dolls.

Smart dolls? I said, baffled by the term.

Yeah, you hook them up to the WiFi and then you can talk to your kid through them. I bet she's been spying on us.

Smart dolls, I said, another echo repeating. The idea was new to me.

Anyway, said Raymond, those ones—I looked—those ones in the shop, they didn't have birthmarks.

Some kind of manufacturing defect, I thought, thinking I'd said it. For a moment I wasn't sure whether I'd said it or not.

I closed my eyes. I was rubbing my temple.

When I opened my eyes, the television was off, gone

into some power saving mode, and I realised its screen
had been the only light I'd had on, because I was sitting in
shadows now.

I'll show you, said Raymond.

Tomorrow, I said.

No, I—

Tomorrow, I said, and ended the call. Then I powered
the phone down and tossed it back onto the floor.

That night I slept on the sofa in the shadows of the
living room and dreamt about the doll.

*

It was the same doll. He wasn't wrong. I could see that
immediately. He showed me the birthmark. It didn't look
like a manufacturing defect.

Jesus, I said, because there was nothing better to say. It
was impossible and it was true. What do you say to that?

I can hardly bring myself to touch it, said Raymond. It's
like it's contaminated. I'll see Sophie playing with it and it
just turns my stomach. But then if you take it off her she just
cries and cries.

What does Mary think?

She'd want me sectioned.

I nodded, shivering. It was cold out on the patio. The
nights were getting even colder. Raymond had propped the
doll up on the white table. It was a baby, of course, but of
an age where it could hold itself up. It looked like it was
holding itself up. In the dark it wasn't hard to mistake it for
a real baby.

It had its slightly stubby nose. It seemed weird to me to
give a doll a nose like that. Its eyes set slightly too far apart.
Who had designed this thing? I thought. And its birthmark.
Why the fuck did it have a birthmark?

Some of Raymond's fear was seeping into me. For him,
the fear expressed itself as revulsion. For me it was a kind

of attraction. There was something compelling about the doll. It made the things around it seem fainter, vaguer, less real. It seemed oddly accentuated. I wanted to touch it but I didn't want to touch it. I sat and peered at it, studying the texture of its bib and the plastic of its face and the synthetic hair glued into its head that, impossibly, wasn't melted anymore, and wanted to look at anything else and at the same time it was all I wanted to look at, the only thing.

What now? I said.

Raymond looked up. I realised he'd had his face in his hands. For a moment I thought he'd been crying but on second thoughts decided not.

Fire didn't work, he said, stroking his beard.

Usually he shaved but recently he hadn't been shaving. Looking at him I saw the exhaustion in his eyes. He looked like he'd been sleeping even worse than me.

I thought maybe I'd bury it.

We did that before.

But deeper.

Okay, I said.

I've got a better idea. You got your car keys?

I tried to calculate the units of alcohol I'd consumed, but the truth is I'm numerically dyslexic.

Yes, I said.

Carefully Raymond put the doll into his satchel. He did it with a kind of gentleness, like he was tucking it in for the night. Then we got in my car and drove to the beach. The night was cold and getting colder, and the wind was getting up.

✳

There's a bronze statue of a donut or something that looks like a donut on the beach, a big green thing, two and a half metres wide, what's called a torus, to the west of the Palace Pier and to the east of the husk of the West Pier. Christ knows why. Public art. On the groin there we stood looking at the waves. The lights of the working pier stained the black waves with their glow. In the winter in the dark with the cold and the rain the sea looked unforgiving. For a moment I thought Raymond was having second thoughts, then he turned and walked back down the groin and skipped over the wall where it was low enough for him to jump down onto the beach, and I heard him land on the pebbles with a groan, cursing his knees.

Where are you going? I said, or maybe thought and didn't say. It was hard to hear even my own voice over the wind.

I walked over to the wall and looked down to see him gathering pebbles, and then I understood. He put the pebbles in his bag with the doll. Then he came back up on to the groin and walked to its end and stood for a moment looking out at the churn of black waves.

I realised he had closed his eyes.

What if it comes back again? he said.

It won't, I said, and wondered if I believed that.

It did last time.

I nodded.

The night really was very cold, but it seemed inappropriate to try and hurry him along.

Raymond, I said.

He sighed and opened his eyes. Then he checked the buckles on the satchel.

How's your throw? he said, and I think I saw a smile on his face. In school I'd never been sporty like Raymond had been. That was probably the reason we'd never been friends back in those days. It gets boring getting beaten all the time.

He stepped back and took a deep breath. Then, frowning, he took a few more steps, giving himself a run up. Then he ran, stopping suddenly at the seaward wall, and for a second I was certain he was about to tumble over it, but instead he launched the bag high, high up into the dark.

He had a good throw. I didn't hear it splash.

I'm going to need a new bag, said Raymond.

Yep, I replied, thinking it would probably just wash up on the beach in the morning.

Oh, fuck, he said, halting in dismay.

What? I said.

What now? I thought. Jesus it is cold, I thought.

My keys were in the bag.

He started patting his pockets. Then he closed his eyes.

Piss.

What?

I think my phone was also in it.

We walked back to my car, parked up on Black Lion Street on the other side of the promenade and the Kings Road. We sat in the car for a while and then I drove us home.

✳

The next day, I don't know why, I called in sick to work and, leaving my car in the drive, got a bus into town. I got off at the stop on North Street, then headed south down East Street, and it was only once I'd reached the beach that I realised what I was doing.

I'd been thinking about the doll, about its stubby nose, its large staring eyes set too far apart, and the fact that dolls came chipped these days, hooked up to the internet, and I'd been thinking about this Mylene.

Did I expect to find the satchel? I don't know. It would be an absurd thing to say, of course, that I expected to find it, but through those last few weeks absurdities had rather begun to accumulate.

The beach might have been a different beach. It was the

daytime now, of course, but the wind had gone, and the sea was flat, and the world felt peculiarly airless. It wasn't hard to imagine some fucker with a Jesus complex trying to walk on it, the sea was that flat. And with the aforementioned accumulating absurdities they'd probably succeed. But it was so cold that you wouldn't want to fail.

I was giving up on the bag, pretending to myself that I hadn't come down here for that, that I'd just wanted some air, nothing unreasonable, when I saw a kid struggling with something on the pebbles. He was maybe seven. I looked around but there were no adults in sight.

I think immediately I knew it was the bag.

Hey, I said, approaching him. Hey.

He glanced up with a look that said he was doing something he shouldn't have been doing.

For a moment I didn't know what to say. He stared at me, and for a moment I thought he was going to try and leg it.

That's my bag, I said, and when I moved forward, ready for a tug-of-war over the satchel, a forty-year-old man ready to grapple with a seven-year-old child, he scrambled to his feet and scurried away.

I watched him leave the beach, disappearing up onto the promenade, kicking up pebbles in his wake. Then I looked down at the bag.

Huh, I said.

There was no doubt.

I crouched down. My eyes widened and I recoiled when I touched it, as if every thread of its fabric coursed with diabolical electricity.

It wasn't wet.

The boy had unclipped one of the buckles but the other was still secure. I unclipped it and opened the impossibly dry top flap, revealing the zip over the main impossibly dry compartment. Under the flap but not in the main compartment there were a few small pockets for pens and things.

Opening one of these, I found Raymond's house keys, and in the other I found his phone. The battery was in the red, in a power saving mode, but it wasn't dead. There were several missed calls from Mylene.

Fucking Mylene, I thought, in Raymond's voice.

In the main compartment, under some pebbles, I found the doll, which was also dry.

I dropped the bag back onto the pebbles and stood up straight. I realised I could hear myself breathing heavily, breathing weirdly. I was trying and failing to think. For a moment I felt short of breath and like a wave of black panic was about to swell out of the calm of my mind, sweeping everything away, but it didn't.

I crouched down again and removed the house keys and the mobile phone from the front pockets of the bag. I fiddled with the phone until I managed to power it off. I looked around for a moment, checking that there was no one nearby to see me, and then running forward I hurled each of them, the house keys and the phone, out to sea.

I'd never had a good throw before, but that was a good one.

When I couldn't find my car where I'd thought I'd parked it up on Black Lion Street, I walked up to Western Road and took a number 1A bus back home.

The house was empty. For a moment its weird airless emptiness surprised me, until I remembered that my wife was at work. I should open some windows, I thought, but didn't.

Instead I went out on to the patio and, standing up on tiptoes, peered over the fence into Raymond's garden. I looked up at the windows of his house. The curtains of the rear extension were drawn and the curtains in the windows of the back bedroom above it were also drawn. The other window on that floor was the bathroom window and that window was frosted for privacy, and was closed.

With the satchel over my shoulder I looked down at

the doll's head poking through the pebbles in the main compartment. Then I slung it up and over the fence, into the garden next door.

Fucking Mylene, I thought, in Raymond's voice.

Raymond didn't come over for a beer that evening or the next, and he didn't ring. The curtains at the back of the house remained drawn and the curtains round the front stayed drawn too. Whenever he watched television he'd have the television on pretty loud, because he was a little deaf, and we'd be able to hear it through the living room wall. Sometimes we'd hear him swearing through that wall. But for the next few nights we wouldn't hear either, TV or swearing, at all.

On the Wednesday, sitting out on the patio on my own, working my way through a bottle of Doombar, I remembered the satchel. Standing up from the camping chair, I went over to the fence, and going on tiptoes stood to peer over into Raymond's garden.

The satchel was gone.

Returning to the chair, I went to sit back down but the damn thing collapsed underneath me, causing me to swear and spill beer. Swearing some more, under my breath and over my breath, I went and took the other chair, which I thought of as Raymond's chair, from the shed. Then after testing the stability of the chair I sat back down and drank what remained of the beer.

Someone was knocking at the door. My wife was out for Sunday lunch with a friend and for a moment I'd assumed she'd forgotten her key and had come back without it, but when I looked down from the stairwell the figure I saw through the translucent glass of the door was shorter than my wife, who's pretty tall for a woman, and slimmer.

That morning I'd heard movements in the living

room next door. I'd stopped to listen, wondering if it was Raymond, but I didn't hear any swearing so had decided it was his wife. Then, later, I'd heard two voices arguing, women's voices, Raymond's wife Mary and another voice I couldn't place. Then the door had slammed.

At that point I'd gone upstairs to take a pee. After a few moments I heard the knocking at the door, and after a small delay I realised it was our door that they were knocking at and not Raymond and Mary's door next door.

I think even then I knew who it was.

I recognised the shape of her through the translucent glass of the door.

Mylene, I said, squinting against the bright diffuse daylight.

Startled, her expression broke out into a smile.

Well isn't it a small fucking world, she said.

What do you want?

Aren't you going to invite me in? she said, staring up at me with big blue eyes set very slightly too far apart. Put the kettle on?

No, I said. I don't think I am. What do you want?

My sister told me the neighbour might know where her useless husband is. I didn't realise the neighbour was you.

I nodded as if I agreed.

I've no idea, I said.

Mylene was leaning against the wall, looking at me sort of sideways, clearly amused by the whole situation.

Okay, she said, suddenly annoyed by what I assumed was her failure to elicit a reaction from me. Well, if you see him, say I need to talk to him.

She turned away. I watched her walk down the drive. At the gate, she turned back, smiling again.

About what? I asked.

Tell him I'm pregnant, she said, and started to laugh.

Fucking Raymond, I thought, suddenly nauseous with what I can only describe as jealousy, and shut the door. It

shook in the frame. When I opened it again, Mylene was
gone.

✻

The next evening when I took a beer from the box in the
utility room and went out to the shed the chairs were gone,
the broken one and the one that wasn't broken. Coming out
of the shed, I saw my wife stood in the doorway, watching
me.

A woman called round earlier, she said.

Oh, I said.

She had the wrong address, she said.

Right, I said.

My wife thought for a moment.

I kind of recognised her, she said.

Uh huh, I said.

I realised I was nodding, but not at anything she had
said, so I made myself stop.

Suddenly my wife smiled.

What's happened to the chairs? I asked.

Oh, I chucked them out, said my wife. One of them was
broken.

She shivered.

And they were starting to rot. Honestly, did the smell
not bother you at all?

Contributors

Seán Padraic Birnie is a writer and photographer from Brighton, England. He holds a B.A. degree from Manchester Metropolitan University in English Literature and Creative Writing and an M.A. in Photography from the University of Brighton, where he works as a Technical Demonstrator on the Photography courses. In 2016 he was one of ten winners of the Magnum Photos/Photo London Graduate Photographers Award. His short fiction has appeared in venues such as *Black Static, BFS Horizons* and *Litro*, and his articles on photography have been published in scholarly journals such as *Photographies* and *Critical Studies*. For more info, see: seanbirnie.com.

Rebecca Campbell is a Canadian writer and teacher. NeWest Press published her novel, *The Paradise Engine*, in 2013, and you can find more of her short fiction online at whereishere.ca

Kay Chronister lives in Tucson, Arizona, where she is completing a Ph. D. in Literature. Her fiction has appeared in venues such as *Clarkesworld, Strange Horizons, Shimmer, Black Static*, and *The Dark*. Her first collection, *Thin Places* (Undertow Publications), will be out soon. Find her online at kaychronister.com

Kristi DeMeester is the author of *Beneath*, a novel published by Word Horde, and *Everything That's Underneath*, a short fiction collection published by Apex Books. Her writing has been included in Ellen Datlow's *The Best Horror of the Year* volumes 9 and 11, *Year's Best Weird Fiction* volumes 1, 3, and

5, in addition to publications such as *Black Static, Pseudopod, The Dark,* and several others. She is at work on her second novel. Find her online at www.kristidemeester.com

Brian Evenson is the author of over a dozen books of fiction, including, most recently, the short story collection *Song for the Unraveling of the World,* and the novella *The Warren.* He has been a five-time finalist for the Shirley Jackson Award, a finalist for the Edgar Award, and has received an International Horror Guild Award. His work has been translated into a dozen languages. He lives in Los Angeles and works at CalArts.

James Everington mainly writes dark, supernatural fiction, although he occasionally takes a break and writes dark, non-supernatural fiction. His second collection of such tales, *Falling Over,* is out now from Infinity Plus. He's also the author of *The Quarantined City,* an episodic novel mixing Borgesian strangeness with supernatural horror—*"an unsettling voice all of its own"* The Guardian—and the novellas *Paupers' Graves* and *Trying To Be So Quiet.* Alongside Dan Howarth, he has co-edited the anthologies *The Hyde Hotel* (Black Shuck Books) and *Imposter Syndrome* (Dark Minds Press). Oh, and he drinks Guinness, if anyone's asking. You can find out what James is currently up to at his Scattershot Writing site.

Kurt Fawver is a writer of horror, weird fiction, and literature that oozes through the cracks of genre. His short fiction has won a Shirley Jackson Award and been previously published in venues such as *The Magazine of Fantasy & Science Fiction, Strange Aeons, Weird Tales, Vastarien, Best New Horror,* and *Year's Best Weird Fiction.* He's the author of two collections of short stories—*The Dissolution of Small Worlds,* and *Forever, in Pieces*—as well as a novella, *Burning Witches, Burning Angels,* and two chapbooks, *Pwdre Ser,* and

Problems in River Heights. He's also had non-fiction published in journals such as *Thinking Horror* and the *Journal of the Fantastic in the Arts.* You can find Kurt online at www.kurt-fawver.com or www.facebook.com/kfawver.

Carly Holmes lives and writes on the west coast of Wales, UK. Her debut novel, *The Scrapbook* (Parthian) was short-listed for the International Rubery Book Award in 2015, and her literary horror short story collection, *Figurehead,* was published by Tartarus Press in 2018, to much critical acclaim. One of the stories within was selected for reprint in *Best Horror of the Year Volume 11* (Night Shade Press) and five further stories were given honourable mentions. Her award-winning short fiction has appeared in many journals and anthologies, such as *Ambit, Black Static,* and *The Ghastling.* Carly works as an editor for Parthian Books.

Michael Kelly is the former Series Editor for the *Year's Best Weird Fiction.* He's a Shirley Jackson Award and British Fantasy Award winner, and a World Fantasy Award nominee. His fiction has appeared in a number of journals and anthologies, including *Black Static, The Mammoth Book of Best New Horror 21 & 24, Postscripts, Weird Fiction Review,* and has been previously collected in *Scratching the Surface, Undertow & Other Laments,* and *All the Things We Never See.*

V.H. Leslie is the author of a short story collection, *Skein and Bone* (Undertow Publications), and a novel, *Bodies of Water* (Salt Publishing), and her short stories have appeared in a range of journals and anthologies. Her fiction has been nominated for the World Fantasy Award, British Fantasy Award and the Shirley Jackson Award and she won the Lightship International Prize. She has been awarded fellowships for her writing at Hawthornden in Scotland and the Saari Institute in Finland, and her non-fiction has appeared in *History Today, The Victorianist* and *Gramarye.*

She also works as a writer for an interdisciplinary project, WetlandLIFE, lead by the University of Greenwich and funded by the Valuing Nature programme, exploring folklore in the landscape.

Alison Littlewood's latest novel, *Mistletoe*, is a seasonal ghost story with glimpses into the Victorian era. Her first book, *A Cold Season*, was selected for the Richard and Judy Book Club and described as 'perfect reading for a dark winter's night.' Other titles include *Path of Needles, The Unquiet House, The Hidden People* and *The Crow Garden*. Her short stories have been picked for several year's best anthologies and published in her collections *Quieter Paths* and *Five Feathered Tales*. She has won the Shirley Jackson Award for Short Fiction. Alison lives with her partner Fergus in Yorkshire, England, in a house of creaking doors and crooked walls. She loves exploring the hills and dales with her two hugely enthusiastic Dalmatians and she has a penchant for Earl Grey tea, fountain pens and semicolons. Visit her at www.alisonlittlewood.co.uk.

C.M. Muller lives in St. Paul, Minnesota with his wife and two sons. He is related to the Norwegian writer Jonas Lie and draws much inspiration from that scrivener of old. His tales have appeared in *Shadows & Tall Trees, Vastarien, Weirdbook*, and a host of other venues. As editor and publisher, he is responsible for the annual anthology series *Nightscript*, as well as *Twice-Told: A Collection of Doubles*, a themed anthology featuring 22 unique visions of the doppelgänger. His debut collection of stories, *Hidden Folk*, was released in late 2018. For more information, please visit: www.chthonicmatter. wordpress.com

KL Pereira's debut short story collection, *A Dream Between Two Rivers: Stories of Liminality*, was published in 2017 by Cutlass Press. Pereira's fiction, poetry, and nonfiction appear or are forthcoming in the British Fantasy Award winning anthology *Years Best Weird Fiction vol. 5*, *Shadows and Tall Trees, vol. 8*, *Literary Hub*, *LampLight*, *The Drum*, *Shimmer*, *Innsmouth Free Press*, *Mythic Delirium*, *Jabberwocky*, and *Bitch Magazine*, among others. She lives in a Victorian garret across from a haunted cemetery with her feline familiar.

Steve Rasnic Tem is a past winner of the Bram Stoker, World Fantasy, and British Fantasy Awards. He's published over 450 short stories. His most recent collections are *The Harvest Child and Other Fantasies* (Crossroads), *Everything Is Fine Now* (Omnium Gatherum), and late 2019's *The Night Doctor & Other Tales* (Centipede). His last novel *Ubo* (Solaris, February 2017) is a dark science fictional tale about violence and its origins, featuring such historical viewpoint characters as Jack the Ripper, Stalin, and Heinrich Himmler. *Yours to Tell: Dialogues on the Art & Practice of Writing*, written with his late wife Melanie, appeared from Apex Books in 2017. In 2018 Valancourt Books published *Figures Unseen*, a volume of his Selected Stories.

Before earning her MFA from Vermont College of Fine Arts, **M. Rickert** worked as kindergarten teacher, coffee shop barista, Disneyland balloon vendor, and personnel assistant in Sequoia National Park. Her first novel, *The Memory Garden*, was published in 2014, and won the Locus award. She is the winner of the Crawford Award, World Fantasy Award, and Shirley Jackson Award. Her third short story collection, *You Have Never Been Here* was published by Small Beer Press in November, 2015. Her story, "Another F*cking Fairy Tale" is forthcoming in *The Magazine of Fantasy and Science Fiction*. A certified yoga instructor, she teaches yoga in Cedarburg, Wisconsin.

Simon Strantzas is the author of five collections of short fiction, including *Nothing is Everything* (Undertow Publications, 2018), and editor of a number of anthologies, including *Year's Best Weird Fiction, Vol. 3*. Collectively, he's been a finalist for three Shirley Jackson Awards, two British Fantasy Awards, and the World Fantasy Award. His fiction has appeared in numerous annual best-of anthologies, and in venues such as *Nightmare, The Dark,* and *Cemetery Dance*. In 2014, his edited anthology, *Aickman's Heirs*, won the Shirley Jackson Award. He lives with his wife in Toronto, Canada.

Steve Toase was born in North Yorkshire, England, and now lives in Munich, Germany. He writes regularly for *Fortean Times* and *Folklore Thursday*. His fiction has appeared in *Three Lobed Burning Eye, Shimmer, Lackington's, StarShip-Sofa, Not One of Us, Cabinet des Feés* and *Pantheon Magazine* amongst others. In 2014 "Call Out" (first published in *Innsmouth Magazine*) was reprinted in *The Best Horror of The Year 6*, and two of his stories have just been published in *Best Horror of The Year 11*. He likes old motorbikes and vintage cocktails. You can keep up to date with his work via his Patreon www.patreon.com/stevetoase, www.tinyletter.com/ stevetoase, facebook.com/stevetoase1, www.stevetoase. wordpress.com and @stevetoase

Neil Williamson is a writer and musician from Glasgow, Scotland. His stories and books, including *The Moon King, Secret Language* and *The Ephemera*, have been shortlisted for British Science Fiction, British Fantasy and World Fantasy Awards. At Halloween he carves a traditional turnip lantern. Just in case.

Charles Wilkinson's publications includes *The Pain Tree and Other Stories* (London Magazine Editions, 2000) and *Ag & Au,* (Flarestack Poets, 2013). His collections of strange tales and weird fiction, *A Twist in the Eye* (2016), and *Splendid In Ash* (2018) appeared from Egaeus Press.

His short stories have come out in many magazines and anthologies, including previous numbers of *Shadows & Tall Trees*, *Nightscript*, *Bourbon Penn* and *Supernatural Tales*. His chapbook *The January Estate* is forthcoming from Eibonvale Press and a full-length collection of his poetry is about to appear from Eyewear Publications. He lives in Powys, Wales, where he is heavily outnumbered by members of the ovine community. More information can be found on his website: charleswilkinsonauthor.com

www.ingramcontent.com/pod-product-compliance
Lightning Source LLC
Chambersburg PA
CBHW031342020726
47499CB00005B/1365